TELL IT ME AGAIN

Poetry
Fairground Music
The Tree that Walked
Cannibals and Missionaries
Epistles to Several Persons
The Mountain in the Sea
Lies and Secrets
The Illusionists
Waiting for the Music
The Beautiful Inventions
Selected Poems 1954 to 1982
Partingtime Hall (*with James Fenton*)

Fiction
Flying to Nowhere
The Adventures of Speedfall

Criticism
A Reader's Guide to W. H. Auden
The Sonnet
The Dramatic Works of John Gay (*ed.*)

For Children
Herod Do Your Worst
Squeaking Crust
The Spider Monkey Uncle King
The Last Bid
The Extraordinary Wool Mill and other stories
Come Aboard and Sail Away

TELL IT ME AGAIN

John Fuller

Chatto & Windus

LONDON

Published in 1988 by
Chatto & Windus Limited
30 Bedford Square
London WC1B 3RP

British Library Cataloguing in Publication Data
Fuller, John, 1937 –
Tell it me again.
I.   Title
823'.914[F]   PR6056.U43
ISBN 0–7011–3288–4

Typeset at The Spartan Press Ltd
Lymington, Hants
Printed in Great Britain by
Redwood Burn Ltd
Trowbridge, Wilts

I

As Hugh approached the bar to order a beer, he realised that he couldn't remember any of the names of the American brands. His eye scanned sign and label for a clue: 'Michelob' was one, but he didn't know how to pronounce it.

'I'll have a beer, please,' he said.

The bartender offered him a list of names that sounded like a line of poetry. Hugh repeated the last word, the only one he could distinguish, and was given a glass of draught Miller. A man sitting at the bar, with both elbows protecting what had been a short, looked impassively at Hugh's beer as he prepared to take it to a table.

'I'll bet you're from the South,' he said.

'I'm afraid not,' replied Hugh.

'North Carolina, I'd say,' persisted the man. 'North Carolina, drinking that stuff.'

'I'm from England, actually,' said Hugh, wondering whether to pick up his change from the bar.

'England,' said the man, speculatively, but without recognition or curiosity, as though Hugh had said 'Tasmania' or 'Rockall'.

'Yes,' said Hugh.

'You're an Englander?'

'Yes, I'm English.'

'You're a tourist,' said the man sadly, looking at his empty glass. 'How long you been in New York? "Actually"?'

'I've been here about a fortnight,' said Hugh.

At this, a slow smile of fascinated disbelief spread across the man's face.

'A fortnight,' he said to the bartender. He looked up and down the bar. 'A fortnight.'

'A couple of weeks,' explained Hugh.

'I know, I know,' said the man. 'You've never been to North Carolina?'

'Afraid not,' said Hugh pleasantly as he escaped with his beer.

The bar was a place of meditation and transit, incongruously decorated with the sombre panelling of committee rooms. At the back the obligatory arcade games shuffled their illuminated windows, beckoning and winking. The flaunted odds, disguised as mere movement of light, seemed shamelessly to defy calculation: simply to lose money, the machines claimed, was a pleasure. Every half-drunk, gratified by his power over such abstract beauty of movement, could be an operator whose largesse made the performance worth while.

Hugh sipped his cold beer, waiting. He had brought the first two movements of the concerto to give to Katey Ottodici. The sheets were loose in one of the prussian blue linen portfolios with flaps that Eskdale's made up specially for him, and he had only finished writing out the last sheet that morning. He was unhappy with the concluding bars of the largo: the violin had exhausted itself in an extended melody and was left with little to do in the coda. It re-entered, vaguely and arbitrarily Hugh thought, as a self-absorbed harmonic unconcerned with the concentrated finality of the orchestral texture. There was something a little kitsch about it.

However, with the first performance only months away it was absolutely necessary to produce something for Boris and his young protegée. And here at least was the elegant majority of the work, fully scored. There would be time for revisions.

A jukebox pulsed out its admonitions and seductions: the teen whine of Madonna, the rough space-age chant of Dire Straits, the wayward sob of Virginia Gerald. The Gerald sound had been in the air ever since he had arrived in New York. It seemed well-established, rooted in the sudden warm days of the early summer but haunted by changeable emotional skies and uncertain hopes. The latest song was 'Tell It Me Again', and it was the most exciting. The words and tempo pressed forward with the erotic momentum of a new involvement, but the voice expressed, within a hectic scattering of slurs and swoops, a contrary of qualifying feeling, a kind of melancholy or critical drag. Whatever the music proposed, its interpreter eloquently undermined. The effect was poised, doubtful, challenging, yet insistently sensual:

> 'A story's going round
> That has a tender sound:
> Tell it me again.'

Hugh allowed his attention to drift with the melody. Backed by strings and urged on by blocks of muted brass, it had a dated air that lent it a faded charm. It evoked the lost riches of the swing band and its girl vocalist, an art perhaps as forgotten as the concerto and similar in its elevated contrasts. He listened to the little tricks of her voice and tried to imagine them on paper, but the song was propelled always just a little ahead of his understanding of the idiom:

> 'You say you've heard it all before, and though
> You may be right, still
> Aren't you curious to know
> What sort of play,
> What role they've given you to fill,
> What words to say?'

The style was a clever approximation of scat, an angular, apparently improvisatory exploration of the singer's vocal range. The voice was all speculation, while the trumpets spat and the saxophones interposed their encouraging caresses. At this climax it fell back with hardly a pause into a more cautious mood into which her note of hurt experience crept, the slowing cadences richly toned and undeniably blue:

> 'I'd like to hear your part.
> I know my own by heart.
> Tell it me again.'

The interpretation seemed to defy the words. It was very satisfying.

Were the other people in the bar listening? Hugh looked round. The man at the counter was staring at his refilled glass. A couple in a booth at the back were laughing with each other quietly. The bartender wiped a glass with a cloth as convention required him to do. It was clear that whatever they heard they could not be really listening.

What chances, then, for the music that was not pressed in millions or transmitted continuously? The blue folder lay on the table in front of him looking already like an exhibited reliquary, a minor opus, an item commanding a biographer's informed interest or an institutional fee.

'The Unfinished,' thought Hugh, with a wry smile. He reduced his beer to a flat pale inch and lit a cigarette.

It was a ridiculous place to meet, but wholly typical of Boris's arrangements, with their conspiratorial informality and theatrical haste. While he waited, Hugh strolled over to the small array of computerised games to waste his quarters. He had been attracted by the insistent signature-tune of the latest model, a mechanical drone in descending thirds and a brief flourish that sounded like a mendicant accordionist's only tune, something wonderfully easy on the ear requiring no agility on the stops at all. He had heard it before, and played the game too, at the airport. The sheer vulgarity of it amused him. The controls manoeuvred a mannikin in pursuit of a girl fleeing down the shifting perspectives of a three-dimensional maze. At some blind turns a stylised gorilla lay in wait, and the occasional spiked gate descended. There were buttons for evading these hazards. If they could be quickly enough manipulated, the girl's lead narrowed and allowed another button to work the mannikin's arms. If he touched her, she deposited an item of clothing and the player's score increased. Success promised further screens and varied adventures, but Hugh succumbed to the second gorilla and scored only 150 points. The game was called *Amazing*, and conversed with the player:

'Bad luck,' it growled tinnily at Hugh. 'Try again.'

Hugh tried again.

This time he foiled the second gorilla and sneaked under a portcullis. In his excitement he took a wrong turning in the maze and lost sight of the girl, but after a few more turns there she suddenly was, only a pace or two ahead. Hugh pressed the grab button, the girl gave a simulated shriek and left her hat behind. 500 points.

'You're getting the idea,' said *Amazing*. 'Enter your name against your score.'

This could be done by producing an alphabet scan on the screen with one button and printing the isolated letter with another. Hugh became flustered in the allotted time and ended up on the screen as H. HOWARF.

'Thank you for playing,' said *Amazing*, and it struck up once more its little tune of invitation, as though eager to be rid of Hugh and be played by someone adroit and macho.

When Hugh turned from the machine, conscious of a false insouciance, expecting to be greeted by patronising stares from the bar, he saw Boris making his way towards him, smiling broadly with a dark tousled teenager in tow.

'Hugh!' exclaimed Boris. 'We've kept you so long, you must be bored rigid.'

He took Hugh's hand and elbow simultaneously and rocked them back and forward. Like the smile, this gesture was without intimacy, performed with the calculation of a Mason or osteopath.

'Hello, Boris,' said Hugh. He looked towards the girl, but Boris made no introduction.

'Margueritas, everyone?' asked Boris, moving to the bar. He seemed to expect no reply. Hugh, who would rather have had another beer, said: 'Fine.'

'I'll have a Michelob,' said Katey Ottodici.

Boris continued his apologies when they were seated with their drinks.

'It was mildly fraught, Hugh,' he explained. 'A late start, to begin with. Then the second trombone decided to take a Florida vacation in the interval and was decidedly emotional when discovered.'

'The whole brass section was plastered,' said Katey. She had her violin case between her knees and kept her hands on it.

'Not unusual, Katey dear,' said Boris. 'But they played magnificently. If you'd stayed to listen you'd have been impressed.'

9

'I never stay,' said Katey.

'She never stays,' agreed Boris. 'Why should she? She gives everything. She's exhausted. Off she goes at the interval. Disappears entirely.'

'I change,' said Katey.

'You were wonderful tonight,' said Boris. 'Absolutely wonderful. They loved it.'

'The third movement was too slow,' said Katey. 'As usual.'

'Ah, now,' smiled Boris, wagging his finger. 'Naughty!'

He turned to Hugh.

'We have our little difference on this point,' he said. 'What is your view, Hugh?'

Hugh looked into his glass. It was frosted with salt and shipwreck-ed with fruit and tasted of anti-freeze.

'Well,' he said. 'I heard you play the Mendelssohn in London.'

He smiled at Katey as a substitute for not having used her name.

'You were very good,' he continued. 'But possibly the third movement was a little slow.'

Katey turned her bright eyes on him and she smiled. The smile was friendly but slightly truculent, made as much with her chin as her lips.

'Thanks,' she said. And to Boris: 'You see?'

Boris shrugged.

'It was maybe slow in London. Here it's O K,' he said. 'It's joyful, not a scramble.'

'I feel it faster,' said Katey.

'If we take it faster, you'll go to pieces.'

Katey didn't reply.

'Anyway, Hugh,' Boris continued. 'We had a bit of a panic about the parts after the concert. Sonia wasn't in the best of moods.'

'And your coach is leaving this evening?' asked Hugh sympathetic-ally.

'It's madness!' cried Boris. 'I wanted to leave tomorrow, but Sonia was convinced that we'd never get everyone there and that there'd be no time for rehearsal. She's quite right, of course.' He grinned. 'She always is.'

'But you won't have time for this yet, will you?' asked Hugh, tapping the blue folder.

'This is it?' asked Boris, with the rehearsed exaggeration of a birthday victim. 'Bless you, Hugh. May I see?'

Hugh handed him the folder.

'Wonderful, wonderful,' murmured Boris, quickly turning the pages. 'We feel privileged.'

'Nonsense,' said Hugh.

'Is it hard?' asked Katey.

'Oh, it's absolutely impossible,' said Hugh with a smile. 'You'll need a sixth finger.'

'Right then,' she said in a businesslike way. 'I'll get one of those.'

'When will the last movement be ready?' asked Boris.

'When do you need it?'

'Yesterday,' said Boris. 'As always.'

'You'll have it then,' replied Hugh.

'Right!'

Boris was delighted. He unzipped a suede case and popped the folder inside. He held the case upright on the table, his fingers stroking the corners. Clearly he was now ready to go.

'It's really for Katey, of course,' he said. 'But I'll get the parts copied straightaway. It takes so long to get these fellows moving. We won't need a run-through till August.'

'You'll have the third movement by then.'

'Wonderful. Hugh, we should be on our way. There's so much to do. How are you enjoying New York? I'm shattered that I shan't be here for the ballet.'

'Oh, don't worry about that,' said Hugh.

'It's going to be quite an occasion. I really didn't want to miss it.'

'I wouldn't mind missing it myself.'

'Now you can't be serious! It's true fame, Hugh. You'll be torn apart.'

'I really don't want to be torn apart,' complained Hugh.

'Don't worry,' said Boris. 'Liz Crail will stick you together again. Give her my love, won't you? And watch her like a hawk. When she sticks people together she usually starts sticking *to* them.'

'I'll be careful,' said Hugh.

'Come on, Katey, we must be on the move.' Boris rose.

'You've only just arrived,' said Hugh.

'Dear Hugh,' said Boris. 'I didn't pretend it would be a social occasion, did I? Another time.'

'I feel like a secret agent passing information,' said Hugh with a smile. 'Or perhaps releasing a hostage.'

'I'll take good care of it.'

'I can't finish this beer,' said Katey. She was standing with it, holding the glass just in front of her as though it were an object in a game that had to be passed to a neighbour before the music stopped.

'Forget the beer, Katey,' said Boris.

Hugh felt an unspoken tension between the two as they prepared to leave since, instead of abandoning her beer, Katey stood awkwardly in her place, half-attempting to finish it. Did the drink represent an unwanted generosity on Boris's part, and was her stubborn struggle with it a rebuke to him or to his attentions? She seemed a nice girl, and Hugh found himself jealous of all the nuances of Boris's Svengali-like role. Observing the conductor's impatience, his charm for the moment put aside, he tried to label the private relationship that was inadvertently revealed: was it irritated father or frustrated lover, he wondered.

Katey smiled at Hugh over her glass.

'I really like your music, Mr Howard,' she said. 'I shall get to *Beatrice and Benedick* anyway, as I'm coming back to New York next month. And I know I'm going to enjoy playing the concerto. Thank you.'

It was quite a little speech, and Hugh felt touched.

'Well,' he said. 'I hope you like it.'

What a foolish thing to say, Hugh thought, as though it were a present. As though it were written for her.

And all this time, behind them, beyond them, the voice of Virginia Gerald hung in the air smokily. The voice was so touching in its proposal of a possible love, so tentative in its approach to the possibility, so doubtful of its pleasure at beginning such a commitment, that Hugh could not help listening:

> 'It's a delicious rumor
> From friends in a good humor:
> Tell it me again.
> They say you've got me on your mind, and though
> They may be wrong, still
> I'm so curious to know
> What do I do?
> Should I stand here and wait until
> I hear my cue?
> Say it. You know I need
> To know that you're my feed.
> Tell it me again.'

Hugh could hardly bear to leave the bar while it was still playing, but somehow they all seemed to be moving out into the street together, even though they parted at the nearest corner.

2

Elizabeth Crail knew that the essence of a successful party was that it should really be several different parties in one, and that none of the different elements should for a moment suspect that they were not the exclusive focus of attention.

'Tikki, dear,' she had said to her daughter, 'I want you to be in charge of the supper table. Yes, I know that Stewarts are serving the party, but they really aren't good enough when it comes to food, and besides I think it would be nice for you to show off to Peter. He probably doesn't realise you can cook.'

'Mother, you know perfectly well that I cook for Peter.'

'That may be,' said Mrs Crail. 'But this will be special. Do your *gigot en croûte*: it's so good cold. And some terrines. I want Peter to enjoy his party.'

'*Mother!*' Tikki objected. 'It isn't Peter's party.'

Mrs Crail was unperturbed.

'People will be so looking forward to seeing you two together. I think you should be seen to be a hostess in your own right.'

Tikki sighed.

'Mother,' she said. 'You can't pretend that it isn't a party for the ballet. It's Tanya's party, and Johnny T's. But I don't mind cooking for it.'

'And you'll do it so nicely, poppet,' said Mrs Crail.

To her husband she said:

'I think Mrs Friedberg will feel very flattered to be asked. And she is definitely unhappy about her portfolio.'

'Darling . . .' protested Roger Crail.

'Be specially charming to her, and she's yours.'

'. . . I really cannot tout for business at your parties.'

She brushed his objection aside.

'It's your party too, Roger,' she said.

To Sammy West she wrote: 'We do so hope you'll agree to play. It would be such a treat.' To the Richardsons: 'You can't get away this time!' To Hugh Howard: 'Everyone is *longing* to meet you.' To Johnny Tierentanz: 'Now you just tell me who you want invited.'

In this way, practically every guest felt privileged, and would never dare to sulk or leave too early with further entertainment in view.

But Tikki was right. It *was* a ballet party. It took place the night after the opening, and all the dancers had been invited. They stood about in corners, beneath flowers, beside the piano, smiling and flushed with athletic achievement, their muscles concealed beneath their sober clothes like the folded wings of birds.

The lift, which opened directly into the Crails' submarine apartment, appeared to disgorge new guests every minute. Exquisite young men in wing-collars hovered with champagne. Groups broke and reassembled at the exclamation of greetings or the insistence of introductions. Pairs joined pairs and wandered into as yet unpeopled rooms. It was all finely choreographed, as Mrs Crail reflected, needing only the slightest effort on her part, a mere word, a gesture, a smile. Johnny T could have managed nothing as perfect.

The principals, of course, needed more direction. Professor Friedberg would do nothing but peer at the paintings if not put firmly into Peter's care and sent to form a stout and serious nucleus in the Red Room. Tanya had to be kept from the bar. Olive Dempster had to be shown the food immediately, to prevent her from talking. Hugh Howard needed constant attention, since he knew hardly anyone except Johnny T, and did little except glare through his lank fair hair in that self-contained and critical way that the English have.

She gave Hugh to Tikki, since she knew that her daughter was impressed enough by him to be willing patiently to point out all the other celebrities. Tikki was tall enough, and Hugh was short enough, for her to look him in the eye.

'I don't know whether I should like you or not,' she said playfully. 'I once had to play your *Holiday Snapshots* at a High School concert.'

'Oh, those,' said Hugh.

'Some of them are lovely,' Tikki went on. 'But some are weird. I never got the hang of the last one, the tinkly one.'

'"Packing"?' said Hugh. 'You just have to play it as fast as you can, and you can put in as many wrong notes as you like.'

'I don't think Miss Corner would have approved of that.'

'Did you like "Scrabble"?' asked Hugh.

'That was the weird one!' exclaimed Tikki. 'You'll think it silly of me, but I didn't know the game then, and I thought it was all something to do with building castles. You know, like scrabbling in sand. It was so slow, and it sounded so funny.'

'I was rather proud of that one,' said Hugh. 'It's slow because it's meant to be me thinking about my hand in Scrabble, you see, trying out all the combinations of the letters in my hand. My seven letters are the seven notes of the scale, A, B, C, D, E, F and G. You never get a concluding cadence because there's no eighth letter, no final A. And those isolated little phrases are all the words you can make, like BAG and FACE.'

'Oh, how marvellous,' cried Tikki. 'I'd no idea.'

'The last bit with all the discords was a sort of parody of Stockhausen. The phrase was DEAF.'

Hugh smiled into his glass. The idea had seemed a good one at the time, rather wasted in a set of children's piano pieces. He imagined all the Miss Corners marking in the fingering for their Tikkis all over the USA, thinking vaguely of sandcastles.

'You do play Scrabble in the States, don't you?' he asked.

'Oh yes,' said Tikki. 'But we're not really what you'd call a games-playing family. Do you have children?'

'Simon, at drama school,' replied Hugh. 'He must be a good bit older than you, but he's destined to be the eternal student.'

'Didn't your wife come with you?'

'We're not together any more, I'm afraid,' said Hugh.

'Oh, I'm sorry,' said Tikki.

'Nothing to be sorry about. All passion spent and so forth,' lied Hugh, as a precise and familiar image of Daisy slid sickeningly into his head.

These images, like all memories, had suffered the refinement of familiarity. Daisy talking at the steering-wheel, Daisy choosing the blue skirt, Daisy tying up raspberry canes, Daisy this, Daisy that. They had all the limited range and arbitrary intensity of a batch of photographs. At times Hugh found himself thumbing through them as if hoping to discover one that he had forgotten taking, one that, because it was a more convincing likeness or a more characteristic activity, could somehow justify the whole process. Or, in more desperate moments, one that perhaps could really explain what had happened. But those were the hardest to find, quite impossible in fact, like photographs that could somehow contain the image of the photographer.

'So,' said Tikki, 'you're all on your own.'

'Yes.'

'Where are you staying?'

When Hugh told her the name of his hotel, a rambling establishment on 32nd Street with a bullet-proof cage for the desk clerk and all the cable TV tuned to Spanish-speaking stations, she was horrified. He had tried to make it sound comic and adventurous in order to disguise his parsimony, but he had put himself beyond the civilised pale.

'We shall have to do something about that,' said Tikki, with the air of promising a treat to a child.

Then, with one of those abrupt transitions common to dreams and parties, Hugh found himself talking to a thin, solemn couple introduced by his host as Jack and Ida Richardson.

'We understand you wrote the lovely music,' said Mrs Richardson.

Hugh smiled and nodded agreement.

'Jack works with Roger, you know,' she said. 'And we're just Friends.'

Hugh wondered how a couple who had the same name and every other appearance of being married could be 'just friends' and was about to say something (what?) when Jack Richardson forestalled him.

'Friends of the Ballet, you understand,' he said. 'We're just cheering from the sidelines tonight.'

'I see,' said Hugh.

'We raised a quarter of a million dollars this season,' said Mrs Richardson.

'So we could pay you people,' said her husband.

'Jack, don't be so boorish, and find me something to eat.'

Hugh was relieved that neither of the Richardsons seemed to want to talk about the ballet or his music, and was happy to be led in the direction of Tikki's supper table. There they were confronted by a stocky little woman in a green dress and red glasses who seemed already to have made a hole in the huge ham. She held up her plate a few inches from her nose as if she could hardly see it, and jabbed her fork at Hugh.

'You're Hugh Howard,' she said, without ceasing to eat. 'Olive Dempster.'

'Hello,' said Hugh. 'Do you know . . .'

'Ida, Jack,' nodded Olive Dempster in businesslike greeting. 'The ham is good.'

Jack Richardson attended gravely to the ham which lay heavily in its bed of endive like a damaged caveman's club. Hugh handed a plate to Ida Richardson and found some pâté for himself.

'You want to watch that stuff,' said Olive Dempster seriously. 'Know what's in it?'

'No idea,' said Hugh.

'You see?' she replied. 'It could be anything. I was served dove pâté once. I ask you. Doves.'

'It doesn't taste like doves,' said Hugh cautiously.

'Well, you're all right then,' said Olive. 'Now this ham is ham. You can see it's ham.'

She couldn't bear to talk with a loaded fork, so took another mouthful, moving the fork in tiny circles at them and making periodic murmurs to show that the conversation was still in her court.

'Ballet,' she said, when she had swallowed. 'Can't understand it. Particularly not Shakespeare.'

'Oh, Olive,' protested Ida Richardson. 'It's so beautiful.'

'Didn't you like the Macmillan *Romeo and Juliet*?' asked her husband. They both looked at Olive sadly with all the reproachfulness of a quarter of a million dollars.

'With all due deference to the divine Sergei,' said Olive, 'and to your good self, too, of course, I simply miss words. Shakespeare, without words! Beatrice and Benedick without words! It's too ridiculous.'

'I think I rather agree with you,' said Hugh.

'Bully for you,' said Olive. 'What did you write it for, then?'

Hugh explained that the whole thing was really a Sinfonia Concertante for oboe, clarinet and strings which had got out of hand. He had happened to call it *Beatrice and Benedick* to acknowledge his inspiration and because he didn't like the plain itemised titles with key signatures favoured by most composers.

'I mean,' he continued. 'You wouldn't want to read something called Novel No. 6 in two volumes by Henry James, would you?'

'Yes!' screamed Olive, spraying champagne over the Richardsons. 'I'd love to! If you're referring to *The Portrait of a Lady*, which I presume you are. That's a title borrowed from another art in any case, and it doesn't tell you a *thing*. At least with Novel No. 6 I'd know whereabouts I was in the canon.'

Tikki's Peter, who had quietly joined the group, laughed gently and touched Olive's elbow.

'You ought to be thankful that James wasn't Trollope or it might have been called something like *She Didn't Know What She Was Letting Herself In For*,' he said.

'Peter, you sweetheart,' said Olive. 'That's even better. But Mr Howard was explaining why he perpetrated this insult to the Bard.'

'There's nothing more to tell,' said Hugh. 'Tierentanz wanted to use it, so I simply wrote more, that's all, using a flute for Hero, brass for most of the other male characters, a badly-tuned piano for Dogberry, and so on.'

'I thought that was so clever,' said Ida Richardson. 'You could close your eyes and still know what was going on.'

'That was, of course, the original idea,' said Hugh. 'Though not much of an original idea in itself, if you think of *Peter and the Wolf*.'

'But that's just a children's story anyway,' said Olive. 'It works perfectly. And what's more it isn't a ballet.'

A waiter came up to fill their glasses with champagne. Almost before he was out of earshot, Olive whispered publicly:

'Tremendous little dandies, aren't they? Oh, Peter, I hope they're not chums of yours?'

'Hired for the occasion, I believe,' Peter explained.

'I wonder if I could hire one,' said Olive, scraping her plate. 'That's one good thing about ballet. You do get to see a lot of well-built men with practically nothing on. Poor Benedick! All those words that Shakespeare gave him and all he could do was leap in circles round the stage like a great circus horse.'

She sighed wistfully and handed her plate to Peter.

'Really, what it is,' she pondered, 'is that without language there is no proleptic interest and only the crudest possibility of referring beyond the particular time and place of the action. It's purely animal. No, Peter, I didn't want you to get rid of it for me. I'd like you to get me some more.'

'The music can do it, Olive,' said Peter. 'What about the Wagnerian leitmotif?'

'You've got a point there,' Olive replied. 'I do grant that Mr Howard was clever in that respect. I don't want any of Tikki's dove pâté.'

'You're saved by the bell, I think, Hugh,' laughed Jack Richardson. 'If Olive is writing all this up for *The New Yorker* you'll have to watch out.'

Olive snorted.

'*The New Yorker*, I'm sorry to say, is more interested in the Baroness at the moment.'

Hugh was about to ask 'What Baroness?' when he was whisked away by Peter to be introduced to someone else.

'I thought you needed rescuing,' he said. 'Olive is very sweet-natured really, but she can seem a bit of a gorgon at times, and I'm sure you've had enough of the Richardsons.'

'You're very kind,' said Hugh. 'Actually I was quite enjoying Miss Dempster, but thanks anyway.'

'Look,' said Peter. 'I'm a friend of Tikki's. Well, Tikki and I are together, if you understand me. She's just told me that you're staying in some crummy downtown hotel. Is that right?'

'Oh, it's not bad,' said Hugh. 'The thing is, I'm staying longer than I need, to work on a new concerto. I'd splash out on someone else's money, but not on my own.'

'That's terrible,' said Peter, as though Hugh had confessed to being bankrupt. 'What I came to say was that you're very welcome to stay in my apartment.'

'Oh, I couldn't, really,' said Hugh.

'Of course you could,' insisted Peter. 'I'm not there myself at all. I've moved in with Tikki, you see. So it's no big deal.'

'I see,' said Hugh. 'But won't you want to sell it?'

Peter laughed.

'That would be like giving away a goldmine. Apartments aren't that easy to come by. No, I'm hanging on to it.'

'Or let it?'

Hugh supposed that Peter's tenure of Tikki's affections was far from freehold, and that he expected to be back in his own apartment before long.

'It's on Riverside Drive, so I can sublet it through the university. I'm at Columbia. I'm not going to do a thing about it till the fall.'

Hugh was glad to agree.

'Well, that's settled. Give me a call at this number tomorrow, and we'll fix all the details. Tell me about the concerto.'

'It's a violin concerto. Boris Reinhardt is conducting it with the Washington Philharmonic in September.'

'Wow,' said Peter. 'That sounds tremendous. And you say you haven't finished it yet?'

'Well, there are a few things . . .' Hugh began, then he smiled and confessed: 'No, I haven't.'

'That's an exciting life you lead, Mr Howard,' said Peter, in admiration.

'Yes,' said Hugh. 'I'm getting a bit panicky about it.'

'Now don't tell me,' said Peter. 'Perlman's going to play it.'

'I wish he would. No, it's a very young new girl called Katey Ottodici. She was the wunderkind at the Juilliard a few years ago. Perhaps you saw the feature about her in *Time?*'

'Oh, perhaps I did. It rings a bell,' said Peter. 'Well, look. Lots of luck to you.'

He laughed, and clapped Hugh on the shoulder with enough genuine bonhomie not to seem dismissive. He looked about him.

'There must be somebody here you really want to meet,' he said.

'Don't worry about me,' said Hugh. 'I'm perfectly happy.'

'What about Liz's prize exhibit? You must know Sammy West, I suppose?'

'I know of him, of course. But I've never met him. I think I probably thought he was dead.'

21

'Oh no, Sammy goes on for ever. Did you know that he was still at college when he wrote *How do you do da?*'

'I might have guessed it.'

'Oh, barbed comment,' said Peter.

'No, no,' said Hugh. 'I mean it's that sort of musical. Full of high spirits. A bit old-fashioned.'

'You don't like musicals, I suppose.'

'On the contrary,' said Hugh. 'I share the poet Auden's view that *Kiss me Kate* is much more fun than *The Taming of the Shrew*.'

'You bet,' said Peter.

'And West is absolutely in the Cole Porter tradition, isn't he? A one-man show, a little less sophisticated than Porter, perhaps. But you mean to say that Sammy West is *here*? Tonight?'

'He sure is,' said Peter. 'In fact, you can see him through there, look. On the chesterfield.'

Hugh peered over shoulders, through a cigarette haze, into the further room where he could just make out a heavy man in a grey suit talking to Johnny T and a black girl with a flower in her hair.

'That's Sammy West?' said Hugh. 'He looks too young.'

'I expect he's sold his soul in return for eternal youth,' said Peter. 'Anyway, his big successes were all in the fifties, weren't they?'

'I suppose so,' said Hugh. '*Fairway Hotel* and *Silver Dollar*, certainly.'

'He's rather gone to ground since, hasn't he? That makes you feel he must be older. He's in his sixties, I imagine.'

'Has he in fact written anything since *More's the City*?' asked Hugh.

'That's just it,' replied Peter. 'It was so panned by the critics that he retired to lick his wounds. Did you know that Tikki's mother was in it?'

'Never!' laughed Hugh, thinking of his hostess's tweeds.

'Yes,' said Peter. 'That's how they met. Shows you how long ago it was.'

'He must be rich enough not to bother. He must get a sizeable income just from "This can't be all",' said Hugh. In a sudden mood of mingled envy, nostalgia and headiness from the champagne he had drunk, he paid tribute to West's most famous song by crooning, 'This . . . can't be all!,' at which one of the waiters appeared at his elbow to fill up his glass.

'Ethel Merman in *Silver Dollar*,' said Peter, in pleased recognition. Hugh nodded.

'Her best role,' added Peter.

'Ah, but you would have been too young to see her on stage. The film wasn't the same thing at all.'

'They never are. The magic evaporates somehow. Come on, I'll introduce you.'

3

Sammy West seemed to be settled on the sofa for the evening with the air of a potentate holding an audience. New arrivals perched where they could, or sometimes others were forced to make way for them, often in mid-sentence. He never moved to accommodate them on the sofa, but sat with one arm along its back in an attitude of self-absorbed and mildly pained exhaustion, like a large relaxed dog. He kept a cigarette between his fleshy lips even while he talked, and his talk was of the anecdotal kind that showed little interest in the guests who were brought to see him, and varied not at all with the make-up of the company. His only acknowledgment of Hugh was a benign glare, an ash-scattering nod, and a brief grunt.

'Nice tunes,' he said, when he was told who Hugh was. He waved his arm, adding: 'This is Hugh Howard, for those of you who don't know. For those of you who want to know.'

He didn't introduce anyone to Hugh, and it was left to Johnny T to indicate briefly a young man perched on the arm of the sofa and the girl with the flower in her hair. She was powdery and plump, and the flower seemed, somewhat improbably, to be a gardenia.

'Chuck,' said Johnny T. 'And the Baroness.'

23

'Hi,' said Chuck.

The Baroness sneezed.

Since Hugh was looking in her direction at that moment, he caught with particular attention that helpless bitter grimace of indrawn breath that precedes its expulsion at speeds of over a hundred miles an hour. There was something about her face at that instant that was childlike and vulnerable, a kind of disbelieving self-absorption that abstracted her from her social self and drew her concentration, and the instinctively alerted features which focused it, into an utterly remote private world which seemed to the outsider somewhere between comedy and pain.

'Bless you,' said Hugh, as the sneeze thumped into her handkerchief.

When she opened her eyes she was still looking at him. For a second Hugh was aware of an unsought intimacy, both in his attention to the involuntary withdrawal of her sneeze and in the exchange of glances which followed it. His first impression of her, albeit brief, vague and generalised, had been of withdrawal or tolerated boredom. In contrast with the leisurely animation of Sammy West, the dapper presence of Johnny T, and the attendant homage of the goggling Chuck, she had presented, in the few seconds it had taken Hugh to approach the sofa, a distinct air of sufferance, of being, however comfortable, somehow apart.

The sneeze seemed to break a spell, however, for without avoiding Hugh's gaze her face broke into a broad smile. It was an accident of greeting that bypassed all formalities of politeness. Its apologetic radiance demanded, and obtained, an instant complicity. Hugh felt the smile as a complex physical symbol, compounded of sexual magnetism, an obscure appeal for rescue and a mysterious gratitude for the token protection of Hugh's watchfulness during the instant of the sneeze. For who, when they sneeze, do not fear that they are about to lose consciousness for a crucial and unspecified period of time?

'Thank you,' said the Baroness. 'I've got a lulu of a cold.'

'That's your Id trying to destroy your voice,' said Sammy West. 'Why are you so guilty about your career?'

24

She rolled her eyes at what was clearly a predictable response and grinned again at Hugh.

'He's a clever man,' she said. 'But he don't know nothing.'

Sammy made no reply to this. He had resumed the story he had been telling when Hugh had arrived, an account of contracts badly drawn up and the mayhem that ensued. The face that from a distance had seemed to Hugh too young for his likely age now betrayed itself as only precariously shored up against ruin. The hair looked dyed, the skin strangely taut across the jowls, the complexion merely a cardio-vascular or alcoholic pink. It was a naturally mournful visage that had been stitched together against collapse. At a theatrical distance the effect was fiftyish and well-groomed; in a *tête-à-tête* the tell-tale details were inescapably septuagenarian, eyes leaking like egg-white into the cheeks, inspired dentistry.

Johnny T was laughing at the story.

'You'd better not be listening to this, Hugh,' he said, 'unless you trust your agent like your own mother.'

'Oh, I do, I do. I think she gets it more or less right,' said Hugh.

Sammy threw back his head and wheezed with laughter.

'"She"?' he exclaimed. 'Perhaps your agent *is* your mother?'

'A lot of English agents are women,' said Hugh. 'They can drive a pretty hard bargain.'

'Don't I know it,' said Johnny T, ruefully.

'It's true of all women,' said Sammy, with a categorical pat of cigarette ash into the air. 'They're in a one hundred per cent fix. They need that overkill to convince themselves that they want anything at all. Otherwise, if you see what I mean, they can't bargain on getting anything they bargain for.'

'Bargain *basement*,' said the Baroness, with an emphatic and contemptuous sniff. She sounded as though she hadn't meant to be heard, and Sammy took no notice.

'But maybe a female agent makes some kind of sense,' he continued. 'Think of all we suffer at the hands of women. Agents and patients created He them, female and male, doers and sufferers! Don't you find it's like being tucked up by a nurse? I expect she draws up

25

your contracts like making hospital corners. When she collects her ten per cent it must feel like giving a blood sample. She's your agent and you're the patient.'

Chuck snorted with sycophantic laughter, as Sammy ground out his cigarette on an ashtray on the table in front of him.

The talk went on, and as long as Sammy had an audience he didn't seem to care what he said or to whom. Hugh was neither perturbed nor disappointed at the performance. In his youth he had sat at the feet of the great and been unenlightened: silence from the folk symphonist, smut from the middle-aged *enfant terrible*. Parties were glittering arenas for such trials of mediocrity and combats of the banal, designed to flatter the untalented and to victimise genius, to level the emperor and saint.

Hugh was much more interested in the girl. Who was this 'Baroness' already mentioned that evening by Olive Dempster as having captured the attention of *The New Yorker*? Although probably not out of her twenties, she had a matronly air; nothing quite like her way of dressing up for the evening could have been seen for thirty years or more. Her bosom was hauntingly generous, her jaw rounded, the chin and throat smooth and full, and yet her fingers were thin and delicate, turning the well-used handkerchief as though it were a second gardenia whose petals must not be shed. Her nostrils were wide, and there was a raffish curl to her lip. Something about the way she seemed rooted to the sofa despite her evident sullenness suggested a girlish uncertainty about how to carry herself at this sort of party, yet she had an unquestionable assurance of her own. She was certainly not gauche or shy, and if she had been brought by Sammy West, nonetheless her manner proclaimed that she belonged to no one. And she had a cold.

If Sammy had brought her, he showed little sign of it. He reserved his most rogueish smiles for Chuck, and after Johnny T had been replaced by Tanya on the sofa it was in Tanya's direction that he most often turned his poached eyes. But wherever he looked, it was less out of interest in others than to make sure of his audience. He used faces as sounding boards, and was impatient at interruptions. Tanya was already tight, and she began to respond to Sammy more positively than his monologues required. At one point he paused to remove her hand from his knee as though it were a spider.

Hugh found himself looking at the Baroness for signs of any reaction to all this. But all she did was give the occasional sniffle. Once when she caught him glancing in her direction she threw him another friendly smile. Hugh smiled back. He realised that he did not much care if she did show signs of jealousy or sulkiness, nor if she saw him looking at her. He felt no need to contrive an expression of conspiracy or sympathy. Hers was simply a face that required to be looked at, and Hugh had drunk enough champagne to look at it without embarrassment.

Perhaps it was as well, however, that he was drawn away from the circle around Sammy West by a tap on the shoulder. It was only as Olive Dempster retrieved him that he realised that he had been kneeling at the Baroness's feet and gaping up at her like a schoolboy.

Olive wanted him to talk to a young colleague of hers who was an admirer of his work and intended to write a freelance piece for a new monthly.

'I almost hadn't the heart to drag you away from the Baroness,' said Olive. 'But you would be doing Ellen a great favour if you could tell her a few little things about yourself. Nothing too technical, I expect. It's a paper about people but not too much about what interests people. Except that they think people interest people.'

'Don't they?' asked Hugh.

'Of course they do, of course they do,' said Olive, clutching at Hugh's sleeve. 'But I like to do my living at first hand. Don't you?'

Hugh could see Ellen standing at an awkward distance from them, too near to pretend to be doing something else, too far to be eavesdropping. She looked as unhappy as a child who can't catch being made to join in a game.

'Tell me,' said Hugh quickly. 'Who is this Baroness? Is she a singer? She's not really a Baroness, I presume?'

'No, no,' replied Olive. 'She's Virginia Gerald. You're bound to have heard her. She's suddenly all the rage.'

Of course, thought Hugh, feeling that he had known it all along. Her music had been in his head all month. It almost had the status of a public commodity, like water or newspapers. And its own special mood of strange chances and erotic possibility, particularly in songs like 'When You're Looking Around For Love' and 'Tell It Me Again', made it all the less unlikely that Virginia Gerald herself should be thrown in his path. His sense of prior knowledge of the encounter rose in his blood like an acknowledgment of agreeable drunkenness.

'Isn't she a strange creature?' said Olive. 'Why do overweight girls always overdress? Look at those white platform shoes, for goodness' sake.'

Hugh had no need to look.

'She has a glorious voice, though,' went on Olive. 'It's no wonder that she's got Sammy West writing again.'

'He's writing for her? asked Hugh.

'Oh yes,' replied Olive. 'He's written all her latest songs. Quite a bit of luck for her, if you ask me.'

In Hugh's head the words and music unfolded as clearly as from a tape:

'A story's going round
That has a tender sound:
Tell it me again.'

Now there was a difference. The song was authenticated by a physical presence which it had also somehow mysteriously heralded, a body and its history alive in a crowded apartment on Park Avenue but fatally linked to the tentative, throaty, inviting performance that had so entranced Hugh. The sound was somehow less strange than the person, as though art were the discovery of a natural state of being which had been lost to the imperfect clumsiness of its approximated embodiment in actual men and women. How lucid, simple and innocent it seemed! The reality borrowed its reflected glory, essentially lumpish flesh transfigured by its captive and eloquent emotions.

Hugh had consented to talk to the earnest Ellen, and did so with that unforced kindliness that is born of perfect good humour. His mind was elsewhere.

Elizabeth Crail decided that her party was going extremely well. Peter had been doing sterling work with all the more awkward guests, quite like an affectionate and dutiful son-in-law. And Tikki hadn't been hanging round his neck all the time, either, which was a relief. Roger was bored, of course, but at least he didn't have to do anything, and she was determined to pretend not to notice that he had slipped away to his study for almost three quarters of an hour. Everyone seemed happy. Even the Richardsons were still here, she noticed. And Tanya hadn't done anything terrible.

Surely it was the perfect moment to ask Sammy West to play something? It gave people a respite from talking (and from listening, too, she reflected, which could sometimes be just as tiring). It lent the evening some shape. It created a sort of parabola within which it provided a focus, a climax of pleasure, and after which the evening, while not ceasing to be as much fun as before, could decently wind itself up. One more filling of glasses, and the bar could close and Stewarts' men go home. Everyone would reflect upon such careful arrangement, she felt, with a wistful gratitude and admiration: 'We had such a *good* time at the Crails', didn't we?'

Sammy was absolutely delighted to protest that his fingers didn't work any more and that no one wanted to hear him anyway and to be almost carried, laughing and dismissive, to the piano stool. He sat there, looking larger than ever in front of the baby grand. He looked as if he were about to drive it away.

He had successfully kept the ballet at bay all evening. He knew that Johnny Tierentanz desperately wanted to choreograph a new production of *Silver Dollar* for the Met, and he wanted to strangle that notion before it was a week older. He knew what they'd do to it, and was determined to have no part in some highbrow put-down. He'd strung Johnny along, and kept him from his chums. He'd shown Tanya where to get off, and snubbed that Howard fellow. Now the evening was his own.

For a moment he looked solemn. His fingers climbed the great stairway of the octaves, paused, and then twinkled down its balustrade in chromatic fourths and thirds. People had moved expectantly into the big room, and there was some shushing.

He looked up at his audience, raising his profile slightly in a parody of theatrical pianism and slightly deepening his upper lip.

From beneath his fingers issued a grotesque and yet scrupulously remembered version, molto andante and with staccato wrong-note harmony, of the wedding march from *Beatrice and Benedick*. There were a few titters at this outrage, and Hugh found himself reddening as one or two smiling faces turned to see how he was taking it.

Sammy bowed over the keyboard in an agony of concentration, the chords thickening improbably, until suddenly he raised his head with a false pert grin and moved into a brightly syncopated medley from *How do you do da?*

There was a delighted burst of applause.

Hugh looked round the room. Tikki and Peter were standing in the doorway with linked arms. Tikki was nodding in time to the music. Ellen, who was still standing near him, seemed star-struck. The Richardsons looked nostalgic.

This is the sort of music that people want to hear, he thought. But he found the familiar melodies too engaging to feel despondent. This music was written before I was born, he then reflected. It was no wonder that its idiom spoke not only feelingly at the composer's hands, but with the authority that pre-existent art borrows from history. Hugh could conceive of nothing that he had actually experienced as being historical, but this facile brilliant tune was a small yet recognisable part of his heritage, a flourish on the contract of his given world. His mother had sung it. It had been recorded on 78s. It was indeed a part of history.

Across the room Olive Dempster gave him an owlish wink, while from the opposite corner a moment later there was heard, distinct though discreetly muffled, another sneeze.

4

Hugh shifted uncomfortably in his bed. He was at the age when sleep was beginning to elude him, though he was not yet willing to admit insomnia. It was like the gradual infrequency of erotic encounters that must precede an unvowed celibacy. Like love, or like the illusion of it, sleep was not slow to appear, although it departed too soon. And since sleep was itself the great stage of rehearsed passion, its fading at odd hours brought Hugh face to face with his small abrupted fantasies. Waking with a slight dorsal cramp, he was immediately in the shaming position of scrutinising some receding accomplishment, like a train he had failed to catch. Similarly, in the reverie attendant upon the expectation of sleep, his mind strayed over hopes as uncertain as rumours, possibilities that only somnolence could begin to verify, and that a sudden wakefulness was forced to dismiss as self-deluding folly. It seemed to him that the body was jealous of the imagination, and would not allow it free play. One hint of a novel delirium, and that sulky organism would pinch itself awake out of pure spite. Was it revenge for those youthful years of circumspection when the body's unbounded stamina had been frustrated by the mind's caution and its fear of puppyish indiscretion?

Half-awake, but not yet ready to enter into full consciousness, Hugh found a more comfortable position. For a moment he assumed that he was in bed at home, and then knew that he was not. Almost simultaneously he remembered that he was in his tiny hotel room and then that that was wrong too: he was in Peter Redmond's apartment, to which he had moved the previous evening. The mattress was wider and harder, the sheets cooler and cleaner. His hand slid easily beneath the pillow.

This slight effort of orientation served to evaporate any precise memory of his waking dream. There remained only the generalised, though still pungent, sense of intimacy and adventure. He had been far away, he knew, reckless of circumstances yet somehow in control of danger, accompanied by someone attractive to him but with whom an embrace, even a touch, could be confidently postponed. The postponement, indeed, was less (he knew) a condition of the unspecified danger than something he himself desired from the relationship. Perhaps the objectified and no doubt elaborately landscaped danger was indeed, in some sense, really the same as the relationship. How devious was the sleeping mind!

'Damn,' thought Hugh, turning again to enjoy a further area of coolness in the bed. He knew now that he would puzzle over the lost detail of the dream, and that neither reason nor bladder would allow him to return to sleep.

On his way back from the bathroom he peered through one of the blinds to gauge the onslaught of the dawn. His resentment was fully satisfied by the ambitious clarity of the morning light and the bulky assurance of the illuminated skyline. Much of New York was no doubt already risen and about its business. It was, in any case, an unsleeping city. At that still and unspecified hour of the night when the sleeper is unwittingly closest to death, roped to the damp sheets of the temporary cradle that is at once a likely shroud and the vessel of his wandering consciousness, there were open stores tiered with the globes of oranges, grapefruit and melons to delight the passer-by, and in the subway the almost-empty cars still hurtled, lit and scribbled, between their terminals. And always there were sirens.

'I have slept through all the alarms of my life,' thought Hugh, climbing back into bed and lighting a cigarette. He surveyed the images of his dream (a quayside, climbing on someone's shoulders, irritation at a lengthy discussion of something) and could not reassemble them into a scenario that explained its undeniable sexual charge.

Whose were the shoulders? Was there a face? All too often the newer faces, incompletely known, dogged him only with their eagerness to be finally fathomed and therefore dismissed. His most disturbing dreams, on the contrary, turned out to have a precise and familiar key: in guilt and regret, and moreover in circumstances of confrontation and explanation that intensified these emotions, he would dream of Daisy.

There was a wardrobe mirror in the bedroom which reflected the sleeper. As Hugh exhaled he glanced into it and was both frightened and amused at what it reflected. The squat and stocky shape beneath the bedclothes, the bony meditating profile angled improbably on the putty-coloured neck and shoulders sunk into the pilllows, the upright arm and fallen wrist with pluming Marlboro attached: these features seemed to him gross and pathetic like a surgical victim reassuming daily habits, like a mortal pharaoh.

Was this the sort of thing that others saw in him, he wondered? There is always a fraction of a second available in which to recompose the expression of the face when a mirror is surprisingly at hand. Nonetheless, one is sometimes caught out in a more or less unguarded approximation of one's public image. Hugh did not care for the solid assertive set of the mouth. It was an opinionated sort of mouth, he felt, less flexible and sardonic than he intended it to be. It was a mouth whose solid contours had been shaped by decades of unconscious response to various forms of social challenge. It was a mouth that too obviously forbade spontaneous interrogation. It was a mouth already looking distinctly old.

Hugh turned again and gave himself a hideously staring and twinkling grin in the mirror. Mirror, mirror, he thought, what a disappointment. You have known more exciting scenes than this, entirely more satisfying offerings to the instantly recording and instantly oblivious deity of silvered glass, perhaps half a century of prolonged and inventive nudity, all the briefest glories of the unrecorded dead. Certainly and most recently the attentions paid by Peter Redmond to the averagely decent upholstery of Miss Tikki Crail, attentions now taking place (with possibly augmented intensity) elsewhere. Hugh imagined making love to Tikki, and could get no further than he would have got if he had attempted to name the English cricket team, and cricket was a game he by no means despised.

He contented himself with the thought that even her actual bodily presence would hardly change this unenthusiastic state of affairs. But what of the really desirable? His mind strayed selectively over those features he had ever encountered which partook of the sexual mystery: the knees of Yvonne Petite, Daisy's smile and encircling arms, Mrs Leathering's bottom, the eyes of the girl in the cheese shop, the whole skin tone of Mary Meadows, Katey Ottodici's chin, Simon's friend Sally's hair. This Frankenstein inventory started to become ridiculous, especially when he began to add guessed-at portions of people he positively hated, like Dixie Polejack, or flatly contradictory anatomies like the flat ribcage and muscled armpits of Tanya Czejarek in juxtaposition with Virginia Gerald's bosom and shoulders. The answer was that the mystery resided in none of these. The key was in the ensemble. And in the reality.

Hugh decided that it was time to get up. He stubbed out his cigarette and padded into the kitchen to investigate once again the refrigerator whose contents Peter had urged him to consume. There had not seemed to be much in it the night before, and there did not seem to be much in it now except for a walnut-sized piece of butter in its wrinkled wrapper, a dead lettuce, some oranges and the end of a bottle of vodka. Some further hunting produced a cardboard envelope of bacon and some taramosalata. Hugh decided against doing anything with the oranges. He put the butter in a pan and unpeeled the bacon into it. It was not what Hugh called proper bacon, which had in his opinion to consist of slices about fourteen inches long and one-eighth of an inch thick from a full side of pig, starting with pure lean at least the size of the palm of his hand and tapering to the rich streak of the belly. The stuff in the cardboard envelope came in wafer-thin uniform strips like bandages and shrivelled to a crisp in the pan as you watched. 'It's the difference between life and death,' thought Hugh.

At least there was plenty of good coffee. After breakfast Hugh washed and dressed and took another pot of it to the table in the living-room on to which he had unloaded his drafts the night before.

For days it had been impossible to get on with the concerto. The hotel had been too hot, and the room at the theatre promised by Johnny T, equipped with a decent piano, turned out to be a sort of *salle de répétition* in miniature, where dancers would come in to collect dumped bags, talk in apologetic whispers, giggle and even unscrew thermos flasks. Hugh did not absolutely need a piano, so was grateful for Peter Redmond's desire to hump Tikki on her home territory. He had managed to trim, at Johnny's insistence, the music for Don John's *pas seul* in the second scene of *Beatrice and Benedick*: its length and complexity had been a constant worry during rehearsals, and now the svelte Belgian who danced the part had put his foot down. Or rather, was refusing to put his foot down. Hugh, who was proud of his bravura writing for tuba, had bridled at first. After all, the tuba player could manage it and it was probably the hardest score he'd ever have to play in his life: why couldn't it be danced? Johnny was adamant, and claimed that it unbalanced the opening anyway. He would have simply made a cut, but the sinuous complexity of the solo part gave no access to his scissors. There had been a few other points needing Hugh's attention, but all in all his work on the ballet was over.

But the concerto was a mess. The first movement, a presto tragico with a rather lachrymose little andantino in the middle, like a soft-centred chocolate, he was still fond of. He conceived it as a tribute to Daisy, and it had turned out to be a sort of sentimentalised portrait in an incongruously ornate and overblown frame, like a child in a storm. The storm was their storm, the storm of their marriage, built upon relentless orchestral ostinati and aggrieved chattering from the violin; but the andantino shone with a bittersweet luminosity, the melody a touch simplistic at first, but deepening on repetition with phrases in canon from the strings alone and some fiendish double-stopping on the fiddle. The resuming presto took on a malicious air, with a version of the andantino melody given to a pair of trumpets with the express purpose, so it seemed, of infuriating the soloist.

The second movement was quite short, consisting of an extended and ruminative melody from the violin played above woodwind alone, followed by an ingenious version of the melody for strings in which the phrases alternated and overlapped or sometimes disappeared altogether in the dense orchestral texture. Finally the soloist re-entered in a higher register and the full orchestra breathed richly beneath it, the effect being like some mythical night bird soaring above a forest on a summer night. There seemed to be nothing for the violin to do at the end except hover and disappear, and Hugh was dissatisfied with this effect. It seemed too 'English', and was certainly old-fashioned.

The third movement, unwritten as yet, needed, Hugh felt, to be a substantial response to the meditative escapism of the largo. The structural temptation was to polish the whole work off with a scherzo, and indeed Hugh had already sketched out a stirring and slightly rumbustious subject, in the character of a fanfare. But it was hopeless. The fanfare was simply an elaborate preparatory flourish for what was inevitable in last movements of this sort, a vulgar rousing tune. Hugh could write such things in his bath, and though it might be perfectly acceptable for a BBC *matinée musicale*, it was not good enough for a serious concerto.

The answer, as he well knew, was that the work was, in his typical fashion, programmatic. It related, as far as was possible, to a crucial emotional staging-post in his own life. The violence and regret of the first movement alone had an achieved reality. Beyond that he had not yet fully travelled. The largo was a sham, a piece of wishful thinking, a self-satisfied display of lyrical twaddle. Since Katey had taken it away and was no doubt at that moment playing it over, perhaps even working on it first as the easier of the completed movements, there was not much that Hugh could do about it. But it might still serve, in its brevity, as a kind of interlude. What, however, was needed now from the third movement was a substantial statement. Where had he come to, in emotional terms? Where was he headed? The next item in the psychological programme was unspecific, confused, non-existent.

Hugh arranged two piles of drafts on the table. On the left a short score in pencil of the first two movements, together with the xerox of the full orchestration that he had handed over to Boris and Katey and a folder of discarded and unused material related to these movements. On the right a small stack of sheets on which he had raced ahead with the facile and over-busy preliminaries of the scherzo, together with some older fragments hoarded for future use, bits and pieces discarded from earlier works which should have remained discarded. A fresh conception was needed. The ending of the concerto had to become, in a sense, a beginning.

Hugh poured himself another cup of coffee, and lit a cigarette. He was mildly distracted by the continuing evidence of Peter's occupancy, books, recently opened letters, a box of chocolates. Would he not suddenly appear to claim these things? Would he not be popping round at all hours to pick up a suit or ask if there had been any telephone messages?

Hugh leaned back in his chair, blowing cigarette smoke towards the ceiling, hearing in his head the last bars of the largo. He imagined the shifting of an audience, a cough or two, the relaxation of the conductor, the soloist's testing of a string. The conductor would, after a moment, raise his baton. The orchestra would be poised for the finale. The baton would descend. What sounds would ensue?

Hugh sensed that he needed troubled strings, the slow working-out of a problem that had not yet been resolved, something dissonant and counterpointed, perhaps even a fugue. A phrase came into his head, a rising flattened sixth followed by a drop to the third, which he scribbled down in case it should lead to anything. He felt like an infant playing with building blocks.

When the telephone rang, he was almost relieved to be interrupted. It was Olive Dempster.

'I'm afraid Peter's not here, Olive,' said Hugh. 'He's moved in with Tikki and lent me the apartment.'

'Yes, I know,' said Olive. 'Young men didn't do that in my day. No one does it now in my day, for that matter, only in someone else's day. Or night. If you see what I mean.'

'I do see what you mean, Olive,' replied Hugh.

'No, dear,' she went on. 'It's you I want. I've just been speaking to

Peter as a matter of fact, and he tells me you're working like crazy on a new piece.'

'I'm crazy all right,' complained Hugh. 'But that's because I'm not working. I mean, I'm trying to. But it's one of those days.'

'Give it a chance. It may yet blossom and be fruitful. I'm hardly up yet myself.'

'Well, I feel like going back to bed,' said Hugh.

'You'll get over it. Make some coffee and shackle yourself to your chair. Don't answer the telephone.'

'I've had four cups of coffee already, and if I wasn't answering the telephone I wouldn't be talking to you now, Olive.'

'Nor you would,' said Olive, unperturbed. 'I'm calling to see if you would like to come with me to Willa's Place next Tuesday. It's a nightclub. Have you heard of it?'

'No, I hadn't,' said Hugh.

'Don't sound so terrified, Hugh,' laughed Olive. 'There's a reason for asking you, and I don't suppose it's what you think it is. I don't know if I made it clear, but I truly am writing that *New Yorker* article on Virginia Gerald, though I rather wish that I weren't. I'm going along to hear her perform and I wouldn't mind a bit of professional advice at my elbow.'

Hugh felt a sudden thrilled conviction of interest.

'But I'm afraid I know nothing about that kind of music,' he said. 'I should love to come, of course.'

'Come then,' said Olive. 'I want someone who knows about music, period. Dan Fleischman is coming to take some photographs, so we'll be a nice little party.'

'Well, thank you,' said Hugh.

'Don't mention it,' said Olive. 'You've got to be shown the sights. Besides . . .'

Here Olive did the best that can be achieved in the way of winking over the telephone.

' . . . we all noticed how taken you were with the Baroness. Don't tell me you're not just aching to hear her sing!'

Hugh protested.

'Don't deny it,' cried Olive. 'It's not gallant. You had eyes for nobody else at the Crails', and who can blame you? And you didn't even know who she was.'

Hugh was privately forced to admit it.

'I'll call for you at eight,' she said decisively. 'We'll meet up with Dan at Willa's Place.'

For the rest of the day he did nothing but work. He actually wrote very little, but he tore up a good deal. The right-hand pile of m s s was considerably diminished by the time that he wandered over to Broadway to buy a spinach blintz at the university delicatessen. By mid-afternoon it had almost disappeared.

Not for the first time he noticed how everybody on the street looked more absolutely like themselves than their counterparts would have done in a London street. It was a matter of self-confidence, he supposed, a superb achievement of self-realisation, a sense of being able to offer to the world a wholly satisfactory image of what you had decided to be. Rich or poor, black or white, beautiful or ugly, young or old, the normal polarities of privilege counted for nothing. It was a matter of style. You could loaf or importune with style. You could walk a basset-hound or hail a cab with style. You could sell a spinach blintz as though it were an uncut diamond.

Did he have to come to New York, Hugh wondered, in order to tear up all his work?

5

There was a marked contrast between the band at Willa's Place and its clientele. Indeed, they almost looked as though they should have changed places: at the tables the young in casual clothes, on the rostrum businesslike men in their late fifties, in suits. It was small, smoky and dark, and the cheapest drink cost $6.50.

Hugh felt overdressed in the suit he had worn for the Crails', the only suit he had brought but felt obliged to wear for any occasion. Olive was in a tartan shirt and boots, looking like a silent film comedian playing a dwarf lumberjack. Dan Fleischman was in a sort of dirty white battledress, and was hung about with beads and photographic pouches. If Hugh had imagined that a nightclub would be anything like its cinema image, he was mistaken. No maître d'hôtel showed them to their table, no one stood up to ask other members of their party to dance, there were no ice buckets on stands. In fact no one seemed to be dancing at all.

'People have forgotten how to dance,' explained Olive. 'In my day you danced, and you danced with somebody. You held on to them. It was wonderful. Then they started flinging you about. And after that they simply danced at you. Well, that's just not good enough is it? They ended up dancing at whoever happened to be within spitting distance. Then dancing by themselves.'

'It's self-expression,' said Dan. 'You want to bring back the foxtrot?'

'Why not!' cried Olive. 'That's what dancing was all about. One man and one woman. And a rhythm.'

'These kids dig the rhythm all right,' said Dan. 'That's what they've come for. The man-woman bit, they can do that anywhere.'

'The beasts,' sighed Olive. 'You're right, Dan. That's the reason.'

'I think it's rather splendid that they come for the music,' said Hugh.

It was true that they came for the music. Nursing their obligatory beer or bourbon like a ticket stub, they greeted the opening bars of each new number with a murmur of appreciative welcome, even a ripple of applause, and listened with a nodding attention. The players performed effortlessly, but not without a kind of private attention to the matter at hand, as though working out a long-pondered problem that it was really no business of anyone else to overhear. They would meet every night to solve it whether anybody turned up to listen or not. Public appreciation was an irrelevance. But not quite. When, after a particularly involved wrangle between the valve trombone and the tenor saxophone, vying the one with the other in argumentative grunts and squiggles, the drummer rapped an insistent call to order and the whole ensemble relaxed into a final and melodically satisfying chorus, the players would smile at each other and bask in the audience's pleasure. Or were those mutual glances a kind of condescension? As if to say: 'They applaud because we've finished, but the problem is still there. They don't know how difficult it is.'

These self-absorbed senior citizens of cool jazz played with a grudging air as if forced to demonstrate some arcane domestic hobby. One of them would bend down and produce some new unlikely instrument (a french horn, say) with a weariness that bordered on truculence. The ensuing counterpoint, though richly inventive, was played so drily, and with so many pauses, that the effect was to minimise the required virtuosity. The texture of the whole ensemble, indeed, was challengingly sparse: the clarinet featured more breath and clacking stops than tone; the tenor contented himself with brief phrases in very low register while the tune was often given to the trombone; the pianist made fierce and isolated jabs at the keyboard, grimacing at the occasional necessity of producing a brief sequence of chorus-identifying chords. And yet the few notes that each instrument produced were somehow welded into a marvellously varied and intelligent whole in which, as in a kind of pointillisme, the argument of the music was, if occasionally elusive to the ear, always triumphantly emergent. It was music that the listener, if attentive, could catch up with, but which for most of the time moved just a few bars ahead of his full comprehension. They played mainstream classics like 'Tenderly', 'East of the Sun' and 'What a Little Moonlight Can Do'.

'Who are they?' asked Hugh. 'There seems something familiar about it.'

'Yeah,' said Dan. 'Some of these characters were famous once. The one with the outsize bandit moustache is Bob Gordon. Played with Bud Shank, Lee Konitz and that crowd. The arrangements are his. The trombonist is Chuck Stolmundsen, believe it or not. You've probably heard most of them at one time or another, old Herman sidemen who had their own groups in the fifties.'

'West Coast?' asked Hugh.

'That's it,' said Dan.

'Didn't Stolmundsen play with Gerry Mulligan?'

'For a time,' said Dan.

'I see,' said Hugh. That explained the cool and colourful style of the band. Unlike the Baroness they were not new, but nor were they a scratch collection of serviceable nonentities. And if they were not on the way up, they had known what it was to be up, and they did not give the impression of being down. The way down seemed unthinkable: they had a different way of measuring artistic success. Perhaps it was precisely for musicians of their collective aplomb that the term 'way out' had been coined. Never really up or down, but out.

'They've really got that old sound together again, haven't they?' remarked Dan, dismantling part of his camera on the table.

'Come on,' said Olive, who was surreptitiously taking notes of the conversation. 'You're making them out to be a whole generation of Rip Van Winkles. How have they been keeping alive these last twenty-five years?'

Dan shrugged. 'You're the one who should know all this,' he said, wiping a filter.

'Listen,' said Olive. 'I'm not the music critic. This is strictly from the sociological angle, you understand.'

'Sure, I understand,' said Dan.

Olive was flushed and excited, and had already finished her whiskey. She insisted on ordering more drinks all round.

'Look, Dan,' she went on. 'The Baroness I can cope with, but I'm not going to interview the band. Give me an angle.'

'Olive, I've told you all I know,' said Dan. 'Gordon was lured by one of the studios out there and wrote a lot of soap music. You know that sort of bongo city stuff when Starsky claps a red light on the roof of his car and burns a lot of rubber, right? Well, Gordon invented all that kind of TV music.'

'What a fate,' said Hugh.

'Maybe he had problems,' said Dan. 'He can still produce this stuff anyway. His old Decca records were re-issued a few years back. Maybe that brought him into the daylight again.'

'Willa's Place isn't exactly the humming centre of things,' said Olive.

'Look around you,' replied Dan. 'Look at these kids' faces. They're all going to be proud of having been here and heard the Baroness. One day they'll be telling their children.'

'You bet,' said Olive. 'But why isn't she at Carnegie Hall already?'

'She's curiously dated, isn't she?' asked Hugh. 'I mean, it's the sound of a singer with a band. She's nothing like your pop star.'

'So what?' snorted Olive. 'It's about time we had some real music again.'

'Oh, I absolutely agree with you,' said Hugh hastily. 'I think she's wonderful.'

Olive grinned at him, and Hugh felt himself blushing. Dan caught the exchange, raised his eyebrows and went on fiddling with his camera.

After the next number there was a longer pause than usual, and the buzz of expectation grew among the audience. What little light there was dimmed further, and a spot came on in front of the band.

'Here we go,' said Olive.

Hugh felt a peculiar tightening in his throat, which he so rarely felt these days that it took him a second to identify as pure excitement. A man wearing black tie in the only concession to formality that Willa's Place seemed to allow came forward adjusting a microphone into which, bending slightly, he spoke haltingly and almost apologetically. He stood too close, so that his words boomed and blurred in the low-ceilinged room.

'Ladies and gentlemen,' he said, scanning the room as though looking for someone. 'This is what you've been waiting for, I know. I don't need to introduce the lady you've come to hear. She's in the charts. She's in your hearts. The Baroness of the Blues. Ladies and Gentlemen, Virginia Gerald!'

As the band struck up 'Tell It Me Again' in what Hugh had barely time to notice was an unbelievably fast tempo, the Baroness emerged from the blackness into the spotlight. The compère touched her elbow, as though straightening a painting, and disappeared. She stood there in front of the microphone, and the applause was total.

What had Hugh expected? He knew this song, which had virtually become her signature tune. He had sat with her at close quarters, almost talking to her. He had been introduced, and she had sneezed and smiled at him. But there was something more, much more, that he wanted from this occasion. It was partly the confirmation of her genius that hearing her in performance would or would not ensure. It was the curiosity to see an artist at the centre of her living mystery. It was this, yes, but it was still more.

As she stepped forward she raised her palms slightly, and, as though choosing the moment arbitrarily, she began the song. The band was with her, and they did not let up. Hugh estimated the difference in metronome markings between the recording he knew and this hectic rendering to be the difference between ♩ = 80 and ♩ = 120. In fact she sounded to be singing it twice as fast, teased by the tenor obbligato into a confiding and infectious enthusiasm that quite transformed the song:

> 'A story's going round
> That has a tender sound:
> Tell it me again.'

Hugh was only vaguely conscious of being transfixed by what was in effect a tremendous *coup de théâtre*. The audience was silent and charmed. He did not care if he was seen to be spellbound too, jaw dropped, insanely and sympathetically smiling. This radically new interpretation of her most familiar song was a challenge conceived and executed in the highest confidence in her art. The subtle timbre of the voice, even at this speed, was beyond question a gift of the rarest kind, and if that lingering cold contributed a touch of sandpaper to the velvet, it fitted the contagious erotic knowingness of the song:

> 'The story's so compelling,
> It thrills me in the telling.
> Tell it me again.

The characters are so familiar
It makes me shy to hear
What they are thinking of and where
They're going to.
The lights are right and you are near:
Perhaps it's true!
You know it's up to you
And how I want you to
Tell it me again.'

Hugh had barely time to notice the new effects produced at this tempo, the mockery behind the naive breaking up of the syllables in 'fam-il-i-ar', the infinitesimal delay at 'shy' that lent an incalculable sexual challenge to the confession, the rough near-lisp of 'lights'. The song was over almost as soon as it had begun, leaving only the drummer's flourish with the cymbals to blur into the enthusiasm of the audience.

But the Baroness was still there, acknowledging the applause with the slight raising of one hand, palm downwards, with a nod or two, with a self-absorbed smile. Like the song, she seemed different. At the Crails' she had contentedly sat in her own portable universe, largely silent, though alert to the conversations that came her way. She had been like a girl allowed to stay up, a girl able to wear her mother's clothes at that one moment when adolescent puppy-fat mimics middle-aged girth, a girl who has unnecessarily raided the make-up. Here she was quietly at one with her environment, riding easily on her instinct for the beat of the music, straying confidently from it and tentatively returning, secure in the public attention and acclaim that her performance deserved. Unlike some singers, who use applause as a drug, she established a genuine rapport with the eager faces at the tables beneath her. Their feelings were not something to be devoured, but to be leaned on, like a friendly arm. Her consciousness of their response seemed to give her just the encouragement she needed to do what there was no doubt that she could do anyway.

And she was beautiful! That, perhaps, though Hugh could not have so simply labelled it, was the essence of the transformation. What near to had seemed a fullness of cheek now took on a boldness of jaw, what had offered itself as a comfortable figure was at the distance of the stage merely stature: Virginia was a tall girl and she hardly needed that fortyish cut to her dress (it was what used to be called a 'gown') to emphasise her shoulders.

Olive cut into Hugh's reverie:

'That girl knows what she's doing, right?' she said, leaning towards Hugh as they applauded.

Hugh nodded.

'Some singers,' she went on in a hoarse whisper as the applause subsided, 'are just creations of the recording studio. Not this one.'

The Baroness spoke.

'Thank you very much, ladies and gentlemen. That was a little song written for me by Mr Sammy West. I'd like now to sing for you another of his songs. It's a very well-known song, from his show *Silver Dollar*: "This Can't Be All".'

There was a ripple of approval at this, and someone at the back of the room called out: 'It's enough for me, baby!' This was followed by laughter, and some shushing, as the band struck up again.

Once more the tempo seemed unusually fast to Hugh, but that might have been due to the racing angular tenor solo with which they unfashionably began. There was no attempt to establish the tune until the Baroness's entry, which was effected without any apparent musical clue from the instrumentalists, bang in the middle of a descending chromatic run from Bob Gordon, who continued his delicious gibbering and squirting throughout the first verse:

'Someone must have told you
Or maybe I cajoled you?
For here you sprawl
Letting me enfold you
Like a waterfall.
It's wonderful to hold you.
This can't be all.'

46

The Baroness freely reinvented the tune and made it if anything more delirious by accommodating it to the narrower intervals of speech. The pianist took over from Bob Gordon, and this time her entry was in the middle of an ascending run:

> 'We share each other's dreams.
> We can recite their themes
> With total recall.
> Our mouths join at the seams
> Like a tennis ball.
> I could write reams and reams.
> This can't be all.'

Next it was the turn of the drummer:

> 'Your breath is sweet and heady.
> Squeeze me, I'm unsteady.
> I feel so small!
> I'm bruised, but ripe and ready
> Like a windfall.
> Down to the core already?
> This can't be all.'

The arrangement allowed for an extended percussion riff on 'bruised' which the Baroness accompanied with a free improvisation on the following syllable 'but'. She was obliged to half-turn to gauge the drummer's intentions, and they were perfectly together as they nodded their way through the distraction and into the rest of the verse, where they were joined by a muted trumpet. The trumpeter was in charge for the following verse:

> 'It must be blasphemy
> To think you'll tire of me.
> I'm walking tall.
> It's physiology!
> It's a free-for-all!
> Can it be good for me?
> This can't be all.'

47

All the instruments entered busily during this verse, and the arrangement continued without vocal accompaniment for some time. The band were pleased with themselves, putting down and taking up instruments, the drummer stirring and shaking his cylinders: it was the musical equivalent of a Chinese kitchen. Towards the end of this mélange Chuck Stolmundsen came in with what in effect was the first clear rendering of the tune more or less as Sammy West wrote it. Hugh found himself smiling out of sheer pleasure. The affectionate distancing of this delayed tribute to the music they were purporting to be playing, turning it into a kind of quotation, seemed utterly simple and charming. Stolmundsen maintained the melody to the end and, within the spare harmonies of the arrangement, West's original conception sounded at once dated and fresh, as though it were the unspoiled essence of what the instruments had been striving for:

> 'I am the pussycat.
> I am the belle dame that
> Hath thee in thrall.
> I am the autocrat
> Of Liberty Hall.
> I know just what I'm at.
> This can't be all.'

The last notes of the song were lost in the cheers, and the voice at the back in a tone of fond rebuke and wonder called out: 'Virginyah!' She sang more songs, mostly familiar ballads from the thirties and forties, but with a noticeable sprinkling of later West items.

'So she's singing Sammy's earlier stuff as well,' said Olive. 'She's really into that old monster.'

'They're good songs, Olive,' said Dan.

'Oh sure, sure,' admitted Olive.

A young black man in a black roll-neck sweater came up to their table and asked them if they were the party that wanted to interview Miss Gerald. When Olive said that they were, he looked uncertainly at Dan and Hugh as if he could not believe that the two men did not have a say in the matter.

'Do you want us to come backstage?' Olive asked.

'Miss Gerald can come out here easy,' he said.

'It might be a little noisy here,' said Olive thoughtfully. 'If you've got somewhere backstage.'

The man shrugged.

'Backstage noisy too,' he said economically. Olive began to talk the problem through, but already he had sauntered away. It wasn't long before the Baroness had finished her session, and had retired, waving and smiling without a hint of effusiveness at the ovation she received. Olive seemed at a loss.

'What do we do now?' she wondered. 'Will she come out here or won't she?'

'Look,' said Dan. 'I think we're being asked to go round.'

He nodded towards the door through which the singer had disappeared. The compère had caught Dan's eye and was beckoning them over. They got up to go, and Hugh, half in parsimony and half in embarrassment, found himself carrying away his drink. As they edged between the tables he realised too late that it was an idiotic thing to do.

6

They were shown to what appeared to be the Baroness's dressing room, except that its facilities were of the meanest and that it also seemed to serve as a general place of congregation. The young black man in the roll-neck sweater was there, with a small thin man in a suit and hat. The compère also followed them into the room and made himself at home, but at a nod from the man in the hat he went out again and soon reappeared with a bottle and some glasses.

'Drinks on the house,' he said. Hugh, still holding his earlier drink, felt all the more foolish.

Everyone was introduced. The Baroness said that she remembered Olive and Hugh from the Crails' party, and Hugh wanted to believe her. She was unpinning the gardenia from her hair, and asked Dan why he hadn't taken any photographs. Dan explained that he had taken two reels, and that the kind of film he used was so fast that it didn't need a flash. She was intrigued by this, and Dan went on talking about the bright unnatural look of flash-light photographs and the way that the subject starts to play up once they know you are taking them. Hugh was thinking that he hadn't really noticed the gardenia, perhaps because he somehow had come to think of it as a part of her.

The small man in the hat, whose name was Goldbein, said: '*The New Yorker* doesn't print photographs.'

'That's right!' exclaimed Olive, as though he were the brightest boy in the class.

Smiling at his discovery, Goldbein repeated it to the young man in the sweater:

'Hear that, Yellow?' he said. 'No photographs in *The New Yorker*.'

Yellow bared his teeth.

'Man's here under false pretences,' he said gleefully. 'Hey, Baroness, what do you say?'

The Baroness didn't know what to say. She smiled inquiringly at Dan.

'Mr Flashman without the flash,' said Yellow.

Hugh felt uneasy.

'I thought I'd explained,' said Olive. 'Maybe I didn't make it clear. Dan Fleischman is hoping to sell his pictures to *Nightbird*.'

'Yup,' said Dan briefly. And then: 'How about a few more, Miss Gerald?'

He adjusted the camera that was hanging round his neck and Hugh wasn't sure that he hadn't managed to release the shutter secretly even as he asked the question. He was certainly quick on the draw. Hugh hadn't noticed him taking any photographs and had quite forgotten that that was what he had come for. He was the silent cowboy of photographers.

The Baroness looked quickly at Yellow, who turned away. He had stopped laughing.

'Shoot them,' she said to Dan.

'*Nightbird*,' said Yellow. 'That's shit, man, you know that?' Goldbein repeated ruminatively:

'I knew *The New Yorker* didn't print photographs. They got no call for photographs.'

Hugh wondered what could be wrong with *Nightbird*, which he'd never seen. No one seemed to mind about it greatly, however, and once Olive had started her interview Goldbein, Yellow and the compère left the room.

Olive's questions seemed routine to Hugh, who would have expected her to be a rigorous inquisitor. The Baroness fielded them with answers she had obviously given many times before, and the standard story of deprivation, talent and opportunity emerged without a single convincing detail lodging itself in Hugh's very receptive mind. Her closely-bitten nails and the gardenia on the dressing-table told him more.

But it looked as though Olive was only interested in the Baroness's relationship with Sammy West. She soon got on to the question of the West comeback.

'Comeback?' queried the Baroness. 'Honey, he ain't *been* no-where.'

'What drew you to his songs in the first place?' asked Olive.

'Well,' considered the Baroness, sucking in her lower lip. 'I always did like those old songs, you know? They got style. They been thought out.'

'Where did you meet him?'

The Baroness gave a broad grin.

'My mother used to say there are some songs just the shape of your feelings,' she said. 'They fit like a glove and once you got them on there's no getting them off. You just got to wear them out. I sing all that stuff: Kern, Porter, West. They're quality. And you know something, honey?'

'What?' asked Olive.

'They don't ever wear out!'

The Baroness seemed as pleased with this as a philosophy lecturer demonstrating a syllogism. She winked at Hugh in a manner which instantly convinced him that she had indeed remembered the Crails' party and the occasion of the sneeze. There was something special about the wink. Hugh, who could not take his eyes off her and felt that his features were sympathetically linked to hers as if by wires or mirrors, winked back.

He had tremendously mixed feelings about this wink. His conscious mind considered it outrageous, as though he had put his hand on her knee. But instinctively he knew it was right. Her appeal was, he vaguely understood, for support in her fencing with Olive's line of questions about her relationship with West, and he was being appealed to both as a man who would understand about, indeed be used to requiring, discretion; and as a person whose likely affections in the course of his professional activities were powerful enough to seek expression without tolerating such public enquiry. Poor Olive, the wink suggested, was quite otherwise.

This was flagrant prejudice, but since Olive was quite unaware of it, Hugh didn't feel too guilty. Their respective positions, he reflected, were probably quite the reverse.

Olive persisted.

'West has been quoted as saying that popular music today is farming music.'

The Baroness looked puzzled.

'You know,' said Olive. 'Country music, folk music. Rock has those origins. Popularity of the ballad.'

'My folks were farmers,' said the Baroness, as if establishing credentials. 'What are you trying to say?'

Olive was unperturbed.

'I just wondered if Sammy West had ever talked about this with you,' she explained. 'He thinks that songs nowadays are refusing to build upon the gains that jazz made in the thirties and forties, that jazz is essentially city music despite its earliest origins.'

'Search me, honey,' said the Baroness.

'I think West's songs,' said Hugh, coming to the rescue. Are what? What on earth was he going to say? 'Are very sophisticated. I like them a lot.'

'You do?' asked the Baroness. 'Well, I sure am glad about that. I guess he's city music all right. A city slicker, huh?'

She made an ambiguous gesture with her hand to her head. Hugh wasn't sure whether she was tipping an imaginary boater forward or indicating brains. Dan, who had been crouching on the floor in search of the perfect low-angled shot, toppled backwards at that moment and the Baroness burst out laughing.

'You are one persistent photographer, Mr Flashman,' she said. 'You know that?'

Dan smiled.

'You got to go out and get them,' he said. 'And I got that one.'

'That's it!' she said. 'Like a song. You got to *get* it. I can get Sammy's songs all right.'

'Somehow, you know,' said Olive, 'you turn them to your advantage.'

The Baroness wrinkled her brow helplessly at Hugh, as if to say, what have I done wrong now?

Hugh interpreted once again.

'Olive means that you have your own distinctive style. It's true. I felt it very strongly. Whatever you sang, it came across as Virginia Gerald.'

'Oh, sure,' she nodded. 'Hey, what do you expect anyway? That's what it's all about, isn't it?'

Olive broke in again quickly.

'What do you think gives Sammy West his particular understanding of your way of singing?' she asked. 'I mean, he does write well for you, doesn't he?'

'He's a clever man,' she said. 'But I have to work on them a little to make them right for me.'

'Do you work together?' Olive asked. 'Where do you work?'

The Baroness gave Olive a sharp glance at this.

'Comes to me in the shower, honey,' she said. And then laughed again. 'He gives me the song. Then I feel how I should sing it.'

She started rummaging on her dressing-table, and found some sheet music.

'See what I mean?' she said, passing it over to Olive. 'He writes it out in his own hand.'

It was West's vocal score of 'Tell It Me Again'.

'Can I see?' asked Hugh. As he suspected, the tune was rather different from the way the Baroness sang it. In fact, cold on the page it had a decidedly simplistic look to it. But then, that had always been West's trademark. He'd set a continent singing three notes, and the whole point was that they were the right three notes. But here was another whole point: when you heard the Baroness singing West you got as much Baroness as West, perhaps more.

'You don't sing this,' smiled Hugh, intending a compliment, but the Baroness didn't see at all what he was going to say.

'Hey, Mr Flashman,' she pouted at him. 'Who these friends of yours taking my songs away from me?'

'I mean, you just use this as a basis for what you sing,' said Hugh. 'I think the result is better than this. It's marvellous. But it's you, not Sammy West.'

'Now you're trying to butter me up.'

Could it be that she wasn't wholly aware of what she did to a song when she made it her own? Hardly. She'd admitted that she had to 'work on them a little to make them right'.

'What you actually sing, Miss Gerald,' said Hugh, eager to make his point, 'is very different from this.'

'Come on, you're joking me.'

'Not a bit. I'll show you.'

Hugh had no need to start a search for music paper. He always carried a special pen which he had made, consisting of a squat wooden holder into which he had fitted five tiny ballpoint refills. On the back of an envelope he made two quick strokes with it, and produced two tiny staves, like the nail-marks of hands across a face.

'Look at this!' exclaimed the Baroness. 'Hey, this is neat!'

Hugh set about transcribing the Virgina Gerald version of 'Tell It Me Again' on to the back of the envelope. He used a 2B pencil with a plug of india-rubber on the end, as he wanted to get it right, and needed to make corrections as he went along. The grace notes, slurs and glissandi had to be indicated, and the precise difference between a sequence consisting of a dotted semiquaver, a demisemiquaver and a quaver, compared with a simple triplet, had to be judged from memory. Not only was everyone still talking while he did it (even Dan, who wanted to get a profile-shot against the mirror) but some of the musicians came into the room during their break and raided the bottle of Jack Daniels provided by Mr Goldbein.

'*We* don't get whiskey laid out for us like this,' they complained.

'Maybe you have to put out to get it?'

'Yeah, that must be the answer.'

The Baroness shushed them.

'Turn it down, boys. This is Mr Howard. He's a composer. Look what he's doing.'

'We're all composers here, baby,' said Bob Gordon, smacking his lips round his gulp of whiskey.

Hugh smiled as he wrote. Dan got his shot. Olive looked disconcerted by the breakdown of the interview, and shuffled through her notes as if to make sure that she had enough material. Mr Goldbein walked sadly through the room with a cup of coffee.

When Hugh gave the Baroness the envelope, she held it out by its edges with both hands and looked at it with delight as though it were a thousand dollar cheque.

'Bob!' she exclaimed. 'Here, Bob. Play this.'

Bob Gordon still had his tenor slung round his neck, as though he could never bear to be parted from it. Hugh imagined him playing it even in his bath, the golden swan's neck with its little lids and levers angled across his hairy chest, blowing blues and bubbles at the same time.

She propped the envelope against the Jack Daniels, and Bob, stooping to it, squeezed out the eloquent phrases that Hugh had transcribed.

'That's your song, you see,' said Hugh. 'And this is West's.'

He pushed West's score across the table to her, but she didn't need to look at it. She was entranced.

'Again, Bob,' she demanded.

Bob once again turned his instrument into Virginia Gerald, and went on to add a few phrases in his own manner. He laughed, and picked up his glass again.

'That's real cute, you know that?' she said, studying the envelope. 'Do you write songs yourself, Mr Howard?'

Hugh thought of his setting of six of Rilke's *Orpheus* sonnets for baritone and wind, and some of his folk-song arrangements.

'No,' he said. 'Not what you'd call songs.'

'You should write songs, you know?'

She was so taken by this crude image of her own voice that she thought there was something magical about Hugh's transcription. But the beauty was all hers, and Hugh's powers were dormant, charged, altogether elsewhere. He felt like Gauguin wielding a Polaroid camera.

The man with the real camera had by now got all he wanted, and was making signs to Olive about leaving. Olive looked helpless and resigned. She had lost the initiative and was ready to go. Hugh could have gladly stayed all night, but as Dan and Olive stood up he knew that the interview was over and that this was perhaps as close as he would ever come to the Baroness.

Her music rang in his head with tantalising fidelity to the emotions aroused by her presence.

> 'Our mouths join at the seams
> Like a tennis ball.'

The song was in essence merely smart. Even its imagery was drawn from the world of yachting blazers and wisecracks with which the young West had charmed the public in *How do you do da?*, though the song was from a show with a cowboy setting. In the Baroness's interpretation it displayed its core of sexual wonder with a fresh concentration, and all the coyness of West's style was subsumed in that intensity.

And her real lips, the lips that had so recently framed the words and the notes, were still there smiling at him, moist, exactly shaped. The eye was drawn to them, as to an incision. And the words that were breathed through them, however conventional in their expression of gratitude or farewell, took on some of the magic of their physical bloom.

As they left, Hugh saw Yellow standing in a doorway leading to some private part of the club, and on his slightly mottled and pockmarked face was an odd expression compounded of studied reserve and pure hatred.

7

During the next few days Hugh imagined that he saw that same look in the eyes of all young blacks he encountered. At the till of the delicatessen, in the subway, on Saturday night at the corner of 116th and Broadway where the next day's copies of the *Times* were being stacked in shoulder-high piles, each copy a daunting two inches thick: always there seemed to be someone who troubled to single him out with a stare of something like accusation or warning. He knew it was his imagination, or the cut of his clothes. He still felt like a tourist, undecided about his immediate destination, over-deliberate about money, calling things by their wrong names.

When he went down to the Public Library to meet Denis Heathfield they were there in force. Cutting through Bryant Park, he was forced to make absurd small detours to avoid being accosted. What did they want from him? It was the middle of the day. The place was full of people. Was he going to be mugged?

Denis laughed.

'Well,' he said, 'it's true that Andrew Porter lost his wallet and wristwatch here on the steps of the library.'

'Here, where we are now?' asked Hugh disbelievingly, looking at the office workers sunning themselves in rows during their lunch break, the secretaries with cartons and sandwiches.

'That's right,' said Denis. 'He just handed them over. A case either of astonishing prudence or simple blind panic. Probably the guy simply wanted to sell him some junk.'

Denis led him to a restaurant where they ordered white wine spritzers and niçoise salads.

'This is disgraceful, Hugh,' he said, hanging his jacket on the back of his chair. 'You've been in New York for what, over a month? And I've only seen you once. I'm afraid the city's made a fool of itself with the reviews of your ballet.'

'Oh, I didn't think they were too bad,' said Hugh. 'Anyway, I wish people would stop thinking of it as my ballet. It's Johnny Tierentanz's ballet.'

'And Tanya's,' said Denis. 'Did you know that we were publishing her memoirs?'

'No, I didn't. Any good?'

'Pretty flat, really. I mean, they'd be sizzling if she'd anything to write about, but instead of being – what? Sizzling bacon? – they're more like sizzling porridge.'

'She can't dance, of course,' said Hugh. 'So what's the appeal?'

'All the political stuff. She seems to have shacked up with almost every member of the government before the Russians invaded. That's good for a book in itself, but you know, nothing else happens.'

He laughed.

'And how are you getting on, uncle? I'm sorry I couldn't come to the Crails'. I appreciated your getting me invited.'

'You didn't miss much. Sammy West was the star of the evening for some reason. I suppose as an instinctive antidote to me. A spoonful of sugar to make the medicine go down.'

'Don't get paranoid. New York is very conservative in some respects, and anyway it would be intended as a tribute to you. He's the grand old man of musical theatre, and the Crails would have been showing him off in your honour.'

'I don't mind him stealing the party a bit,' said Hugh. 'I hate parties.'

'Olive Dempster tells me you were a great hit with Virgina Gerald. You must have been talking for a change.'

Hugh was conscious of a thrill of pleasure at the mention of her name, but remained non-committal. Denis toyed with a piece of lettuce.

'She's too good for success, that girl,' he said. 'I hope a few weeks at Number 3 doesn't give her grandiose ideas. She's a blues singer of the traditional kind, and that's not the kind of music that makes it.'

'It seems to have done so this time,' said Hugh.

'It's bizarre,' said Denis. 'There must be a reason. It can't go on.'

'Why not?' protested Hugh.

'It's what she would call "lagniappe", and I hope she's philosophical enough to realise it.'

'What's that?'

'It's New Orleans for happenstance, serendipity – God, why are all the words for it so peculiar. You know what I mean: an unexpected plus.'

'She comes from New Orleans, then?'

'Oh, somewhere in Louisiana, I think.'

'I'd got the impression she'd lived in Texas.'

'Hey, why the third degree? I'm no expert on the Virginia Gerald biography.'

Hugh grinned.

'Sorry, Denis,' he said. 'I expect you're right about it being a fluke.'

'You bet I'm right,' said Denis. 'She hasn't the pizzazz to become a star of that kind. Look at the clothes she wears. She just stands there and belts it out.'

'I wouldn't put it like that.'

'Well, how would you put it? She's a Sammy West creation, and it's all in the music.'

Hugh knew better, but he wasn't going to be able to prove to Denis Heathfield in a crowded lunchroom that even if it was 'all in the music' then that was the Baroness's creation as much as Sammy West's, perhaps more than Sammy West's. He'd proved it to himself, and perhaps he had proved it to the Baroness. He let it go.

'What did he create her for?' he asked. 'Is it the old Pygmalion story?'

'Hardly,' said Denis. 'He's as queer as a hand pump, isn't he?'

Denis didn't seem particularly interested in any of this, so they talked about the friends they had in common, about the state of publishing in England and the US, and about that perennial topic, money.

'I hope you're getting a fat royalty for the ballet,' Denis remarked, as he welcomed the ice cream with a close scrutiny and a quarter-turn of the plate on the table cloth.

'Yes, but not yet,' said Hugh. When he explained that his presence in New York was self-financed, Denis was horrified. Hugh had to explain that it wasn't quite as disastrous as it seemed because Peter Redmond had lent him his apartment and the ballet had paid for his air fare (the royalties would come later).

'I'm quite an object of charity,' he went on. 'They'll be passing on their old suits next. The latest contribution to the Howard Benefit is the use of the Crail Ranch when I give my lectures at Dexter.'

'A ranch, yet,' exclaimed Denis. 'How the rich do live!'

'They call it their ranch,' said Hugh. 'But I don't think it is one, really. More like a country cottage. They go there for riding and boating. And it has a piano.'

'Lucky you.'

'I don't normally need a piano. It makes you compose in a certain way if you rely on a piano. It can be awfully limiting. But I must admit that it would be a help at the moment. I'm getting in a bit of a fix with the concerto.'

'Don't tell me you still haven't finished it?'

'I'm afraid not. And giving these lectures is a bit of distraction, too. But I can do with the dollars, you see.'

60

'I bet you can. How many to the pound at the moment?'

'$1.20 or so.'

Denis closed his eyes in pain.

'Hugh, don't!' he winced. 'That's criminal.'

Then, after a moment's reflection, 'It's wonderful, too. I must try to come over to London this fall. I could live like a king!'

After that particular conversation it seemed entirely appropriate for Denis to pick up the cheque, and Hugh made no effort to fight over it. They parted on Fifth Avenue. Denis was returning to the library to continue his search for illustrations for a book on nineteenth-century American hostesses. 'We should have assistants who would do this sort of thing for us,' he complained. 'But they never get it right. Goodbye, Hugh. Good luck. You must come round for dinner before you go.'

Hugh wandered down the avenue looking in the windows of the radio stores. He was mildly cross at having agreed to come downtown to lunch with Denis when he could have continued working. Wasn't Denis in any case Daisy's friend? Or, rather, wasn't Dorothy Heathfield Daisy's friend? And hadn't Denis studiously avoided asking about Daisy, as though Hugh had murdered her or something? The only positive outcome of the meeting had been Denis's view of the Baroness's relationship with Sammy West, which had left him feeling strangely exhilarated.

On an impulse he went into one of the stores and asked to see some pocket tape-recorders with headphones. He and Daisy had given one to Simon when they were first available, and he thought of them still as ostentatious toys. He didn't think that he ought to be satisfied with their quality of reproduction. He always felt guilty when proposing to spend money on himself. And perhaps most pervasively, though with less possibility of rationalising it as a serious objection to going ahead with the purchase, he wanted to surround himself with the sound of Virginia Gerald.

The salesman was a comedian who kept producing unlikely and outlandish headsets in the form of Martian antennae or oversize white sunglasses with tiny radios in the earpieces. But eventually Hugh bought a classic red Walkman, and some tapes.

The salesman was intrigued by his choices. The Prokofiev violin sonatas. The Stravinsky violin concerto and *Suite Italienne*. The Chuck Stolmundsen Quartet. And Virginia Gerald.

'Has she made any other recordings?' asked Hugh.

'I got some singles, but I guess most of them are on the tape, and this is the only tape,' was the reply. 'How about some Nina Simone?'

Hugh politely declined Nina Simone, and left with his purchases. The streets, though presumably now empty of office workers, were no less crowded. Walkers gathered at crossings and were admitted by automatic signs to the next block, drifting like grains of sand through the neck of an hourglass, crossing each other at intersections like halma pieces. Cabs lurched at lights. And at every corner the sharp smell of the pretzel sellers' grills attracted knots of stray pedestrians, men dissatisfied with their first lunch, men pretending not to be trying to find a cab, men who actually liked the pretzels.

Hugh walked down 42nd Street towards the subway. Here he was obliged to run a gauntlet of nude encounter booths, lounging blacks, and triple-X-rated cinemas (*Happy Nuns*, *Cherry Valley*, *Dirty Girls*) and wondered if he could have managed this with greater credibility if he had been wearing his Walkman rather than carrying it in a plastic bag. In one doorway a policeman was waiting beside an inert figure on the sidewalk in some embarrassment, professionally unconcerned in stance but evidently conscious of playing an unpopular and symbolical role, like a centurion in a Pietà. From another doorway could be heard the sounds of mechanical amusements, including, indeed predominantly, what Hugh was shocked to recognise as the fugal motif of the current problematic bars of the third movement of his violin concerto.

How could this be?

It was as arresting and summary as the phrase that introduced each movement of the Stravinsky concerto as a kind of 'call to order', indeed was rather too like that phrase, as Hugh had half-realised when he bought the tape. Normally he avoided listening to music that he liked in any genre he happened to be working in, but here he was aware of the operation of the guilt of influence and the secret morale of emulation. However, it was not Stravinsky coming from the amusement arcade, and of course it could not be Howard, as yet unperformed, unpublished, even (alas) unwritten. It was the signature tune of *Amazing*.

Am I writing street music without realising it? thought Hugh. Will I be introducing tram bells and electric drills next?

He returned to the apartment in a state of depression, poured a glass of iced tea and looked at the pages of his concerto that contained the outline of the bustling fugue based on the offending phrase. After the tranquillity of the largo was it credible that he should have conceived as a fresh departure the vulgar scampering of the *Amazing* mannikin? Wasn't it even worse than the original fanfare and the music-hall high-jinks that were to have followed?

Or was there some point in it after all? Perhaps it had representative value as something both mindless and erotic, part of an eternal quest, momentarily debased by circumstance. Hugh doubted if anyone would actually recognise the motif, but what if they did? And where would the fugue lead?

'Ama-zing!' purred the machine. 'Come and play me!' It was embodied on the page as a challenge and its presence there seemed no more mysterious than its duplication in public places throughout the United States.

Hugh walked about the apartment wearing his Walkman, tuned in to the Baroness. He knew he could have listened to her sitting down. For that matter he could have bought discs and played them on Peter Redmond's record player, but he had wanted to be able to listen to music anywhere, in the streets, in the plane, in Dexter, or wherever he happened to be. The music surrounded his head like a swarm of bees, an impregnable helmet of sound. It actually encouraged him to keep moving, as if to remind him that it played only for him, a confidential whisper from the depths of borrowed space, an aural definition of an alternative universe whose three-dimensional axes converged in his receptive brain. He played it while making supper. He played it in his bath. He played it while walking about in his bathrobe with a whiskey.

Night deepened behind the buildings that Hugh could see from the apartment window. The lights that were switched on and off created a perpetual though barely noticeable shift of texture on their façades, a continual slight adjustment of a meaningless pattern. In the windows just across the street he could see parts of rooms across which a pair of trousers might walk before a hand pulled down a blind, or which remained strangely empty though half-illuminated. Further away, windows were yellow or white, containing or not containing movement, or they were black. The related positions of the windows were like some code punched out against the night-scape, ready to be fed into a giant machine that was programmed to divulge a calculus of night activity, an explanation of all that was happening in Manhattan, and why.

As an observer, Hugh felt a surge of painful abstraction from this established routine of petty or meaningless events. He knew that he had no need or reason to demand a share in them, and that if he somehow had a divine knowledge of what occurred in each and every one of them, he could still be convinced that his own cube of living space contained all that at that moment he could possibly require. And immediately he knew that this knowledge was false, bred of habit and narrow horizons. It was not that the multitude of individual lives in the multitude of lit cubes out there were in themselves desirable. How could they be? It was that his own was incomplete, and that his curiosity about the others was a product of his feeling of distinction from them, and that this distinction, this haunting separateness, had an ordinary name which, as in a fairy tale, it would be fatal to remember. He felt like a giant or a king who had never known the simple pleasures of ordinary people, and who only lived for the moment in the story when his life would be changed.

When the buzzer sounded, it broke in upon his solitude in several distinct ways. He was not, as a vagrant in someone else's apartment, expecting to be visited. He was startled by such a summons from the speculative world. And the buzzer, heard not in a receptive silence, but through the aura of private Walkman sound, itself had a kind of detached air about it, as though it were something he could simply listen to and not act upon.

But remembering the complicated instructions left by Peter Redmond about both locking the apartment and vetting callers to it, he immediately went to see who it was. He pressed a button and spoke into the little grille which served as a microphone to a similar grille in the lobby. Like all the services and fixtures in the apartment it was an archaic affair, heavy, decorated, and in technological terms not far removed from the speaking-tube. Everything, including plumbing and central heating, had the appearance of having been fitted once and for all, at immense cost, at the turn of the century and never having needed to be replaced.

The reply was indistinct, something about a letter. Despite Peter's warnings about who to let in and who not to let in, Hugh felt obliged to press the release button. It was the automatic response that always prevented him from hanging up on cold-callers, the politeness that led him to accept invitations that promised an inevitable boredom. After all, he reasoned, the apartment door was triple-locked and equipped with a spyhole. If the caller was an evident brute or drunk he could simply not open the door.

After a while the bell rang, and Hugh did look through the spyhole. Though the image was distorted and foreshortened, the face looming bulbously like a forlorn aquarium specimen, staring blankly and expectantly in his direction, Hugh could hardly believe that he in turn could not also be seen. This feeling of vulnerability was increased by Hugh's recognition of the face above the black roll-neck sweater. The face was cocked at an angle and sucking its top teeth. It was a black face, at once alert and indifferent, careless and insouciant, and it belonged to Yellow.

8

Hugh was used to English hospitals: Victorian iron-master mansions decayed into asylums, Portakabin warrens behind the furthest housing estates, dusty red-brick havens of gentility in leafy London squares, timeless prefabrications of glass and concrete like a barracks or seaside pier. The possibility of a hospital in black reflecting glass with massive security and receptionists like TWA hostesses had never occurred to him. He was directed to the Baroness's room as cordially as if he had come to buy something. Only the occasional presence in the corridors of men in spotless green gowns and caps reminded him that he was not in an expensive hotel.

It was of this that he first spoke after greeting her shyly. She was propped up in her bed looking perfectly well, directing at him a smile of such radiant complicity in his presence that Hugh felt an instant certainty, with a little inner lurch of excitement, that his life had irrevocably changed from that moment. It had required no action or over-eagerness on his part, no risk of rebuff or abject self-recrimination. She had wanted him to come and he had come without question.

'This is very civilised,' said Hugh. 'In England I'd have had to wade through the ward to get to you. It'd have been like leafing through a textbook of surgery and I'd have been thoroughly demoralised.'

'Oh, they protect visitors from all that,' said the Baroness. 'But there's plenty goes on behind the scenes.'

Hugh was standing awkwardly by the window, and she made him draw up a chair close by her bed. She made a sandwich of his hand, without drama or hesitation, like a grandmother about to impart some grandmotherly wisdom, and then simply smiled again. It was a smile of frank recognition, relief, curiosity, and tenderness. It was a smile that wonderfully contrived to seem like a continuation rather than a beginning.

But there were as yet no intimate things to say.

'Had he opened the letter?' she asked.

'No,' said Hugh, remembering Yellow's ostentatious and ill-tempered detachment from the message he had brought. 'At least, I don't think so.'

'I told him not to,' she said, 'so there was a good chance that he wouldn't.'

'I can't think how you knew where I was living,' said Hugh. 'That was almost as mysterious as your writing to me at all.'

She laughed.

'That didn't need no Sherlock Holmes,' she said. 'You wrote my song out on the back of a redirection. Look.'

She had the transcription on her bedside table, and she took it up carefully.

'Well,' she considered, cocking her head on one side. 'Maybe I was a little bit smart, seeing as how they got more addresses on this thing than you got notes. They got Novello here, printed along the bottom in green. Borough Green. Sevenoaks. Kent. That sounds kind of pretty. Then there's this London address, Willingham Square, maybe it took a horse and cab to get to before someone put some more postage stamps on it so it could fly to Mr John Tierentanz of the Manhattan Ballet, and even then it wasn't through. I reckoned you must have ended up where it ended up. On Riverside Drive.'

Hugh had never heard her say so much at once, and was riveted by the way her mouth and tongue controlled all those perfectly ordinary words without the benefit of sung pitch or interval.

'Yes, I'm a vagrant,' he said. 'And soon I'll be going to Texas as well.'

Her eyes widened at this.

'Is your ballet opening there?' she asked.

'Oh no,' said Hugh. 'The New York performances are about as much as they can manage, I think. I'm going to deliver some lectures at the University of Dexter.'

67

'Say, you're a professor, too!' said the Baroness, admiringly.

'Not a very serious one,' said Hugh. 'It helps me to earn my bread and butter.'

'I guess only a professor could have written out my song just like that,' she pondered. 'And maybe only a not very serious one would have wanted to.'

'Well, I wanted to,' said Hugh. 'I hear it all the time. I can't think of anything else.'

She simply squeezed his hand, and Hugh was suddenly over-whelmed, as if at a great distance, by the unlikeliness and inevitability of this meeting. He felt like a general who surveyed a field of battle only briefly reconnoitred and known to be disadvantageous on which, surprisingly, the first distant advances had already been made, and whose purely theoretical calculations had now yielded to the urgent need for deployment and command.

He covered their hands with his free hand, and briefly pressed them as if to establish a reliable frontier outpost of touch. That alone, if it could be held, would for the moment be enough.

Light from the window slats fell broken upon the bed. Outside in the corridor someone called, and there were frequent sounds of footsteps.

'How are you, then?' asked Hugh. 'What's wrong?'

She sighed, and looked at him seriously and intently.

'You don't need to know about it,' she said. 'I don't want you to know about it. I sure am getting the hell out of here, anyway.'

Hugh nodded.

'They're no place to be if you can avoid it, hospitals,' he said.

It seemed a pointless thing to say, because she laughed again at its obviousness, and he smiled too. He wasn't sure that this was what they were talking about, important as it must be, since while they talked he found his hand touching and retouching hers, the hinges between their thumbs and fingers gently interlocking and turning and retreating, the fingers bending and their tips touching knuckles, a restless cautious diplomacy of abstracted greeting and exploration.

Suddenly he found his lips on her cheek and a hand awkwardly on her shoulder. He said something, but he hardly knew what it was, and her mouth came round to meet his, and it all seemed easy. On her bedside table were knitting-needles to which was attached a foot of white cable-stitch knitting. Hugh felt that he had never seen any knitting before in his life. It seemed extraordinarily sensuous, touching, unnecessary, beautiful and strange. A bottle of pills stood next to it, some Kleenex and deodorant, and an issue of *Nightbird*.

Why, at this surprising moment, as the feelings ran back beneath his ears and over his scalp, was his head full of Sammy West?

> 'Our mouths join at the seams
> Like a tennis ball.'

What had West's gross dismissive genius to do with the reality it pretended not to mock? And why had Virginia Gerald so irrevocably lent West's music the warm tongue that was necessary to give it life?

Hugh was suddenly aware that someone was standing in the open doorway. It was a man in a white coat, holding a clipboard. His face was an impressive assemblage of glasses, nose and five o'clock shadow, a mask of imperturbable solemnity. He spoke.

'Five minutes,' said the mask, and disappeared.

'That's Dr Listener,' she said. 'You're going to have to go. He's always in a rage.'

Hugh felt exhilarated, bewildered.

'This is all so strange,' he said. 'I don't even have a name for you.'

'I got a name all right,' she smiled. 'Sometimes I got too many names. My real friends, from way back, they call me Gin.'

'Gin?'

'There used to be a reason.'

She laughed.

'And if you hear someone call me Gerry, then watch out because that person is up to no damn good!'

'Why are you in here, Gin?' asked Hugh.

Gin's smile wavered for a moment, and her fingers moved along the folded sheet as if seeking an answer perhaps as if proprietorially straightening it, as though if she were indeed there, despite her will, she had to keep control.

'No questions asked, honey,' she said, and she looked at his eyes in a small pleading of trust and hope. 'This is one of the places you got to get me out of, and I don't want you looking back or I may just end up as one pillar of salt.'

'I can't stop thinking about you,' said Hugh helplessly.

'Don't see why you should.' She shrugged.

Had Dr Listener's interruption broken the spell? Had anything of significance really taken place between them? She seemed restless now, distracted. He had been summoned on some kind of errand, he realised, one that he was to say nothing about to Yellow. She wanted him to take her from the hospital.

Why?

There were movements outside the door, metallic sounds. Gin suddenly grasped Hugh's hands again.

'Will you help me, Hugh?' she asked, using his name for the first time, with an intonation that thrillingly seemed to turn him into a different person, someone entirely capable of doing anything at all.

'Yes, yes, of course I will,' said Hugh.

'They'll turn you out in a minute,' she went on. 'Listen. Give me your phone number, and be ready to come round with a cab when I call you. It'll be maybe tomorrow, or Wednesday. Will you do that?'

'Of course, yes. Anything,' said Hugh.

'Anything,' she repeated with a smile. 'They all say that. Then it's want everything. And do nothing.'

He grimaced.

'Try me, anyway,' he said, writing out Peter Redmond's telephone number, which he had to copy from his diary. 'How can I get in touch with you?'

'I'll call,' she assured him.

A nurse bustled into the room, wheeling a trolley. Hugh stood up and prepared to leave. Almost as an afterthought, Gin said:

'Can I come to Texas with you? Please?'

And with equal carelessness, but with his mind ablaze with excitement and objections, Hugh said:

'Yes!'

'You don't mean it.'

'I do mean it! Of course you can come. I've got the use of the Crails' house there.'

She smiled up at him, settling herself more comfortably in bed, like a child being promised a treat. Only then, and in the admonitory presence of the nurse, did Hugh imagine he saw a shadow of pain cross her face and remember that there must be some reason for her being in hospital.

The farewell seemed public and insufficient, and the image of her that he took from the room, the smell of her, the feel of her lips and fingers, was like a party challenge to his memory, a kind of erotic Kim's Game, elusive because artificially assembled, confusing and unexpected. The inquisitorial Dr Listener was in the corridor. Hugh felt obscurely that if he were to give the doctor an account of his intimate feelings, were it possible, he would merely write them down on his clipboard as useful evidence of the disordered state of things that it was his profession to put right. There was no place for kissing in a hospital. It was a symbol of all that antisepsis was designed to protect. It was the locus of the real life that admission to hospital suspended. It was flagrant rebellion.

Dr Listener made no response to Hugh's nod and smile, but merely looked at him over his clipboard and watched him, unnervingly, down the corridor, as though he were an unlawful intruder, or someone who himself showed symptoms of illness. No hospital visitor escapes the feeling that he, too, is really a patient. The glances of the nurses in the corridor, the concern of the receptionist to check the signature on his pass, the attentions of the doorman: was it not possible to sense an irony in the way they were trained to treat the visitor? Didn't their attitude acknowledge an impending helplessness in the lives of the presently well? Was this not the politeness of society itself, in its performance of shallow arabesques upon the icy lake of the treacherous human organism?

In the outside lobby of the hospital exit (itself not identical with the entrance, as though information gained by visitors should not be passed on to new visitors; as though the experiences of shock and bereavement were not to re-enter society but be channelled onwards and outwards, to spend themselves in isolation) Hugh discovered an area of play designed to detain, distract, perhaps even in a sense to rehabilitate. One of its features was by now perfectly familiar to him.

'Ama-zing!' crooned the gremlin voice. 'Come and play me!'

Lights winked around the rim of the machine's casing. The interior glowed black. It invited you to do what almost appeared to be possible: to step inside and disappear. It was like a sentry-post on the border of some physical dimension.

Hugh did not pass by. He felt that he needed to unwind, perhaps, or to postpone mental analysis of his new psychological state. He was transformed, he knew, as radically as the erotic transgression of the human boundary can transform us. He wanted to sustain and suspend the first impact of this transformation, to relish it without entertaining any proviso. He did not want, for the moment, to take it back into the world of his planned life. He carried it with him like a fragile trophy.

The hospital's version of *Amazing* was more complex than those Hugh had seen before. It may, he reflected, have been a newer model with improved technology, which would eventually replace the older *Amazing* in all bars and arcades all over the country. It took more quarters, and required the insertion of the player's hand in a kind of metal glove that not only contained finger-buttons coded for play, but recorded pulse and blood-pressure as adjuncts to the pursuit of the girl which was still the main purpose of the game. The graphics were greatly improved, too, allowing a varying angle of view down the racing walls of the maze, a more naturalistic representation of the human figures, and a wider range of physiological control. The maze was more complex, and more of it was shown, so that there was every opportunity to take short cuts to narrow the lead of the escaping girl. There were new, and more realistic, hazards such as stretches of water which required a fiendish tattoo on the finger-buttons to enable the mannikin to swim across them. Hugh's instrument was the viola, so his fingers soon learned the necessary adroitness. He had removed the girl's scarf, earrings and jacket, and notched up 1725 points, before running out of quarters. He still, however, could not cue in his name on the scoring panel accurately.

'Well played, H. Hovarc,' said *Amazing*, in a dry monotone. 'Bills may be changed at the side of the machine.'

But Hugh was not going to start spending all his money on an arcade game, even one that had unwittingly lent him a musical theme.

'That's enough for now,' he said, absently. 'Cheerio.'

'Cheerio, H. Hovarc,' said *Amazing*.

9

When Hugh rang the Crails to confirm that it really would be all right to go to their house in Dexter right away, they insisted that he came round that evening for dinner. Warned that it would be pot luck, Hugh nonetheless found Roger marinading fillet steaks the size of pocket bibles, and Liz looked dressed ready to be photographed for the society pages. Hugh reckoned it must be a token barbecue, for when it was time to grill the steaks Roger put on an apron and cooked them with much publicity within sight of the dining table. Liz was radiantly concerned to appear relaxed and well-adjusted in the matter of her daughter's domestic arrangements.

'Tikki's tremendously sensible,' she said more than once, as though this quality were somehow a protection against seduction by a personable young man actually living in her own apartment. Hugh himself, somewhat flushed with male self-esteem in the matter of his tryst with the Baroness, felt obscurely insulted by these confidences, as though he could not be classed, with Peter Redmond, as an unattached threat to maidenhood. He made some fatherly noises, however, and felt a fraud.

'Peter's a fine boy,' said Roger. 'It's the way the young do things nowadays.'

He was keeping their glasses filled. Liz looked up at him.

'I know, I know,' she mourned. 'And I've no objection to Peter.'

'It was extremely kind of him to lend me his apartment,' put in Hugh, slightly embarrassed at being included in such a family conversation.

'Oh yes,' admitted Liz. 'He's sweet and generous, isn't he? Has your work gone well?'

'Terribly,' said Hugh. 'But it's no fault of the apartment.'

'New York is impossible in the summer,' said Roger. 'You'll find the ranch quite different.'

'Oh yes,' said Liz. 'It's lovely there. We shall be quite jealous of you. Europe will be just as tiring as New York.'

Peter and Tikki were forgotten for the moment as she concentrated on dramatising the prospective toil of their European holiday.

'Roger!' she wailed. 'Why on earth are we going? Did I say I wanted to go?'

Roger smiled patiently.

'Yes, darling,' he replied. 'You've been wanting to go for two years, and quite often talk of nothing else.'

'I know, I know,' she said abjectly. 'What an idiot I am. I'd much rather be at the ranch.'

'Never mind,' said Roger. 'Hugh will keep the place aired for us, won't you, Hugh? Did I tell you to mind out for Jed Finch, by the way? He does know you're coming, but he can be very over-protective.'

'Jed looks after the horses, Hugh,' said Liz. 'He's got a heart of gold and not a grey cell in his head.'

'I hope you don't ride, Hugh,' said Roger. 'Jed can hardly bear to let us use the horses, so it would probably be better if you didn't attempt to. Sorry.'

'That's perfectly all right,' said Hugh. 'I've never been on a horse in my life.'

Roger looked relieved.

'There was also a favour I wanted to ask you,' he said. 'But you must say no. I expect you to say no.'

'Why ask him then, Roger?' put in Liz. She stubbed out her cigarette in a space between her broccoli and half-eaten steak.

'Because it might conceivably appeal to him, darling,' said Roger. 'Hugh, what it is is this. We've bought a new car and want to use the old one in Texas. We have a station wagon there, but a second car would be useful and it seems crazy not to make use of this one.'

'He doesn't want to spend a week driving to Dexter, does he?' said Liz.

Hugh wasn't sure that he did, but was very conscious of the favours he had received from the Crails and felt that he ought if possible to agree.

'Could I do it in a week, in fact?' he asked.

'It shouldn't be impossible,' said Roger.

Hugh calculated the number of days before his lectures. Then he calculated his saving on the air fare. Then he remembered hotels. Then he was forced, not for the first time, to wonder if Gin really intended to come to Texas with him or whether it was not all an illusion or joke. And if she did want to come, would she want to travel in a car? And if they flew, would he have to buy her an air ticket? Why did she want to come? How could she possibly be interested in him?

The two sets of calculations, practical and emotional, were not absolutely distinct. Each bore upon the other. Once Hugh had agreed to drive the Crails' car to Dexter it seemed no longer a foolhardy and exhausting trek, nor even simply a way to save money (not so much), but an appropriately romantic method of travel, a fly-by-night escape from a world where it was only a strange dream that Virginia Gerald should summon Hugh Howard to her bed to be kissed.

Equipped with the keys to both the Crails' ranch and car, like the hero of romance awaiting supernatural instructions, Hugh lived the next day in a state of enchantment and suspense. He drank nothing but iced tea and ate nothing but biscuits and salami. He wondered if Gin had already rung, while he was at the Crails'. He didn't go out, in case he missed her call.

When Boris rang, with expansively friendly but quite precise enquiries about the state of the third movement, Hugh was disappointed enough to be uncharacteristically brusque. For a moment Boris was amused.

'Hugh dear,' he laughed. 'The ballet must be even more of a success than I thought. You sound positively grande-dameish.'

'Do I?' asked Hugh.

'Here I am,' said Boris, 'absolutely bursting with pleasure at your concerto. What we have of it. Which is not, by any means, all. And you sound as if nothing was further from your mind.'

Hugh thought of the by now fantastically protracted rigmarole of the *Amazing* motif, and of how uncertain he was that it either related significantly to the first two movements of the concerto or itself led anywhere in particular. He felt a slight panic at its state of unreadiness.

'I've been working on it,' he said lamely. 'It's a fugue.'

'Tremendous!' exclaimed Boris. 'Is there anything for me to see? Should we meet? Katey is already back in New York, as you know. Perhaps you two should get together in any case to discuss the first two movements. I'm still in Philadelphia, of course.'

Hugh explained that he would be in Texas for several weeks, and Boris began to sound peeved.

'Well, Hugh dear,' he concluded. 'I hope you are planning to return at some point with the rest of the great work. A lot of people are relying on you.'

Eventually Gin did telephone. Her voice sounded more distant and cautious than he had somehow been expecting it to be, and he was struck again by the absurdity of this assignation. She greeted the prospect of the car eagerly, implying that it would be more discreet. Hugh wondered what she could mean by this: did she think she would be recognised at the airport or in any way subjected to unwelcome attentions? He didn't know if she was famous in that sense. He had seen none of the popular musical papers. Her pictures had not yet appeared in *Nightbird*. He arranged to collect her at the hospital at 5.30, and to take her briefly to her apartment. She seemed anxious to leave New York as soon as possible after that.

Oh, it was an assignation all right, almost an elopement. As Hugh went to collect the Crails' Cadillac, wondering how on earth he was going to be able to drive it away in the Manhattan traffic, he was reminded of nothing so much as a student date with its attendant uncertainties and bravados. Peter Redmond's apartment had come to seem stultifying to him, with its cupboards full of correct suiting rarely worn, its Daumier prints, its fencing foils. It had taken on that recognisable identity for Hugh, nervy, smug, oppressive, of a place where he could not work. It was true that Peter had called back only once, to collect a bank book or something, but his presence could be sensed nonetheless. Hugh felt that the very lampshades were looking over his shoulder. He hoped that the house in Dexter, being only periodically inhabited, would have a more accommodating character. He was eager to get there, for a change of air. He must finish the concerto. But what imp of erotic egotism, he wondered, stoked up the furnaces of his glands against a season of loneliness that he must whisk off a strange girl to live with him there?

He fumbled at the controls of the Cadillac as he was beckoned irritably out of its narrow parking space in the underground garage by a burly sweating man whose job it was to keep them as tightly packed as possible and to manoeuvre them for release like a Victorian conundrum. He felt like shouting through the window that he had never driven an automatic Cadillac before. He almost felt like crashing it deliberately just to show the burly garage-man how unfair he was being. It was the frustrated rage of an adolescent suffering from calf-love: he knew it, but he suffered it. Then suddenly, as he found himself in blessed freedom at the base of a ramp on which there was no other vehicle, and no beckoning man, and beyond which lay the relatively easy manners of the public street, he realised that an automatic Cadillac more or less drives itself, and he prepared to enjoy it.

At the hospital Hugh was subjected to further indignity. Gin was not waiting in the lobby as he had expected, but was still in her room, though now dressed and sitting in the armchair with her overnight bag beside her.

'You got to spring me from this place, honey,' she said. 'Seems they don't let you go by yourself.'

She smiled ruefully, looking more tired than when Hugh had last seen her. He noticed that her ankles were wrapped in gauze. She was wearing a loose white jacket with lapels, on one of which was a purple flower of carved wood.

'Who do I see?' asked Hugh.

'There's a nurse down the corridor with a big complex,' said Gin. 'The one that looks like that film actress, the grandmother that got her head cut off, you know?'

Hugh did know, and went off in search of a nurse who looked like Angela Lansbury. He passed an expensive old lady who was being wheeled down the corridor like a trolley of nitroglycerine. Surely this wasn't an institution that trivialised the rights of its patients?

Angela Lansbury consulted what was clearly Gin's file, and looked at Hugh with eyes of half-smiling ice.

'Would you please wait a moment, sir?' she said, operating the intercom.

A younger nurse looked up at Hugh from behind the desk with curiosity, and Hugh, in turn, while waiting for what turned out to be quite a long moment, did not know where to look. He felt a kind of fugitive embarrassment whose source he could barely locate. It was no business of nurses in a hospital to speculate, however subliminally, on the relationship between patients and their visitors, surely? Hugh was beginning to feel once again that sense of victimisation that had come upon him on his previous visit, not so much now as the bizarre illusion that he himself might not be able to leave freely because he was no healthier than any patient, but as an odd visitation of guilt. Seeking the formalities of Gin's release, he had acknowledged himself responsible for her. Yet he knew nothing of the reason for her having been admitted in the first place, and the nurses would imagine that he did. Their eyes said so, and beneath their guarded intermittent glances Hugh shifted uncomfortably.

When Dr Listener appeared, to look over the file with his impassive mask and to look from the file to Hugh and from Hugh back to the file again, as if to establish some relationship between them, the feeling of guilt increased. Hugh recognised his predicament as one he had not often felt since youth. It was the secret and hopeless self-righteousness of the schoolboy facing his teacher's pained presumption of complicity in events too shocking for open acknowledgment. Dr Listener held the file in strong hands whose tanned hairiness was uninterrupted to the biceps except for a massive watch on a strap of linked gold. The short sleeves of his white coat were cuffed and neatly creased to the seam at the shoulder, and he smelled of an exhaustive routine of soap.

'You're the guy who's been coming here,' said Dr Listener categorically, as though this were entered on the file.

'I was here yesterday,' said Hugh, more in the interest, he felt, of accuracy than of exoneration. There was nothing, surely, that he could be accused of by this summary judge? What was the bond between medicine and bureaucracy that allowed this leisurely and unfriendly interrogation?

'I know,' said Dr Listener. 'I saw you, didn't I?'

'I mean,' said Hugh, with a faltering persistence that he realised sounded lame, 'that I've only been once.'

Dr Listener raised his eyebrows.

'Once?' he queried. 'You're here again today.'

Hugh began to explain his explanation, but the doctor talked across him to the Angela Lansbury nurse.

'This is an SA2 case, right?' he demanded. 'You finished the paperwork? Miss Gerald signed, right?'

The nurse nodded.

'No complaint filed?'

The nurse shook her head.

Dr Listener wearily turned his heavy sterilised features towards Hugh, and regarded him with contempt.

'Listen, fellow,' he said. 'It's advisable that Miss Gerald takes the treatment. You understand? But if she doesn't want to, then we have to release. For myself, I don't want to let you take her away. Maybe you'd like to think about that. Then you can witness: name, address, identification. Then Miss Gerald has to pay. That's the way it has to be. This time.'

He flung the file down on the nurse's desk, having himself first contributed some authoritative hieroglyphic to the corner of one of its contained papers.

The procedure of release, as sketched by Dr Listener, was as lengthy as the hospital authorities could contrive it to be. Hugh played his part effectively, but in a state of partial perplexity and mild fury. He noticed that Gin, too, was not as relaxed about it all as she seemed to be, for she made several mistakes when writing out the cheque.

Hugh contained his feelings, for their expression could only involve the sort of interrogation of Gin that did not seem appropriate. She walked unsteadily, and was quiet in the car. In profile she looked younger and more vulnerable, her nose thinner and more retroussé. She laid one hand on Hugh's as he drove, and he had a brief glimpse of its dimpled knuckles and tapering fingers.

'This is maybe crazy, isn't it?' she said.

'It isn't something I make a practice of, I must admit,' said Hugh. 'I didn't know you had to fill in so many forms to be a knight errant.'

'Yeah,' she replied. 'Errol errant.' She had the habit of making these trivial remarks so decisively that they achieved the status of symbolical fixatives.

'I hope it was wise to leave the hospital,' Hugh remarked.

'I'm not going to collapse on you, if that's what you're worried about.'

'No, I was concerned about you.'

'Me, I feel better already. I'll feel even better away from the Big Apple.' She gave a shudder, and added: 'Don't you ever feel you want to get away from everything?'

Hugh pondered.

'I think I have got away from everything already,' he said. 'You can't get away from away.'

'Well, honey,' she said. 'If it's good for you, it's good. But there sure is a worm in that apple that you going to taste sooner or later. I bit me a big piece and I thought it tasted real good, but there was the little fellow waving at me, and oh boy, then . . .'

She laughed, and made a dismissive gesture with her hand, as though shooing away a whole Pandemonium of apple-worms.

They were making for her apartment in a somehow relaxing evening light that bathed the tide of traffic with a glow of expectancy. Hugh had by now got the measure of the traffic signals and seen how the car handled. He felt less tense, but still needed to keep his eyes on the bumpers ahead. As she talked, he felt a comfort of intimacy that he could not remember having felt for a long time. The pedestrians walked with an artful informality and precision, like film extras, as though fleshing out the dramatic scenario that was Hugh's superb drive through the city. Three young girls working off their enormous bottoms in grey jumpsuits, a man in a hat slowly and carefully folding a newspaper, a little woman muttering over her grocery bags and stopping to sigh, these were details of a design which Hugh felt he was in the process of creating. The whole city was playing at being itself, ignorant of the identity of the hero. He was pleased to allow the world its illusion of free will, content that it should have yielded him his prize.

At the lobby of her apartment, the attendant looked up from his paperback and said: 'Nice to see you back, Miss Gerald.'

'Hey, Shaker,' said Gin. 'How do you know I been away?'

'Well now,' said Shaker. 'Quite some visitors disappointed not to find you in.'

'Don't want to know about them, Shaker,' she said, taking Hugh into the elevator.

'Right you are then, Miss Gerald,' chuckled Shaker.

The apartment was painted all over, ceilings included, in shades of mocha and cherry, and there were Indian spreads on several of the walls. Hugh felt it was like being inside a chest of drawers. They touched lips briefly, but Gin gripped both his arms and held him away.

'Get myself a case and some things,' she smiled.

Hugh nodded.

'Fix yourself a drink,' she called over her shoulder as she went into her bedroom. 'Through there.'

Hugh wandered about, looking at her things. The room was an odd mixture of the plain and ornate: beaded cushions on a studded leather récamier; a big oak table against the wall with a china lamp as big as a wash basin; a stuffed mynah bird in a cage of dulled brass; a painting on glass of the Alamo; a mirror with a broad wooden frame of stripped oak; a mirror in a metal frame of stamped tin; a glass-topped coffee-table with a large Mexican candlestick of pink, yellow and vermilion plaster cherubs, two bottles of Comte de Neufchâtel *mousseux*, one empty, one a quarter full, an ashtray in the shape of a china lung, dirty glasses, a bowl of black liquorice, some paperbacks (*The Gourmet Diet*, Alice Walker, Peter de Vries, the latter with Sammy West's name on the flyleaf), a menu card for a take-out restaurant called Starvin' Marvin, a programme for Hugh's ballet; on the floor a heavy wool cardigan with a kind of metallic sheen to it; a drinks tray; a stereo unit with records loose on it (Coleman Hawkins, Lester Young, Bob Gordon's 'Looking Up'); a shelf with framed photographs (the Baroness about eighteen, very distinctly plump, performing with what looked like a college band; a group of monumental stones, with tourists posed in front of them; a middle-aged couple, uneasy in a photographer's studio; a young saxophonist in action).

Hugh took a glass from the drinks tray, but decided against whiskey. He filled it instead with the remains of the bubbly, which was quite flat and tasted, not altogether unpleasantly, of marzipan pigs.

Gin came into the room, picked up the cardigan and caught Hugh with the bottle.

'Hey, man,' she said. 'That wine is days dead.'

'My parsimony,' said Hugh apologetically. 'It's quite drinkable.'

'Not to me,' said Gin. 'You can fix me a bourbon and club soda.'

While Hugh was pouring the whiskey there was a voice from the hall.

'Gin honey, you there?'

'Myrna!' called Gin. 'Come in. We're in here.'

The voice belonged to a middle-aged woman of comfortable shape and friendly disposition with leaf-shaped spectacles, Gin's neighbour. She was given a whiskey too.

'Gin, now I've told you a hundred times it ain't safe to leave your front door open,' she said.

'Myrna, we just got in.'

'That don't matter,' Myrna said, shaking her head. 'Why, Royce would blow my head off right away if I left the door open for one second. You should shoot all them bolts again before you even take your hand off the door handle.'

'Sure, Myrna, I know,' said Gin.

'Well now,' beamed her friend. 'It is one good thing to see you back. I called Willa's Place like you said, and the Arquebus. I got your mail, too. And that Yellow came round for your messages. I told him what you said but I didn't tell him nothing else.'

She looked at Hugh and nodded and smiled at him raising her glass. Hugh raised his marzipan pigs in return. He wondered, as they exchanged this silent toast, how much Myrna knew about him, and quite what she thought they were toasting. There was not much, after all, to celebrate.

'Gin, I don't like that Yellow,' said Myrna. 'I just don't trust him somehow.'

'Yellow's all right, Myrna,' said Gin. 'He'd do anything for me.'

Myrna pursed her lips.

'I can see that,' she said. 'It's the way he does it, like a blind thing. Ain't no affection in it. Half thought he'd rough me up when I told him I didn't know where you'd gone.'

'Myrna, you're a real good friend,' said Gin warmly. 'I don't know what I'd do without you.'

'Well,' said Myrna. 'Times you need a friend when friends ain't friends, know what I mean?'

'Yes, I do,' replied Gin.

'What you going to do now, honey?' asked Myrna, putting her hand on Gin's. 'Just what you going to do?'

Gin told her about Texas, and got Hugh to give her the address so that mail could be forwarded.

'How long you going to be away then?' asked Myrna. 'Ain't you going to turn up for your engagements?'

'Don't know how long, Myrna,' said Gin. 'Reckon they'll not mind if they think I'm sick.'

'You just call me if you want me to deliver any more messages,' said Myrna. 'Maybe while you're gone you'd like Royce to fix that washing machine for you?'

They chattered on, as neighbours do, and Hugh drained his glass, feeling rather like a guest who has arrived too early, or a waiting taxi-driver. Across the room the young photographed Virginia lifted her arms as though holding an enormous balloon which had just burst to her infinite surprise and delight.

The living Virginia moved on her bandaged ankles back to her bedroom to finish packing, telling Myrna to take her time with her drink. Alone with Hugh, Myrna became grave.

'What are you going to do, mister?' she said.

'What do you mean?'

'About Gin, I mean.'

Myrna sighed and shook her head.

'Oh, I know what you'll say. It's what Royce tells me twice a day. None of my business. I know.'

Hugh cleared his throat.

'I'm sure I wouldn't say that,' he said.

'It's what you hear when you live so close,' she went on. 'You just know when something is wrong.'

Myrna finished her drink and stood up.

'It's not for me to say anything.' She looked at Hugh sharply. 'You're a foreigner, aren't you? English?'

'Yes.'

'So polite. So gentle.'

84

She gave Hugh's arm a little squeeze.

'I know all men aren't the same,' she laughed. 'Thank goodness! My Royce wouldn't hurt a fly. And it's a relief to me that you look the same.'

For a moment her face darkened, and she added:

'And they call it love!'

10

The shape beneath the sheet was like a landscape, and the extreme stillness of its breathing like the slightest susurration of wind in the crest of a wood from which a protective mountain rises. From his own bed Hugh watched the slopes and ridges for signs of movement, but nothing stirred. The darkness was a sufficient disguise of the presumed dilation of lung and expansion of breast, the tiny gale that might make a fold of sheet tremble if one were close enough, or small enough, to see it.

For the best part of an hour Hugh lay alone in wonder at the pleasure he could feel in enjoying his desire without taking it any further. He imagined being small enough to adventure in that feminine landscape, a strange counterpart to the decisive full-scale acts which always heralded the disappointing achievement of desire. Aroused but undemonstrative, charged but untense, he entered the alternative gardens of the imagination, discovering that contrary to popular delusion the imagination has no future, merely an unfulfilled past. He was like a traveller arrived at last at the main route he has long sought, who sits by the roadside to sketch a map of his wanderings.

Their own wanderings on the first day of their linked time had begun promptly, for Gin had shown no desire to linger in her apartment.

'Now! I want to leave right away! Why not?' she had exclaimed, and Hugh, who had somehow expected a preliminary clarification of their relationship, was compelled cheerfully to agree. What precisely the clarification might have consisted of he had no time to work out. At the least, it would have needed some kind of territorial decision, a symbolic acceptance, a token toothbrush. Some part of him, urged on by the precipitous and preordained aspects of their surprising entanglement, had hoped for a momentous sexual encounter, emotional, dramatic and prolonged beyond credibility. But he was enough of a realist to accept that whatever the Baroness might want from him was limited by her essential ignorance of him, and that outside fiction a sudden conviction of passion did not usually issue in immediate escapades. It would have to be enough.

Thus they performed their nocturnal flight. Hugh, already rootless, was ready enough to leave for Dexter. The reason for going had mysteriously become hers, the romantic submission his. She was like a female Othello.

It was not yet eight o'clock when they had taken the Lincoln Tunnel to New Jersey. The flat industrial landscape lay in the suspense of an uncertain convalescence in the rosy evening light. From the tollgate on the New Jersey turnpike Hugh could still see the Empire State Building as they waited in line, and felt a strange pang of uncertain anticipation as he realised that he was in fact leaving the hectic civic concentration that it symbolised. His adventure was bred of Manhattan's culture. Its very possible confusion of art and life was a product of that cultural intensity. Its assumption of freedom belonged to that rootlessness. Its trust in an unpredictable future derived from a city of haunted pasts. It was a city that belonged to adults and to the experiences that they hourly needed to recreate.

And yet, even as Hugh in a moment thought all this, he knew it was only part of Manhattan's accumulated myths. He was experiencing a kind of *Heimweh* for an environment he had known only for a matter of weeks, an environment that had bestowed upon him, however temporarily, the human form now dozing beside him who had become its yearning voice, even in a way its soul. This sudden love for

86

Gin: was it no more, then, than a cultural infatuation, a recognition of the myth? What would he do with this tender fragment of Manhattan in Dexter? What would he make of it anywhere else? Could it ever belong anywhere else?

Gin had switched on the car radio, but he did not know whether she was listening to it or not. Her eyes opened once or twice to stare out into the dusk, or to meet his eyes with a small smile of comic complicity and reassurance, but soon she seemed to be really asleep. Hugh retuned the radio and found a listener-supported radio station from the Delaware Valley at 91 FM broadcasting *The Pirates of Penzance*. Its ingratiating melodies and decent fun wormed another kind of nostalgia out of Hugh, for Simon had once come home from prep school able (almost) to sing 'I am the very model of a modern Major-General' to his own accompaniment on the piano, and Hugh, taken unawares by the demonstration of independent will and uncertain competence, had been moved to surreptitious tears. Moreover, there were aspects of the Englishness of Gilbert and Sullivan which Hugh still felt that as a composer he could share, and they were, after all, ancestors of the musical theatre of Porter, Rogers and Hammerstein, and West. He listened with an attention he had never before given it, taking in not only the familiar tunes, but all the absurdities of the plot. The pirates were, for example, orphans to a man. He was reminded of Barrie's Lost Boys, and thought how tough Gilbert's vision of pirates (or fairy guardsmen for that matter) was compared to Barrie's, whose cloying mother-fixation denied him the rumbustiousness of High Victorian comedy. The Victorian myth of the 'orphan' and the 'orphanage', he reflected, was based less on the mortality than on the sexual irresponsibility of parents. To that extent Simon himself had become some kind of orphan. Was Barrie right in claiming that it was motherlessness and not fatherlessness which obsessed the lost boy? Had Simon been unfairly claimed by Daisy as her divorce-right, or had he chosen to go with her willingly, in preference to his father? Was every Mr Darling a potential Captain Hook?

Hugh did not want to think of these things, and was glad when Gin

87

woke up shortly after ten o'clock just in time to exclaim in delight at the delicate and glimmering panorama of lights as they crossed the Delaware. Hugh enjoyed explaining the music, for it was completely strange to her. She listened to it with a serious enthusiasm, as though Hugh had invented it spontaneously for her amused wonder. She refused to believe how old it was.

Later, somewhere between Baltimore and Washington, they decided they were hungry and had stopped for a meal that was more like breakfast than it was like anything else.

Gin looked at Hugh over a cup of coffee which she held with both hands.

'You're a real Englishman, honey,' she said. 'Not like some, who think they are or would like to be.'

'It's what it says on my passport,' said Hugh.

'It's all there for you,' she went on. 'It doesn't change.'

'Oh, lots of things change,' protested Hugh.

'Not much,' she said. 'Like that Gilbert and Sullivan. Say, is that what you call pantomime?'

'No,' said Hugh. 'It's not pantomime.'

She frowned, as though disbelieving, or sorry to be wrong.

'I thought maybe that was pantomime.'

'It's better than pantomime.'

She nodded.

'What I mean is, you belong to all that. You don't need to learn nothing new.'

Hugh wasn't sure whether to take this as a compliment or not.

'A lot has happened since Gilbert and Sullivan,' he said. 'Even in English music.'

'Yeah,' she admitted. 'But it don't faze you none.'

They had paid their bill, and bought some cans of soda to take back to the car. Gin adjusted her reclining seat and made a pillow of her cardigan, so Hugh put on his Walkman to avoid keeping her awake on the rest of the journey. He had had no idea how long the rest of the journey would be. Gin was tired. He was tired. Yet they had not yet discussed where to stop for the night. For Hugh such a discussion would involve the unvoiced plans about sleeping together which he presumed were as much in her mind as his. He was willing to go on driving for the moment, and she seemed willing to go on being driven for ever.

When she saw Hugh's Walkman she insisted on listening to it herself so that she could hear his tapes. He put on the Stravinsky for her.

As they had continued on their journey he had kept glancing at her to gauge her reaction, but she was now just a little too far behind his sightline. Perhaps Stravinsky was not really new to her. Perhaps it would not faze her, even if it was. Hugh did not really know what kind of music she had been raised in before absorbing the tradition represented by Sammy West, who was probably the kind of would-be Englishman she had had in mind.

After a while she leaned forward into his line of vision.

'Hey,' she exclaimed, with an air of discovery. 'This stuff is like you!'

Hugh laughed aloud in demurral and secret delight.

'No, I mean it,' she said. 'It's like your ballet. It has those same crazy intervals. This guy a friend of yours?'

Hugh told her all about Stravinsky, and tried to explain Stravinsky's importance for his own music. His pleasure at her observation lent his explanation an urgency and fluency in which he took some pride, until he realised that she had fallen asleep again. She continued sleeping as they crossed into Virginia, and though he wanted to point out that they were now in her name-state (as if to prove that he could please her with a foolish sentiment as well as bore her with a musical lecture) he did not in fact wake her.

To drive without an immediate destination is a strange suspension of will, or of anxiety. The moon was flat and theatrical. Their headlights swept past wooden houses with dead blinds and empty porches, sleeping shells of suspended life. Once Hugh had to slow down suddenly for a deer that bounded in front of him across the road. They passed motels still lit for business, and passing them did not seem reckless. The night was neither young nor old. It was more like a state of mind.

And so it had gone on. Gin would briefly resurface, and they would exchange a few drowsy words. Another small town would surround them for a moment, vacant and purposeless as an abandoned film lot. Once Gin put the Walkman back on his own head, and Hugh was amazed to hear her voice coming, not from the car-blurred, window-rattled ambience of the passenger seat, but richly and precisely from within his own head:

'But if you touch it I say broken,
If you break it I say sold.'

She squeezed his arm at this, and Hugh felt that she was trying to tell him something. But did she know that it was those words he had heard, or was it the whole song he was meant to be thinking of? Or was it simply a joke, the accessibility of a mechanised wooing voice when too tired to speak? The song, like so many of the Baroness's, was at once an invitation and a warning:

'When you're looking around for love
It's something you'll find there's plenty of
Or so I'm told,
But if you touch it I say broken,
If you break it I say sold.'

In this way they reached the limit of their endurance for travel, and at some time after two in the morning, and at a place not certainly nearer either to Arlington or Lexington, they turned off for the Faint Heart Motel. They prepared for sleep in unembarrassed haste, and fell into the twin beds as if into the embrace of a mother, or as an example of gravity.

And yet five minutes later, Hugh was awake and listening for Gin's breathing.

It was like some dreamed deliberation of delay. Everything he could think of doing was less intention than act undone, less to be hoped for than something not yet regretted. But he did not want to wake her.

90

Perhaps he wanted to have nothing to regret. He had to give her time.

His eyes travelled again and again round the motel room, searching in its shadows for some palpable consciousness of the sexual, but he was not sure that it did not merely offer a trivial history of restlessness in its over-mirrored solicitousness, its disposable travellers' aids, its fake baronial veneers. His presence in the bed displaced the ghosts of all others. Their feelings were unimaginable. The motel might have been built that very morning, perhaps expressly for them to act out this scene of slumber and vigil.

Damn it, thought Hugh. Was he not going to get any sleep at all?

He tried the reliable distraction of composing in his head, but his own music could not easily displace the vigorously implanted seed of 'If You're Looking Around for Love'. He allowed his mind to wander more theoretically over his future *oeuvre*, a form of fantasising normally inducive of immediate drowsiness. He thought of his plan for a series of musical portraits, all of women, all with a psycho-erotic flavour, exploiting a bizarre and recherché orchestration, but departing not very far from a relatively simple lyrical base. The point would be that the real portrait to emerge (and the cycle could in fact be called *Portrait*, in the singular) would be of the composer himself. The variety of texture would itself be a novel treat (a trio of alto flutes performing athletic arpeggios for Mary Meadows, a melancholy cornet backed by violas and cellos for his mother, a violin for Daisy with harp, treble piano or celesta, a chamber organ and snare-drums for Dixie Polejack, a couple of baritone saxophones for Mrs Leathering) and the necessary unity would be a thematic one. They would all, perhaps, be variations on a theme which (representing Hugh) would not be revealed until the end of the piece, or perhaps not at all. Hugh's mind drifted irresponsibly sideways into the reception of this future work, its critical acclaim, the difference between the recorded versions of Haitink, Rozhdestvensky and Simon Rattle, its frequent performance at Promenade concerts, and so on. Just before he finally fell asleep, he realised, with more rueful amusement than dismay, that something rather like this work had already been written, that it was deservedly popular, and that he could hardly embark on writing it again.

In the closing seconds of wakefulness, therefore, he was blessedly free of any obsession with either the Baroness's voice or body. He drifted towards sleep, as secure in his talent as in an ocean liner, wrapped in the noble elation and Edwardian tenderness of Elgar.

II

Hugh didn't really know whether it was in the morning or still in the middle of the night that the Baroness slipped into his bed. Her initiative removed the occasion from all taint of schedule. It was altogether outside the demanding patronage of time. He could think coherently of nothing at all and did not wish to. Only two or three ideas flickered intermittently across his mind: that this, after all, was what he lived for and was worth any sacrifice or risk; that he had never been in bed with such a big girl; that none of the many things he found to do with her was, in the end, quite final or extreme enough. These glimmerings seemed quite distant and theatrical, for there was, after all, a great deal to do, and an unusual amount of it, he realised, was being done by the Baroness.

After that they lay back and talked. Hugh noticed that it was after 9.30 am, but as far as he was concerned he was ready to stay in the Faint Heart Motel all day if necessary. Behind the thick brown pleated curtains car doors slammed and engines started up. They drank some soda, and Gin found a bar of chocolate in her bag.

'I guess I must kind of like you,' she said, laughing into the sheet that was drawn up beneath her chin, her head angled awkwardly against the headboard, propped up to receive the squares of chocolate that Hugh fed to her. 'You reminded me who I am, that's what.'

'I didn't know you had amnesia,' said Hugh. 'Is that what Dr Listener was treating you for?'

'Ssh,' said Gin, putting her fingers to Hugh's lips. 'I'm serious now. You gave me some self-respect. I mean, you treat me like I know what I'm doing.'

'Well, you do know what you're doing. It doesn't take much to perceive that. You're a wonderful singer, one in a million.'

Hugh felt that he was searching for the right phrases and not finding them. But she seemed to know and to appreciate what he intended to say.

'That means so much to me. Hugh, you're a real musician. And you make me feel real, too.'

'Look, Gin. Everyone loves your singing. You're on the way up. It doesn't need me to tell you that.'

'Honey, nobody tells me nothing. You think anybody bothers to say that? Why, they just too busy making sure they get their *piece*.'

She pronounced the last word with a distinctive emphasis and scorn which gave it an equal sexual and financial meaning. Hugh, who did not want it to appear that his readiness to boost her artistic morale depended in any way on a deficiency of sexual interest, moved his lips from her shoulder to her cheek and took her ear lobe between his teeth.

'It's that Backman,' she continued. 'He's that percentage comes right off before you see a dollar. He's that worm in the apple. You got to slip him his piece before anyone will smile at you.'

She shook her head and sighed. Hugh settled his head once more on her bosom and felt the following inhalation as a sideways pressure so sturdy and momentous that this reminder of the bulk and shape of her body visibly renewed his own. She pretended not to notice.

'Mr Backman takes his piece all right,' she said. 'He got his creatures out there working for him. He makes sure you know where your bread is buttered. He's going to use you so you can't help yourself, that Mr Backman.'

'Who is this obnoxious fellow?' murmured Hugh, with a fake drowsiness, moving his hand stealthily across her stomach.

'Everybody knows Mr Backman,' said Gin. 'He's the one who keeps your secrets. He's the one whatever you do makes you feel like nothing 'cause you always going to owe him everything. He's clever, Mr Backman, and he's dirty, and no one's going to let you fight him.'

Hugh did not notice the tear that had gathered in the Baroness's eye as she spoke, the merest glistening and deepening of the lens that surveyed the dimness of the room without focusing on it. She stubbed out her cigarette, hardly noticing whether she had hit the target of the ashtray or not, and turned to him.

'Honey,' she said. 'You sure are the sexiest white man in Virginia.'

'Not quite there yet,' murmured Hugh, parrying the unnecessary flattery with an unnecessary joke.

When the stillness of the morning convinced them that they were the only motorists not on the road, and when the cleaners with their wire trolleys of linen had twice rung their doorbell, they decided that the world must be allowed to reclaim them. They took their time over coffee and pancakes in the diner, and bought a wide-mouthed thermos which they filled with ice-discs that spilled out from a machine in the motel in response to an inserted quarter. They filled the car with gasoline. They bought a newspaper. Finally, they were ready to leave, and Hugh could think of nothing but their next motel stop. Where would it be? Somewhere in Tennessee? Now that he was travelling, the distances seemed less daunting. The roads were straight, and he could keep up a constant speed. At this rate they could be in Texas in a day or two.

Driving by day, the car windows rolled down, the sleeveless arm resting on the lip of the warm steel shell of the car where it protected the retracted glass, the wind ruffling the small hairs and entering the tunnel of the sleeve to cool the armpit, Hugh felt completely relaxed. Gone were the confinement of the dark, the loneliness of radio voices, the weary sense of leaving a busy day behind. The day was brand new. The sun had created it afresh. The body was new, shed and spent, showered and tuned. There was nothing to do but travel.

Gin talked for a change not of the uncertainties of her career, nor of the predatory Mr Backman, but of her childhood. She had been born in a small town between Lafayette and Baton Rouge. She had never known her father, who had upped and left at the first challenge of responsibility towards the girl he had seduced. She lived with her mother on the citrus farm run by her grandfather, who himself had, it seemed, a relatively young family by a second wife.

'We sure were a whole dangerous swarm of little creatures in that house,' she said. 'There was Sam and Ellie, and blind Ida. They were Sarah's children.'

'Your grandfather's wife?'

'Yeah. Grandpa pretended to take no notice of them at all. I guess he liked them pretty much though and just wanted to spare Ma's feelings, and Richard's. Richard was Ma's brother, but he was maybe ten years younger than her. So when I was little he was still a child. All these kids were my aunts and uncles!'

Gin chuckled at these memories, and Hugh, guiding the car at what seemed an unnecessarily sedate maximum legal speed down the straight highway, settled back comfortably as though he were being read a story, not sure that he quite understood all the relationships.

'They never behaved much like aunts and uncles, though, and I guess that says something for Sarah. She was pretty relaxed about it, and she seemed to love Grandpa all right. We were all crowded together, and in the early days that included my great-grandmother. She gave Ma a lot of talk from her about having me and being unmarried and all. Ma told me how it used to get her down, being called a sinner and a disgrace to the family. But there was nothing that little Richard could do wrong. Well, Ma weathered that all right, and she looked after Richard as well as me.'

Gin lit a cigarette, and the exhaled smoke swirled and vanished from the car window like a terrified spook.

'Sam was the real devil. He sure was old enough to know the difference between little aunts and little uncles. See him strutting around like a savage after his bath-time, come right into our room as if he didn't know what shape he was. Pretended he'd left something in there, Dick Tracy maybe; he was always reading Dick Tracy. Never dare do it if Richard was around, but Richard had this gang over in

95

Henderson Swamp. God knows what he did there, but he was out all hours. Strutting around too, I'll be bound.

'My time was with Ellie and Ida, begging flour for food pies under the kitchen table, Oh, those de-licious food pies! Ellie would tie my great-grandmother's shoelaces together and then say Ida did it. Ida never got whopped. In the evenings Grandpa would play his guitar, and sing. He knew all the old blues, and sometimes his foreman Clarence would bring his cornet and we kids would beat out a rhythm on the back of the chesterfield, you know? It was leather and hollow, you could raise the dust, like beating a carpet. I guess we didn't keep very good time, but that didn't worry Grandpa none. He'd keep on playing with his eyes shut tight like he was trying not to cry and Clarence sat there bolt upright with *his* eyes popping out of his head. I used to love those evenings. Ma and Sarah would look at each other like they were sisters and smile over him. They couldn't be that close. She was Ma's stepmother, you know? She knew all those secrets, all those bed secrets.'

Hugh tried to imagine such a family.

'What happened to them all?' he asked.

Gin loked at him with amusement.

'I'm boring the pants off you with all this stuff,' she said.

Hugh protested that she wasn't boring him at all.

'My uncle Richard was killed in Vietnam,' she said. 'Ida died, too. In an automobile accident. She was a real sweet kid, could do cats' cradles like you never seen though she was blind as a stone. Ellie married a store-keeper in Butte la Rose. Sam took on the farm. Hell, you don't want to know all this.'

'Yes, I do,' said Hugh. 'What happened to you?'

'Well,' said Gin, flipping her cigarette butt out of the window. 'The great event in our lives was Jack Gerald. He was a sergeant in the Air Force down on manoeuvres from Fort Randolph near San Antonio. Seemed like our local swamps were fine training ground for the boys they were sending out to Vietnam. They sure had some fireworks out in those swamps. They dropped those boys from low-flying helicopters. It was like dropping lumps of sugar in strong tea.

Two of Jack's company died in those manoeuvres they took so seriously.

'I guess I was about eight or nine then, and beginning to take care of myself. Anyhow, Ma had started to go out now and then in the evenings. I guess she needed a good time. She wasn't as old as I am now. So she used to go to these dances at Baton Rouge and kick around with teenagers. Guess it was some way to go, near an hour on the bus, but my great-grandmother wasn't around to complain any more and Grandpa was real pleased to see her dressed up again.

'Strutting Sam was beginning to be a pain in the ass. He'd taken to coming into my bed to read me Dick Tracy at night once Ma was out of the way. There were one or two things I didn't like about that. I wanted to get to sleep for one thing. For another he couldn't hardly read. I could read better than he could, and I didn't like Dick Tracy. *And* what's more, as you may have guessed, Dick Tracy wasn't the only dick he brought into my bed.

'Oh I wasn't so innocent, and he sure thought I was fun to play with with my new breasts and my pigtails and all. He liked to pull those pigtails. "I'll pull these and you pull this," he'd say. But I arranged with Ma for Ellie to sleep with me, said I was scared of the dark. Sam sure wasn't going to try anything on his own sister. Things quietened down after that.

'Meanwhile Ma was getting very thick with Sergeant Jack Gerald. He came to the house and brought us all presents, and no one could resist him, not even Richard, who had been bawling Ma out for going to dances in the first place. In fact Richard fell for him in a big way. That's the reason he joined the Air Force nearly a year before he was due to be conscripted, when most of his friends were doing all they could to get out of it. I suppose he might be alive now if it hadn't been for Jack.

'We moved to Texas when Ma married Jack and we had a name and a father and a real brick apartment and all. I didn't know the difference before that, you know? But when we visited Grandpa I realised the difference all right. The old house looked like a shack. Well, it was a shack: flaked whiteboard walls, tin roof. And when

Grandpa took out his guitar he couldn't hardly play, his hands were so bad.

'Jack was real good to me. He knew it was no use babying me so he treated me like a little old lady. And when Jimmy came along he was specially good, because he knew I might be jealous. Well, I don't know why they talk about jealousy. I was proud as anything to have a baby brother. I remember that sour smell of the skin on his head when I kissed it. I thought Jimmy would always look up to me, and I wouldn't have to stand no nonsense from him. Back in Cecilia I'd been the youngest. Sometimes that meant good, sometimes it meant bad, but it was always someone handing it out. Now I could give, as well. I suppose what it was, I was old enough to have a baby of my own, though I didn't think of that at the time. Yes, I'd matured pretty early. I worked it out the other day, you know, one of those fool things you get to doing when you look over your life. Over two hundred periods already! That's some trouble, I hope you realise that?'

Hugh realised that there was no social sympathy appropriate to such quantified pain. He searched for a formula, found none, and reached over for her hand which he squeezed. She laughed.

They were passing town after town where lives like the one she was recounting were being lived, but the streets seemed empty to Hugh; the few signs of human presence (a man mowing a verge, a group in discussion around a jacked-up van, a school bus) were like careful representative symbols, sinister alien imitations of normality, perhaps, or placing shots from a film.

They stopped for an alien imitation lunch, and filled up again with gasoline. Hugh heard how Jack Gerald, gripped by political enlightenment and personal depression, refused to renew his engagement with the Air Force, and after a period without work eventually set up a small tourist operation in San Antonio. The lucky basis of this operation was a part-time job as caretaker of an Indian monument just outside town. The Scattle Stones were the oldest human artifact in the county, perhaps in the whole state. Jack Gerald put his release money into a couple of buses and went into the business with another ex-airman to put the Scattle Stones on the map, taking in other tourist attractions on the way, the Mexican Governor's house, the mansions of the German Cattle Barons in the King William district, and always, of course, returning to the hub of this sightseeing circuit, the Alamo. Jack and his friend drove the buses, and since her mother was busy keeping house and looking after Jimmy, it fell to Gin to sit in the Scattle Stones kiosk and collect the quarters.

The lineaments of such an existence possessed a directness and simplicity which Hugh, searching for ways to describe Manchester Grammar School, could not begin to match. Gin had not progressed beyond fifth grade. At an age when he was still collecting bus numbers she was performing sexual favours in the back of borrowed pick-up trucks. When he was taking his O-Levels she was singing in bars for five dollars an evening. At an age when his scholarship to the Royal Academy seemed more like a schoolboy trophy than the threshold of a career, she had already moved to New York, discovered and manipulated by the legendary Mr Backman.

For her, driving south was a key that unlocked these experiences. For Hugh it was an adventure that took him even further from the calculated arc of his own ordered life. As the landscape changed he seemed to leave behind the safe trajectory of his ambition. Merely to move (as now, absurdly, past bunched and lightly wooded hills, a scattering of seeded spruce, a splay-tailed unnameable bird bobbing on a fence, and a sign that read MARION, HUNGRY MOTHER PARK, TAZEWELL) was to acknowledge that real experiences could after all lie in ambush for him. The sky became overcast and cleared again. The soil turned orangy-red. Roadside holdings were replaced by cabins peeping from high wooded bluffs. Trees crowding the highway were weirdly draped with dead creeper. They stopped. They ate. They slept. They made love. And in the morning the land would be flat again as if in response to renewed energies.

After one stop, when Hugh yawned and grinned and said that he needed to stretch his legs, he returned from a twenty-yard stroll back along the highway to prod a frayed rim of blown tyre that might have been a snake, to find Gin sitting in the driver's seat.

'My turn,' she said.

Hugh was amazed.

'Why didn't you tell me you could drive?' he asked.

'Sure I can drive,' she said, starting the engine. 'Get in, unless you want to be left in Tennessee.'

Hugh climbed in, and off they drove again. The opportunity for telling her more about himself was missed, for the angle of the passenger seat as she had left it was too tempting and Hugh began to nod off. The last thing he saw as they sped along in the late morning sun was a sign advertising 'The World's Only Guitar Shaped Museum'. He was curious enough to look out for the unique object itself, but before they reached it he was fast asleep.

12

Hugh had, despite himself, expected the Crails' ranch to be a low wooden building bolstered with stockades and much fencing, set in a dusty plain stretching to the horizon. However much he had modified that view when consulting the map, he was still not quite prepared for the newish stucco mansion with deep-set green roof, verandah and balconies, reached by a fresh-cut mountain road rising above the lake and giving astounding views of Dexter not more than a couple of miles away, embosomed in trees, the tower of the university as gracious as a Tuscan campanile, the river winding in broad masses across the whole landscape. There were other houses on this wooded ridge. A sprinkler here and there, a station wagon with a boat trailer, a fenced orchard, and other signs of habitation, gave it the air of a determined and well-to-do settlement carved out of a mountainous wilderness in the way that only money can contrive. The scenery had a farouche beauty that somehow had not yet surrendered its innocence by pretending to be a suburb. Its inhabitants had too much leisure to regularise it as a commuting district of the city. It was charted by no bus-route or mail delivery. These houses were recreational encampments, sending up the smoke of barbecues. Teenagers roared down the dusty road to the lake on expensive motorbikes. The middle-aged woman in the white house up from the Crails' seemed inseparable from her chestnut mare, and rode solemnly among the trees like a well-tailored centaur.

The Crail house was built on a strip of open land that had been settled earlier. There were fields behind it, and an old farm a couple of hundred yards further down where the Finches kept a dozen or more horses. Some belonged to absentee pleasure-seekers like the Crails, but the rest were available for riding-lessons and children were driven out from Dexter at weekends to be led by Jed Finch along the wooded trails with hard hats and little crops. Jed was also keyholder, trashburner and handyman for a number of houses on the ridge, jobs which he performed carelessly but with fierce pride. He was somewhat indignant when Hugh and Gin arrived.

'Didn't let on there was two of you,' he grumbled.

But there was nothing very much for him to do, and he kept out of their way. Hugh wondered how much the Crails paid him.

In those lazy days when they first arrived there seemed to be nothing to do but sleep off the journey, drink freshly squeezed orange juice and drive down to the lake. Hugh would wake to the glare of the sun leaking from the edges of the roller-blinds and to the self-righteous or delirious calls of birds outside their window. The lateness of the hour would send him from the bed like a sleeper of Ephesus eager to enjoy the reformed world. He would bring juice or coffee for Gin, who would simply sigh and turn over, and then he would sit outside, matching the birdsong with the fragments of music in his own head. Somehow they bought food, but it was never enough and it didn't matter. Hugh felt that they could live on air. The air was delicious. The morning haze, dizzying as a spritzer, settled to a noon clarity that allowed, it seemed, a vision of the whole state looking west towards the plains, an area larger than France to be gulped down by the thirsty eye. The birdsong caressed and penetrated the air as if to give it a voice.

Why should any of the flora and fauna be recognisable, Hugh wondered, or at least as recognisable as they were? In fact, there was so much that was not only strangely distinct, as in the time-warp of a continent's drift, but absolutely alien, like the ball-moss freely mobile and living on the moisture in the air, that Hugh felt an elation of novelty in the slightest observation of nature. That whinnying above the trees that might have been a distant horse, that abrupted shriek: the bird voices deceived by claiming a naturalised status in the colony. That claim was reciprocated by the whine of speedboat or chainsaw, utterances of the pleasure-seekers occupying the ridge. Both expressed a joy in untranslateable sounds that might, nonetheless, be mistaken for things unlike them. Bluejay, mockingbird and whinnying grackle seemed, therefore, vagrant, ingratiating, human.

He was right about the piano. He found that a version of the third movement fugue in piano score, laborious though it was to produce, and fudged though it had to be for his fairly small hands, did tell him more about this material than his inner ear could tell him, and he was able, with confidence, to add a further voice with a much better notion of what the resulting texture would sound like.

The first time he played the opening over, with its Amazingesque chase theme transformed into a confident exploratory exchange of parts, gathering and accelerating into a massed and busy machine of sound, Gin trailed into the living room and stood against the piano wearing nothing but a sheet and a mock-tragic expression.

Hugh had to break off and laugh.

'I just don't know how you make all that stuff up,' she said sleepily.

'Neither do I,' said Hugh. 'And I'm not doing enough of it, either.'

'If I'm in your way, honey, I'll just go on up back to bed.'

'What, at half-past eleven?'

'Yeah, at half-*past*, goddamn and *blast*,' said Gin, with long English vowels. 'You ain't tuned into my schedule yet, you know? What's a girl to do with a man who's snoring already when it ain't turned one in the morning?'

'I was thinking we could take a sandwich down to the lake.'

'Sure thing,' said Gin. 'Give me five minutes. I can go to sleep there.'

'Come as you are,' said Hugh. 'You'd be a sensation.'

'I'll be a sensation anyway,' retorted Gin, throwing the end of the sheet across her shoulder and stalking away as though auditioning for Yves Saint Laurent. Herrick was so right, Hugh thought, about the female anatomy. A paltry gesture towards duty made him turn from the vision of 'that brave vibration each way free' a second or two before she disappeared through the door, to pencil in three quavers on his draft. He felt no virtue, only a renewal of excitement, like rumbles of thunder after a storm. What were these marks of his on the music paper anyway? They were nothing more than the ink in a barometer: if they dried up and the graph revolved as a blank it would have absolutely no effect on the weather.

But he did try to work for a lot of the time, sometimes reading through the typescript of his lectures and pencilling in the margin little opportunities for off-the-cuff aphorisms, sometimes forging ahead with the concerto. If he worked when the Baroness was awake she would inevitably gravitate towards the living room, perhaps lying on the sofa in the way she did with one foot still on the floor, reading old numbers of *Vanity Fair*, sometimes coming to lean on the piano and listen. Once, to amuse her, he modulated his fugue at a complex moment of overlapping voices and key changes into the racier section of 'Tell It Me Again', and she exclaimed aloud like a child who has, or thinks she has, outwitted the conjuror. But then Hugh turned the bass voice into a version of 'America the Beautiful', in octaves, pomposo, and Gin hammered him on the shoulders until he was forced to stop.

'How come you can't play songs?' she would ask. 'Can't you improvise none?'

Hugh's response was to tinkle an accelerated version of 'This Can't Be All' in the harmonies of a Bach chorale, but after some more hammering he was forced to admit that he couldn't swing. He quickly picked up a walking left-hand accompaniment that Gin had learned in the bars of her girlhood, but when he tried to hint at chord-sequences with his right hand in the necessarily reserved manner the style required, he simply collapsed with laughter.

'Come on, Howard,' said Gin decisively. 'We got to get down to some serious playing together, you know?'

She found a pile of music in the piano stool, which she eagerly sorted through. There was Grieg, and Selim Palmgren, Chopin and Poulenc. Most of it seemed to belong to Tikki Crail and was covered with the neat exhortations of Miss Corner. Hugh's *Holiday Snapshots* were in the pile, and Gin made him sit down and play them through. Hugh felt they sounded very dry.

'Kind of fun,' said Gin, unconvincingly.

They found a couple of albums of popular songs, clearly from their date belonging to Liz rather than to Tikki. They played 'Night and Day', 'No One But You' and 'Time To'. Hugh was fascinated to hear the Baroness getting on to terms with this last song, which she had never performed.

'Milton Baxter, I don't know, he's too thin, too whiny,' she said. 'I never like to sing him.'

Hugh played over the simple arrangement, adding the notes that he felt were necessary to give it life, notes that had been omitted for the benefit of the amateur drawing-room pianist. Some of his chords sounded more like Britten than Baxter.

'Hey, man,' cried Gin. 'What you doing with that tune? You making it sound like afternoon tea. Hey, take it down a bit, will you? I can't sing in that key.'

Hugh transposed it a whole tone, and Gin began:

'It took me time to get through to you.
Now time is heavy on my hands . . .'

Hugh's stylistic hodge-podge of thickenings and augmentation was immediately lost beneath the deep melancholy authority of Gin's rendering, but she was not satisfied.

'See what I mean?' she complained. 'Those first three notes, they're all over the place. "It took me time . . ." What does the guy think he's writing, a baseball march?'

She sang the first line over several times, trying to get it right. In the end she settled for a heavy monotone, singing the first four words on the same note.

'How about that?' she asked.

'It's economical,' said Hugh, putting his hand round her waist.

'Yeah, but look,' she said. 'The climax of the verses comes in the third line, "All that" on B flat. I don't want to hit B flat till then, do I? It takes out the sting.'

She pushed his hands away from her bottom and on to the keyboard.

'Listen, Howard,' she said good-naturedly. 'You play those black notes not mine.'

He struck up the introduction to 'Time To' once again.

'Slower!' she yelled. 'What is this? Try to pretend you're fucking the goddamn piano, can't you?'

Hugh gave the keys, black and white, all he could give them. Gin closed her eyes and sang:

> 'It took me time to get through to you.
> Now time is heavy on my hands.
> All that you taught me,
> All that I know, is due to you.
> Nobody understands.'

She nodded.

'OK now, Howard,' she said. 'We got to pace this tricky little chorus right. Not too slow, not too fast.'

They picked up the song again:

> 'Time to love,
> Time to despair,
> Time to move
> To another chair.
> Time to spend,
> Time to start,
> Time to mend
> Your broken heart.

Time to leave,
Time to cry,
Time to believe
It's time to die.'

Hugh broke off with a flourish.

'Gin, that's perfect,' he exclaimed. 'You make everything sound perfect. It's just not the same song.'

'Yeah, well. Milton Baxter sure as hell couldn't sing,' she said. 'So what *is* the song till someone sings it?'

Hugh, accustomed to being consulted by soloists and conductors alike about metronome markings or the possibility of using three instead of four bassoons, could only admire this wholly reasonable liberty with her musical material. He wondered what would happen if someone like Katey Ottodici were a self-taught genius instead of a highly-disciplined prodigy: would all the problems of his concerto simply be solved in rehearsal? He had heard of playwrights who left it to the actors to write the play. No, it could not be done. But what the Baroness did with Baxter was truly original, and as they played through the whole song Hugh did his utmost to produce a discreet and idiomatic accompaniment, hinting at the elements of the melody she cavalierly omitted, predicting her rubatos, keeping the tempo as Gin had ordered it, 'strong and smooth as beef gravy'.

'It took me time to get through to you.
Now time is heavy on my hands.
All that you taught me,
All that I know, is due to you.
Nobody understands.
Time to, &c.

There's always time to claim there's time to
Find the time to say to you
All that needs saying
Before I shrug and climb to
Some cold and distant view.
Time to, &c.

I needed time to get to know you
And there was never time enough.
All that you gave me
Turns into what I owe you.
You left when the going was tough.
Time to, &c.

And if there's time to say goodbye
There still is time to try again
All that you showed me
Of love that will not die,
Of love's demanding pain.
Time to, &c.'

The Baroness was quiet after singing this song, and for the first time Hugh noticed the glistening in her eye that sometimes occurred in moments of reflection. His tact was stretched by his instinctive curiosity about the world she had left in order to enter his, but he maintained silence. She had said nothing about her bruised ankles, which she now hid in white socks that gave her an oddly athletic air. She did not want to talk much about her interrupted engagements, except to dismiss Goldbein with that characteristic shooing motion of her fingers, saying: 'I don't owe him *nothing*.' She had finished her life story precisely at that adult threshold that most tantalised Hugh. She did not explain Mr Backman. She never talked of Sammy West.

Whenever he did probe, at those philosophical moments when he could prepare himself for doing so, as if to remind both of them that he expected her ultimately to return to the world she kept from him, she would touch him on the nose and say: 'When I take up with a fellow I don't ask too many questions.'

The lake was always the key to unlock their claustrophobia. Gin was a strong swimmer, and would without hesitation plunge in and strike out as if intending to reach the other shore, oblivious of the speedboats dangerously unzipping the water just in front of her. There was a boat station, and a lawn with a picnic area, and in the afternoons people would gather there for their pleasure. Boats would be unhitched from cars and scooted into the water. Young men in plaid briefs brought files of work, but ended up chasing each other into the lake until it was time to return to Dexter for a class. And always the birdsong continued whether the people came or went.

Hugh had dozed, and woke suddenly to feel his face locked motionless against the sun, the shouting resumed in his ear like a soundtrack, a busy texture of energy, a distancing vocal babble. Damn it, he thought, he would burn. He raised his head to look for Gin, but she was beside him, beads and film of lake water glistening on her thighs, back and shoulders. She must have woken him, but she had already shut her eyes.

There was an oiled girl stepping from a bobbing prow, angling the outboard motor towards the opposite shore like a gun. Shaking the curls free from her bandeau, she called again and again to a wonderfully deaf dog who scampered and snapped after the only things he did hear, the busy grackles, with their alarm and chatter. Boys splashed.

Elsewhere heads barely turned from their attention to the sun, little lidded profiles, like rehearsals for a tomb.

Everything was so green. Everything was so recently settled. There was a sense of waiting for something to happen. The lake, which had been river before it was flooded at the civic will, had an air of unlocated satisfaction. No extravagant claims were being made, but in the chatter of the waters there seemed, Hugh thought, to arise a perfectly reasonable riverly notion that although there may finally be no such thing as success (successes being simply those few mistakes that you have managed to live with) nonetheless to create a lake where before was none, and to pose before it with one relaxed hip, is really something to make a noise about. Yes, Hugh thought, I know what that strange-familiar aerial song is, after all. The birds are singing in American.

He felt that broad inner unifying sweep of perception that he knew was a preliminary to musical conceptions. He did not know whether to resist them or not. English pastoral was played out, surely, and probably the pitfalls of American pastoral would be no less frequent and unexpected for being unfamiliar to him. Really, he did not want to write any sort of half-obligatory 'American' tone-poem.

'Do you want to go?' murmured Gin, beside him.

For a moment he interpreted this lazy remark as facing a more decisive departure than simply leaving the lake to the pleasure-seekers and returning to the Crail house. Did he want to go? Where did he want to be? And did he want to be there with the Baroness? At the back of his head was an angular musical motif, a jaunty sort of tune, like a smalltown neighbourly greeting on a weekend morning. It was not his, and it did not take more than a moment to identify it as by Charles Ives.

'No,' said Hugh. 'I'm quite happy here.'

And he wondered if he really were.

13

Some of the outside world caught up with them. Since his lectures were now only days off, Hugh felt obliged to ring Professor Prinzhorn, the Chairman of the Music Department at Dexter, to let him know that his prize lecturer had not forgotten the occasion, was already at hand, and was organised enough to require some details of the arrangements.

'Why, Professor Howard,' cried the aggrieved Prinzhorn, 'you should have let us know when you were coming so we could have met your plane and shown you around.'

Hugh made suitable excuses, but was left with an invitation to drinks which he did not absolutely refuse and to which, therefore, as he realised as soon as he put down the telephone, he was now more or less committed. The precise timbre of voice and excess of academic enthusiasm of the previously unbelievable Prinzhorn had the effect of making Hugh look yet again at the typescript which by now he had almost memorised. Gin made him say some of it to her and responded by simply roaring with laughter at her own helpless incomprehension of it.

'Thank you very much,' he said, in a state of amused rebuff.

'Oh, don't mind me, honey,' she said. 'I guess I do my thinking in other parts of my body.'

Gin had befriended a small dog that had come nosing for food one day. On one of their rare visits to the nearest shopping mall across the river she had insisted on buying dog food for it.

'Where those folks of yours then?' she would demand of it, in playful anger. 'Why bother us, now?'

And she would give it great cylindrical gobbets of Master's Menu, which it wolfed mistrustfully before scampering off. She called it Sam, and when Hugh raised an eyebrow at this name, she chuckled and said it was a perfect name for a dog.

Jed Finch brought round a pile of mail, something that he wore the air of being entitled to do. Most of it consisted of communication between local utilities or the state bureaucracy and the absent Crails, but there were a couple of letters for Hugh and, more surprisingly, one for Gin. It was a typewritten envelope, but Hugh noticed written on the back of it: 'He came round but I never said your address.'

Hugh read his letter from Daisy first, for the handwriting gave him a tremendous excitement and sense of exclusion. It was like waiting in a crowd, hardly able to see anything, for some fairy coach which had already, as he really knew but did not want to admit, passed by. He tore open the envelope slowly, like a famished man being closely observed. It was, of course, about their agreement to give Simon some money, a perfectly practical letter in that careless italic hand with ambiguous risers that always gave him the old twinge of irrational expectations. He scanned it fiercely, as though he had missed the crucial sentence which revealed its real purpose, such as 'When you come don't forget to bring a bottle of Bell's.' He did not know if he wanted such an impossible assignation or merely expected it, as the kind of remark that her handwriting had been invented for. He could not imagine anyone else reading that writing and finding such a message, someone for whom it would now have a natural validity.

The other letter was from Katey Ottodici, eager to consult him about the concerto. It was a dry, simple letter, in a girlish hand with circles on the 'i's instead of dots, and Hugh noticed that she had signed herself with 'love' and a cross that indicated a lip-greeting in that way the young have without really meaning it. The few points that she raised were realistic ones, though, and Hugh felt a sudden urge to expound them to her, to explain himself at length, which was the closest he ever came to the genuinely pedagogic.

Unlike the fool lectures, he thought, which the more he looked at them seemed to be nothing but empty and pretentious theorising. How much better he could make them if he had time to introduce more real discussion of his own work. Why did everything happen at once? He had had months in England to prepare something new for Dexter, years (almost) to write the concerto: and now something as overwhelming, personally valuable and time-consuming as this unexpected affair with the Baroness had turned up, complete with an idyllic location. He had no idea what it could lead to, or what it really meant for him. His professional life, so much of it too like itself to be uniquely absorbing, might tick over while he sorted out his feelings. But not quite yet. The lectures hung over him oppressively. The unwritten movement made him feel sick to contemplate: it was like the dreamed cue for an entrance for which he had not yet learned the part.

Had he learned his part with the Baroness? He realised that he was thinking of her, as he had always done, in the compulsive terms of the song:

> 'I'd like to hear your part.
> I know my own by heart.
> Tell it me again.'

That was her challenge: whatever it was she was doing with him, she knew why she was doing it. Sometimes it seemed as if she might just as easily stop doing it. But what did Hugh think he was doing? He had been taken up and spirited away by a song. He was in love with the embodiment of a romantic attitude. He had been hypnotised by a part of American culture reborn in the vocal chords of a large girl from Cecilia, Louisiana. It was her art, which was also the impersonal ghost of American popular music, which had seduced him. Was it a trick like the aggressive whinnying of the grackle, or the plot to get Benedick married? Was it simply the next available object of a biologically programmed appetite, like a new screen of *Amazing*?

Hugh looked at Gin, smiling as she read her own letter held in both hands like a billet doux in a stage comedy, and knew that it was not so, or did not feel it to be so. What he felt for her belonged entirely to the whole which no single reason could explain nor its own explication destroy.

'Hey!' she exclaimed. 'They want me on TV!'

'Gin, that's marvellous,' said Hugh. 'But surely you've been on TV before?'

'Oh sure,' she said. 'Everyone gets to be on TV. But this is different. This is Freddy Connor.'

'Well,' said Hugh, who hated Freddy Connor. 'You'll be so famous that you won't want to talk to me any more.'

Connor's show reduced his guests to the accessible, exposed their weaknesses with all the fierce enthusiasm of hasty research, faced them with anyone they had ever quarrelled with, made them pretend an interest in the affairs of the other guests, and then allowed them, in a kind of grudging postscript, a minuscule exhibition of their talents.

'Honey,' said the Baroness, drawing herself up to her full height. 'I'll make sure that *you* get on the show, too.'

'Not me, you won't,' shuddered Hugh. 'There are some secrets I want to keep.'

Gin had put the letter back in its envelope without offering to show it to Hugh. Nor did she ask him about his own letters. She seemed suddenly thoughtful. Had his remark about secrets somehow offended her?

It seemed not, for she walked over to him and gravely kissed his forehead. That evening she played him as many of her Grandpa's blues as she could remember, long rigmaroles of self-pity and outrageous sexual boasting that delighted Hugh with their posturing weariness and jabbing repetitions.

'Yeah,' she said. 'That's the way music should be. No Mr Backman for him. He just played for himself and for his family. No strings.'

After that, although it was getting late, she wanted to go down to the lake. She appeared with blankets and a bottle of the Crails' wine.

'Come on,' she said. 'We can walk round aways. Everyone will have gone by now.'

Hugh agreed with less than alacrity. He would have been happy working on his concerto, happy for Gin to have brought out the knitting. But she was restless. She seemed always slightly ungainly indoors. If she sat in a chair she looked as though she had been put there. She craved for the physicality of the lakeside, lying not sitting, with the possibility of flinging oneself violently into water.

'You know?' she said on the way down. 'I don't want that Freddy Connor thing after all.'

'Why on earth not?' asked Hugh.

'You can bet it's going to have its price,' she replied. 'It's Mr Backman with a vengeance.'

'Come on, Gin,' said Hugh. 'You know it will be good for your career.'

'My career?' she said. 'Yeah, and Mr Backman's career. And Freddy Connor. Watch them all come round, the vultures.'

They passed time on a rocky ledge further up by the lakeside as any lovers would do. The wine turned out to be an entirely inappropriate Californian burgundy, mouthfilling, like a hothouse. Hugh realised that it must have been an expensive one, the kind that beats Château Latour hands down at a blind tasting.

'We should be drinking this with steaks and béarnaise sauce,' he said.

'Hey, I can cook, you know,' said Gin, punching him in the ribs. They had defrosted a pizza earlier.

'So can I,' said Hugh. 'I just mean that this is a dinner wine, not a lakeside wine.'

'Maybe I'm a dinner girl, too, more than a lakeside girl,' she replied. 'Why don't you take me out?'

'I will,' said Hugh, absently. He had noticed something up on the ridge that took his attention.

'You don't sound too eager, Howard, you tightwad,' she said. Then: 'What's the matter?'

'I keep catching a glint up there,' said Hugh.

'Where?'

'Up on the road there, look, just before it curves into the trees. Just above the first house, the one with the gables.'

'Oh sure, I see,' said Gin.

'It's someone with field-glasses, and they appear to be looking down here.'

'Down here?' exclaimed Gin. 'You mean at *us*?'

'Looks like it,' said Hugh. 'There it is again. It catches the sun back there because it's so low on the horizon.'

'Maybe he's watching birds,' said Gin.

'A Peeping Tom, more likely,' said Hugh. 'Bloody hell, what a nerve!'

Gin was buttoning her dress.

'Maybe it's that Jed fellow,' she said with a shiver. 'Let's go back, honey. Least in bed we can draw the blinds.'

'Doesn't look like Jed,' said Hugh. 'Too heavy-set. Dark clothes.'

The setting sun was large and still, as though it lay at the bottom of the lake itself. It performed none of those baroque farewells that a cirrus-streaked sky encourages. It flooded the ridge with red light and the reflection of the binoculars was like a spark from a banked fire.

They drove the mile or so back up the hill, and as they passed the curve in the road where the man had been, there was nothing to be seen. Back at the house they were greeted by the dog Sam, snapping and bouncing, eager to renew his acquaintance with Master's Menu. Hugh felt sure that it was Jed Finch's dog, let loose among summer visitors to save the cost of its upkeep. It was probably even specially trained not to accompany Jed in public.

While Gin was in the kitchen he switched on the television and watched the end of a frightening programme about FBI harassment of Church-sponsored visitors to Nicaragua. One of the speakers was Gordon Liddy, of Watergate fame, asked for his views as a former functionary of the FBI. He was straight out of *Dr Strangelove*, bright-eyed, jaw-flexing, single-minded, dangerous. Questioned about the admiration he had expressed for the SS in a recent book, and how this squared with his former federal work, Liddy replied with candour that the FBI was in fact the SS of the US, was indeed, and was intended to be, its élite cadre of protection. The programme, insufficiently edited or compèred, left the great American public fully in possession of this and other edifying thoughts. It was succeeded by a quiz game of a greed and banality ('Win a wardrobe of watches for every occasion') that kept Hugh staring in appalled disbelief until it was over. He switched the set off, called for Gin and discovered from her distant response that she had already gone upstairs to bed.

Before he went up himself, he lingered in the living room looking for something to read. There were novels by American authors of the less obvious sort (Willa Cather, Sinclair Lewis) that he had never read, and knew that he should. He was tempted by some collections of photographs and, more dutifully, by a book about the history of Texas. The photographs were of the kind in which the grain of the film and the angle of vision reduced skin and sand to a single riddle of texture. He decided to read Lewis's *Main Street*. Then his eyes fell on Gin's letter, lying where she had left it, on the window seat.

He had no scruple in reading it, hoping to find out just what strings she feared might be attached to appearing on the Freddy Connor Show, to discover the degree of her commitment to Mr Backman.

The letter was not from Connor, not from Backman, but from Goldbein of Willa's Place. It began by complaining about her absence ('I can fill your spot like I did many times before but now you're so heavily advertised there is real disappointment and naturally this reflects on the reliability of the club') and went on to refer to the

Freddy Connor appearance only incidentally in connection with some proposed filming at Willa's Place, and the question of fees for Bob Gordon and his group ('If a facility fee and something for Bob is not forthcoming I have told Mr West that the question of using Willa's Place cannot be taken for granted').

Hugh was puzzled. It seemed then that the Freddy Connor appearance was not news, or at least not news to Goldbein, who presumed that Gin knew about it. And it sounded as though it were all in some mysterious way being masterminded by Sammy West, who had some relation with Goldbein. What was West's interest?

The prior decision on his part to ask no more questions about any of these matters, or about the Baroness's hospitalisation, was a kind of mesmerised wonder, inertia, or even superstition about ruining a fragile liaison. The gift of Virginia was accompanied by a tacit injunction, as in a fairy tale, not to break the spell.

He put the letter back, and vowed to forget about it. He didn't believe that the worm in Gin's apple was impossible to spit out. He knew that he himself had to make some decisions, but perversely he didn't want to know too much, as though if in perfect possession of all knowledge he might not only be unable to come to these decisions, but after all not wish to come to them. He took his book up to bed where Gin was waiting for him beneath one of the Crails' sheets, shaped like the Americas. The story of Carol Kennicott's frustrations in Gopher Prairie remained unopened.

Later, he himself lay transformed and fulfilled, his heel at Cape Horn, Panama cradling the Caribbean of his stomach, his arms flung out north of Canada to the snows. Somewhere ahead a figure driving a team of huskies came lashing furiously towards him. In the dark aperture of the fur hood only a mouth could be seen and it was shouting some warning, even though he could hear nothing but the barking of the dogs.

Then Hugh was suddenly awake and tense. He lifted his head from the pillow to listen to what he thought he heard. Gin shifted drowsily and asked him what the matter was.

'What's that barking?' he asked.

'Sounds like Sam,' she replied, turning over.

'Sam's in the house?'

'Yeah. He didn't want to leave.'

Hugh got out of bed.

'What do you think he's barking at?'

'How do I know what he's barking at,' she murmured. 'Perhaps he wants to go now.'

Hugh went downstairs, after slipping on his trousers. The house was dark and still, the air still very warm after what had been an extremely hot day. The Crails' expensive ethnic rugs felt like fields of stubble wheat to Hugh's feet.

The dog was in the kitchen, staring at the back door with its ears flattened. From its bared teeth there came a low continuous growling, like an old-fashioned alarm clock almost run down.

'It's all right, you idiotic dog,' said Hugh. 'There's nothing to bark at.'

But Hugh wasn't at all sure that that was true.

14

The days drifted by freighted with a sexual immediacy that Hugh had never quite experienced before. He supposed that it was due to Gin's happy acceptance of physical companionship as the essential basis of their relationship. They had no domestic plans, no relations to please, no cautious staking-out of intellectual positions to effect. She had sought his protection and was content to bask in it, like a lazy animal in the sun. There was a kind of withdrawal in her presence, a reserve, a proviso. It was as though she were tacitly agreeing to be free with her body, because it was particularly her body that he had rescued from Dr Listener.

But that was the whole point. If she were to make over to him more than her body he would surely discover who he was really rescuing her from. In his mind's eye he always visualised the loitering presence of Yellow, the face brazen and distorted as he had seen it in the lens of the peephole in the door to Peter Redmond's apartment. Was he the agent of the parasitic Backman? Was Backman indeed her agent? Was Backman Goldbein, for whom Yellow clearly worked?

And who did the Baroness sing for?

This question, which led Hugh directly into the heart of her fascination for him, was, he knew, essentially unanswerable. The emotion of her performances derived from the whole of her experience, which flooded back from her presence with Hugh like a long shadow, darkening the route she had travelled. Only her childhood, uncomplicated by passion, lay fixed in light. He could understand her chatter about her early life. It was all she could freely give him. And Hugh had given her no more, for he saw more piercingly than ever his own life as a muddle and a desert. He could conceive of no way in which he could offer her any of that. Whenever a particularly forceful image offered itself (Mary Meadows pretending to give him tea and show the photographs of her holiday, and simply having to stop, helpless, until he had taken the difficult decision to put his lips to her neck and await the consequences) he had to abandon it as being too foreign to her experience. He might as well have attempted to explain the dialect of his grandmother as she attended to the stove, or the jargon of his fourth form. He realised that his experience of love was as foreign as any of the more obviously bizarre forms of English social life. It was with a pang of regret and jealousy that he realised how freely Gin had learned to take (and to bestow) the love that for him was so hedged with hesitations and circumspection. A season of adolescence for her was perhaps equivalent of his half a lifetime of longing and botched experiment.

Not talking about *The Freddy Connor Show* became a distinct bother to him. If she were going to do the preliminary filming she would have to leave Dexter before he gave his lectures. She continued to be dismissive about her television opportunity, almost as if to please him, while at the same time behaving as if she were living towards a crucial deadline. She would sit at the piano and sing her lines with an odd mixture of technical exactness and wayward experiment, like a schoolgirl bored with copperplate. She wrote to Goldbein.

'Have you fixed it up then, Gin?' Hugh asked.

'Fixed it?'

She smiled inquiringly at him with that outward curling of the upper lip that made him want to lie down and be trodden on.

'With Goldbein.' As he said this he realised that she would know that he had read her letter, but it was too late.

She turned on her heel, tapping the envelope that contained her reply on the palm of her hand.

'Old-time Goldbein,' she said, musingly. And left the room.

Later they were due at the Prinzhorns', and Hugh had promised to take her out to dinner at last. He felt that he had been in hiding with junk food for weeks and it was time to look around and see what Dexter had to offer. Gin had prompted him more than once. Now they prepared for the evening in unusual silence. What might have been a matter of conspiratorial comedy (whether either of them had brought anything like the right clothes) became for each of them a trivial private worry.

Prinzhorn was a clean, heavy and unsmiling man, whose hand-shake and manner in pouring whiskey belied the impression of effusiveness that he had given over the telephone. His wife was small and nervously talkative. She smiled with exaggerated interest at Hugh's slightest remark and was motherly towards Gin.

Perhaps half an hour elapsed before Hugh understood with a surge of puzzled fury and embarrassment that his hosts were themselves embarrassed by the presence of the Baroness. A further embarrass-ment was almost immediately provided by the assumption that they were expected for dinner. The other guests, a lean young buttoned couple with faculty connections called Moffat, said nothing that engaged Hugh's attention. He timed his theft of pecan nuts (from a bowl that was never actually handed round) with a regimented resentment, and noticed that Gin, in the absence of their hostess in the kitchen, had picked up a copy of *The New Yorker* from the coffee table and was paying no attention to Prinzhorn's long account of the misuse of electronic equipment in the music workshops at Dexter. From the intensity of her reading, Hugh suddenly realised that Olive Dempster's article must have appeared at last. Already perturbed by the uncertainty of Gin's plans, and divided in his attention by the claims of politeness and academic duty on the one hand, and a desire to escape with her on the other, he was now gripped by a curiosity to know what Olive had written and how it was affecting her subject. As Prinzhorn's sentences continued to occupy the space between him and his guests like an electric current that could not be tackled except at the source, Hugh was transfixed as in a dream. Gin was beyond the dream, in a strange world of her own where some spurious image of her own life was confronting her from the public prints. It was like the telling of a spell that might enchant her, transform her, put her beyond his reach for ever, if he did not manage to reach her in time.

Dinner was a nightmare of further monologues and silences, and it was not until they strayed back into the living room like football players at half-time that Hugh had a chance to look at the article. Prinzhorn was investigating the drinks cabinet, and Hugh did not care if he offended the Moffats who in any case were deeply involved in apparently lighting the same cigarette.

The article predictably (except that Hugh had failed to predict it) was about Sammy West. It was about the West phenomenon, his prodigious fame, his survival of newer musical fashion, his continued secret influence. The Baroness appeared simply as his creature, his Eliza, hypnotised into the elocution of a style of singing that could never have occurred to her naturally. Hugh flipped over the irritatingly meagre columns of text crowded out by the ads for cashmere twinsets and mail-order tournedos in his search for some fresh or illuminating attention to the ostensible subject of the article, but he did not find it. Virginia Gerald was safely docketed as some cult toy, the eighties in fifties clothing, a throwback of nostalgia, like Popeye caps or the films of Bogdanovich and Spielberg. Olive's style was impetuous, confident and buttonholing, the prose equivalent of talking with her mouth full.

Hugh put down the magazine in disgust as Mrs Prinzhorn came into the room with a tray of coffee. Gin would not meet his eyes. It was his fault, wasn't it, this sophisticated calumny? This was Hugh's world, his friend, his style of analysis, where everything could be explained, even the things you didn't believe in.

The wooded lake, which had seemed a million miles from anything that could lay claim to them, now contained alien presences, like objects in a puzzle picture. Even the politeness of Mrs Prinzhorn, dispensing doll-sized cups of coffee, suddenly took on the banal mask of the spy, like a telling close-up in Hitchcock.

'And are you staying long in Dexter, Miss Gerald,' she asked, shunting a box of chocolates across the glass-topped table. They nudged the corner of *The New Yorker*, and Hugh wanted to pick it up and show it to Mrs Prinzhorn, and say: 'Look, she's famous! She actually does what your husband only writes about. She does it better than any of us.' But there was something about Mrs Prinzhorn's teeth and hair that reminded him of Olive.

'You're staying for the lectures, presumably?' she added.

'No,' said Gin. 'I'm going tomorrow.'

As they drove home, these words, long buried by the later trivialities of the evening, rose up in his head like a storm, forecast but ignored. He felt as though he had run up the steps of a tower to prevent some disaster, and now saw it already happening at a distance, powerless to do more than observe.

Part of him was furious. After all, the things that had come between them (his lectures, Olive's article) were nothing more than slight hazards in their professional lives, already set in motion before they met. But the idyll of the lake had to be fatefully circumscribed, he knew. It had that sort of unlucky unreality, doomed from the start.

'Are you really going?'

'It's all going someplace, honey,' was her dry reply. The rest of the evening was gripped by the frost of something like a quarrel. It hardly needed words to define it, for both of them knew what it was about. An airline reservation was made, her scattered possessions gathered up, the bottle of bourbon raided, separately, for their nightcaps.

In the bedroom Sam was slobbering over something on the rug.

'The Crails are going to bless us for letting that dog in here,' said Hugh. 'It's eating up the house.'

He rescued the object from Sam's jaws and wiped it on his handkerchief. It was a piece of rectangular tin, embossed with a frieze and the letters 'SS' on it.

'He could cut himself on this,' said Hugh. 'Whatever it is.' He straightened it and put it on the chest of drawers.

'Let me see that,' said Gin suddenly. She picked it up, and looked sharply at Hugh. Then she examined it as though it were a counterfeit coin.

'OK, OK!' she shouted, flinging down the piece of tin. She strode to the window, and stormed at the screen as though she were a character in a play unable to contain rage. It was little more than a frustrated release of breath from a body gripped by tension, but Hugh stood expectantly for the speech that seemed sure to follow.

Gin simply turned towards him, her eyes glistening with tears.

'There ain't no escape, is there?' was all she said. 'And no place to go but out.'

'Stay, Gin!' pleaded Hugh. 'Stay, then.'

But why should she interrupt her career to linger with him in Dexter? Whatever they both thought of *The Freddy Connor Show*, Hugh knew that her life had to continue.

'Come with me, Howard,' she said. 'Let's cut out together!'

Hugh had a momentary vision of an audience of Prinzhorns and Moffats waiting expectantly in formal rows in front of an empty podium, and shrugged helplessly. A bug that had somehow crept by the screen in a crawling ecstasy of infiltration was now hurling itself angrily against the lampshade, a metallic whirring of blacks and greens like an elastic toy. Hugh envied its energetic acceptance of such an artificial environment, envied its lack of choice. It sailed tremendously to a corner of the ceiling with a faint drone, leaving the mere human inhabitants of the room to their inconceivable deliberations.

15

They drove in silence to the airport. The Crails' Cadillac, whose colours and fixtures and surfaces had once seemed in themselves so conspiratorial, an almost human agent of their adventures, now seemed alien, efficient, businesslike. Hugh wished it would break down. He imagined it sputtering to a feeble stop. He would kick its front tyre and laugh, and they would climb up the bank of bluebonnets that bordered the freeway, kicking off their shoes, running and running, eager to possess the land of which they were momentary tenants. Flowers coloured the roadside grass like poppies in a field of wheat, but the Cadillac did not stop.

It was as near to a real quarrel as they had had. Gin made efforts to establish some practical arrangements for meeting again, which Hugh in an agony of wilful self-denial pretended to ignore. At the putting-down place he was waved irritably on by a policeman: a bus honked at his tail, waiting to draw in. Gin stood by the glass doors of the entrance, expecting him to join her. Her bag with her knitting was balanced on her suitcase, and Hugh drove on, his stomach lurching in obstinate sacrifice and resentment, he could see in his driving mirror that it had slipped off, spilling its contents, and that she was stooped awkwardly to rescue it. Her face was puzzled, harassed, beautiful, and Hugh spoke his frustration aloud as he accelerated down the exit ramp, looking for short-term parking:

'Shit, shit, shit,' he howled at the unfamiliar concrete maze. By the time he had left the Cadillac, with a slightly grazed bumper, in a third- floor bay and returned to the entrance, Gin had of course gone inside.

The lobby was crowded with the usual mixture of brisk executives and wan migrants, each programmed to move at different speeds so that movement between them was impossible without weaving and dodging. Hugh headed left, scanning the concourse impatiently. He couldn't see Gin anywhere, but on reflection realised that he could hardly expect her to be waiting for him inside. He found the TWA desk and asked the clerk if Miss Gerald had checked in. The clerk obligingly keyed the computer, and said, No, she hadn't.

At once relieved and slightly puzzled, Hugh walked back more calmly into the throng of passengers. He had time now to observe the individuals who moved about the concourse with the calculated pace of film extras: the immaculately powdered stewardesses, the Chinese family with two little girls who giggled and turned round and round like dolls, the old lady with seven items of matching green leather luggage on a trolley, the security guards, the lovers constrained by saying goodbye in a public place. Gin was somewhere in the crowd, but he could not see her. Was she looking for him? Had she not found the check-in desk? Perhaps there was another check-in desk?

As the minutes went by, Hugh became more puzzled and irritated. There was no other check-in desk, he discovered. Gin had still not picked up her ticket, and now the New York plane was being called. He looked at his watch and was alarmed to discover how much time had gone by since they had arrived at the airport. He must have taken far longer to park the car than he had thought.

The clerk at the desk was interested when Hugh asked for the second time.

'Is that the singer?' he asked.

'Yes,' said Hugh.

'You a friend of hers, then?'

'Of course I am.'

Hugh was vaguely annoyed at being asked these questions. They seemed to identify him as someone the Baroness had made moves to avoid, or as someone who was importuning her.

'She better hurry if she wants to catch the plane,' said the clerk. He had a small, slightly pig-like face that seemed to Hugh to be smirking.

'Are you sure she couldn't have collected that ticket?' frowned Hugh. 'I mean, couldn't she have picked it up and it not have been recorded on your computer?'

'You telling me I don't do my job?' asked the clerk.

'Of course not,' said Hugh.

'What are you, some kind of fan?' said the clerk.

'What do you mean?'

'What's it with you if she takes a plane or don't take a plane? How come you're so concerned?'

Hugh was gravelled by the outrageous remark. The clerk continued, sorting papers and labels on his counter with a smug air:

'A person like Virginia Gerald is free to come and go,' he said. 'She's entitled to privacy.'

'I'm a friend of hers,' snapped Hugh.

'So you said,' returned the clerk, 'but I don't know that.'

'I brought her to the airport,' said Hugh in a despairing fury. 'Why do you think I'm here?'

'Look, mister,' said the clerk, with a chirpy smile. 'I couldn't give a damn why you're here. Virginia Gerald ain't here, that's for certain. Maybe you're some kind of nut, talking funny and asking all these questions.'

Hugh turned away, saddened and angry. The clerk took further confidence at this.

'I don't even know that she made this reservation,' he said. 'Someone could have been fooling around.'

'Nonsense,' said Hugh absently, his eyes once more searching the concourse. 'It's her reservation. I made it myself.'

The clerk laughed shortly.

'Well,' he said, perhaps uncertain as to how rude he could really be. 'There you are.'

Hugh moved away from the check-in desk, and walked up and down. Flights were leaving all the time: might she for some reason have taken a different plane for a different destination? Might she have taken a cab back to Dexter? He knew with a sinking certainty that she was not here. Had she gone to look for him? Might she be in the car park?

As a last resort he went to Information and had her named called. He felt embarrassed and resentful as the loudspeakers announced his loss in dry and unconcerned tones. The New York flight left, and nothing happened. After another quarter of an hour he collected the car and returned to the Crails' house, convinced that she somehow must have gone home.

Home! How could he think of it as home? The white walls and green Italianate roof gave it the air of a toy or model of a grander sort of house than it was, seen too close, the architectural detail fudged. It was furnished in a bizarre combination of items handed down, abandoned or purchased expensively to fill a space. It was markedly more ethnic than anything in the Crails' New York apartment, but it lacked simplicity. There was a Zanussi washing machine, but there was also a custom-made wooden dish-rack. It was the domestic equivalent of stone-washed pre-shrunk designer jeans.

Hugh wandered through all the rooms, knowing that not only would Gin be in none of them but that she would have efficiently removed all trace of herself from them. And she almost had: there was still, however, a dampness to the shower curtains, a torn shampoo sachet in the soap dish, a single black hair on the tiles. It was not that he could not prove that she had ever been there, but that there was no one except himself to whom it could possibly matter. Certainly not the Prinzhorns, who did not reckon on entertaining black girls, nor Jed Finch who had two visitors to complain about instead of one. What about their mysterious prowler, if he existed? Hugh had some idea at the back of his mind that Gin's disappearance and the prowler were connected, that the prowler could not now possibly return, and that Gin would not return either. Sam, who at that minute was snuffling and whimpering at the back door, would sleep easily if Hugh were to let him back into the house, which for Gin's sake he did, for Sam at least would miss the hands that most regularly put down bowls of Master's Menu for him, and plucked at his ears like fruit.

'We've been abandoned, you and I,' said Hugh aloud to the dog. The dog was not sentimental. It trotted upstairs to bed, while Hugh poured himself a drink and looked around for some food. 'Abandoned,' he repeated, as he cut a piece of cheese and ate it by itself. Already the refrigerator had unnervingly acquired a bachelor sparseness. He opened a tin of ravioli, and ate it with a spoon, unwarmed. The little doughy envelopes stuck to his gums, and the tomato sauce was too sharp. Like Sam, he wanted to go upstairs to sleep. He wanted to crawl into a corner and hide. He finished his drink and poured another.

Later, he rang the airport. The ticket had not been collected. The afternoon settled around the house like a spell, the ultimate in stasis. Even the birds seemed too lazy to make themselves heard.

Where was she? Why had she not gone to New York? Perhaps, if she had for some reason been eager to elude him, she had simply bought another ticket under another name, or from another airline, and gone to New York after all. She could be anywhere. Thinking over his last sullen hours with her, Hugh felt ashamed and helpless.

The last sight of her, stooped over her spilled luggage, seemed infinitely incomplete. It required some tender resolution, a finishing cadence. He did not know how he managed to pass the rest of the day, but when he finally slept, the bottle of bourbon was empty.

16

Hugh threw himself back into his work with an obstinate and mindless fury. He wanted to cut his mind off from his body, or rather to enslave the body, as Prospero had enslaved Caliban. He drove it with a punishing fervour, denying it food, not even going to the kitchen shelves to see if there was another tin there of the adhesive ravioli. He would have eaten it if there had been, and he did not want to eat. His fingers were clenched round his soft pencil so tightly that he felt that he was not putting down marks on the page, but tugging them out of it. It was a kind of wrestling match with the small traditional technology of graphite and paper.

The tide of music in his head seemed self-begetting, like a system he had once seen illustrated in a museum model whereby methane from sewage drives machinery for processing sewage. Well, that was all the human body was, wasn't it, after all: a machine for processing sewage? A phrase of Yeats came into his head: 'the fury and the mire of human . . .' What was it? '. . . veins'? Yeats had claimed to embrace the static immortality of becoming a mechanical singing bird like the Emperor's toy in Hans Christian Andersen. He could understand that. Blood was an imperfect medium for emotion.

But when the Emperor lay dying, his toy couldn't console him. He needed the real nightingale.

Oh yes, there was a long history of pretence of that kind. Keats had heard the real nightingale, and confused it with immortality, and perfection. Emperor and clown. Music and sewage. Blood and begetting. Fresh images.

The pencil bit into the paper, down into the fivefold frieze, surprising as spring bulbs in a border. Little purple stabs of crotchets, yellow quavers, fragile white semi-quavers.

The concerto was going disgustingly well, the aimless Parnassian fugue enlarging itself effortlessly into an organic and irrefutable theme as a chattering village river somewhere finds the cold sea. The gong-tormented sea. The pile of mss thickened as the music unfolded in his head, and what had perhaps been taken up as a distraction soon successfully distracted him. Hugh was not conscious of working round the clock, but as the quality of light changed behind the blinds so the intensity of his effort deepened. He could almost smell the paper. He was on to his fourth pencil.

The movement now lay fully bathed in the light of his attention and imagination. It was as though he had finally walked on to the stage and found the words forming at his lips that all along, even in the fear of the wings, were his to say. Slowly, he learned to feel easy saying them, and just as naturally beneath the culminating complexity of the fugue there formed his new theme.

Oh God, prayed Hugh, let it not seem obvious. It would be so easy to do a Tippett, incorporating the blues into a symphonic texture with cultural innocence and pastoral condescension. Perhaps impossible not to. But Tippett in his Third Symphony was using not only a trumpet but the human voice which was so heavily implicated in language, and Hugh was using a violin. And when at bar 63 the violin finally took up the theme that had been rehearsed on the cellos as a ground to the fugue's climax, it was with as little sense of being a wordless voice (he hoped) as it was possible to be.

That was the purity of strings, after all. It was emotion apparently divorced from utterance. Whereas Bob Gordon could lend his reed an expressive vocal character which was directly related to his own breath, the violinist had to rely on touch. Bob could mime Gin's melodic line, but the fiddle couldn't, whatever you did with it. Hugh hated the spurious jaunty scrapings of jazz violinists like Grappelli. To him it had always seemed too polite; tea-room comfort without the dangerous aura of smoke and liquor that belonged to jazz.

The theme was required to evoke no actual echo of any known melody, but to be as far as possible the quintessence of them all. Hugh did not dare to listen to any of them while he wrote, and he wrote without distraction for two days, and for much of the third. He came to bar 85 when the soloist required a pause; then he made a jug of coffee, turned on the lights and drew down the blinds (ineffectively) against the whirring night insects. He did not much care about them any more. Their self-immolating excursions even comforted him, providing as they did the slight noises and activity that filled an otherwise oppressive void. His pencil sketched an orchestral response in great surges like an immovable force momentarily calmed, the bar-lines like breakwaters, the notes themselves like only briefly identifiable nodal crests of sound, repeating their effects but never in quite the same way.

Thus he reached bar 102 and the next pot of coffee. At this point the resolution of the movement seemed plain sailing. All the orchestra had to do was to acknowledge, with as little bluster or regret as possible, all that had taken place. He wanted a quiet conclusion. He wanted, if possible, to suggest that such statements could be made, and that was all. They led nowhere in particular, just as they came from nowhere in particular. The orchestration would be of the plainest, just the strings, with an obbligato cor anglais, the most wistful of the woodwind, Hugh thought.

Eventually, with most of the movement plotted, Hugh had to drive out in search of cigarettes and food. He turned by the forgotten lake, crossed the freeway and made for the nearest mall. He moved down the supermarket aisles in a foolish but contented stupor, pulling random items into his basket, things he did not care to eat but which he did not care if he did eat, because it did not seem to matter, an iceberg lettuce, canned apricots, a marshmallow-textured sliced loaf, chocolate. The evening shoppers strolled or stopped at his side with a deliberation that affected him. He observed their purchases with a secret friendliness. It pleased him that a man in shirtsleeves and red canvas shoes should be buying four six-packs of local beer. It pleased him that a very old woman wearing black slacks and nail varnish should be buying a bag of ice.

On the way back he put Gin's tape into the car cassette player, feeling that he could now control whatever emotion it induced in him, pretending to a studied observation of an example of that essence he thought he had captured in his third movement, pretending simply to listen. Side two began with 'Too Late', a simple Rivers and Schuyler ballad that Gin had revived and made her own, breathing it intimately with only piano and bass to take the melody along, her version economical as usual, barely using half an octave:

> 'I was a fool that night,
> A fool to get excited.
> Why did you let me tag along?
> Why didn't you tell me it was wrong,
> That I was uninvited?
> I was a fool that night.'

The car lights on the freeway were like fireflies flickering in the dusk. Hugh was conscious of his tired and ineffective body, the pathetic bag of groceries on the seat beside him, and the disturbing directness of the song. It was as though Gin had been waiting in all the wisdom of her art to make this comment on their relationship, waiting patiently for him to remember her, and simply switch her on.

> 'I wanted us to meet.
> The meetings were repeated.
> Now, when I see you smiling there
> I know you want to be elsewhere.
> Why should I feel defeated?
> I wanted us to meet.'

Was it true? Was he flattered by the episode, and ready in his heart to accept its ending? Should he have made a better effort to make her stay? Should he have gone with her? Certainly they should not have quarrelled. The piano agreed, casting down its tender but terse clustered cadences like a losing hand at cards. And the Baroness sang on:

> 'I came to you too late.
> I thought you might have waited.
> You were a world ahead of me
> So how could I think that you'd break free
> From the life you had created?
> I came to you too late.'

Bathed in this wonderful sound, Hugh arrived back at the house stony, abject, restless, in that uncomfortable state so close to, but somehow resolutely opposite to, tears. He knew he must get back to the concerto, filling in that still sketchy passage from bar 102 to the end, settling the orchestration in his mind at least, even if the actual scoring was still to come. But first he made a phone call to New York. It was as fruitless as his earlier calls, but behind it was a new determination.

17

On the morning after he had completed his lectures, frosty affairs for the most part, his jokes delivered with the straight face of total nerves and therefore not understood, the applause dutiful, with only two dull questions, Hugh took the Greyhound bus for San Antonio. He had woken with a fresh sense of alarm at having found no solution to Gin's apparent disappearance, and had got through once more to Denis Heathfield.

'Hugh,' Denis had yawned, 'you do realise that however early it is with you as you munch your buckwheat pancakes or whatever down there, it is even earlier here. Dorothy is still asleep.'

'I'm sorry, I'm sorry,' said Hugh. 'I just had to know if there was any news.'

'I can't help being mildly amused at all this, Hugh.'

Denis's voice did indeed sound amused, and cruelly so.

'I feel like a Grand Vizier making enquiries on the Sultan's behalf about some absconded slave girl,' he went on. 'Well, Hugh, the bazaars have been thoroughly searched and your little piece of treachery is nowhere to be found. Not a sawn-through manacle in sight.'

'Don't, Denis,' said Hugh wearily. 'It's not very funny.'

'Nobody's amours seem at all humorous to themselves, old fellow,' replied Denis. 'But how is it that everyone else's do? Eh? Answer me that.'

'Do they?'

'Of course they do. It's the very warp (or do I mean weft?) of comedy and gossip. You should hear Olive Dempster on the subject. On second thoughts, perhaps you shouldn't.'

'Did you see this Myrna woman?'

'Oh, the stalwart neighbour? Yes, I did see her. She made me feel

like the worst sort of heavy from the FBI. You know, Broderick
Crawford in a straight little snap-brim hat. I felt so awful I almost
enjoyed it.'

'What did she say?'

'She said almost nothing at all at great length and very accusingly. I
believe she thought that you had abducted her.'

'Gin hasn't been back?'

'Not to her apartment at any rate. Nor to that drab little nightclub
you sent me to either. I spoke to a cheerful fellow called Goldfish who
was so busy sucking on a pickled gherkin that he had no time to tell
me anything.'

'But had she turned up for the filming they were doing for the TV
programme?'

'I think not,' said Denis. 'Or maybe it was simply that the filming
never took place.'

'Well, it couldn't do, could it, if she wasn't there?'

'Don't snap my head off, Hugh,' said Denis. 'I spent quite some time
gumshoeing on your behalf. It seems clear to me as a result of it all, and
this is my considered conclusion, right on the line, QED and all that,
that Miss Gerald is not, as they say, in town. My bill will follow.'

'I'm sorry, Denis. Thank you. I'm really extremely grateful.'

'That's all right, uncle,' said Denis. 'I'm sorry it turned out like this
for you.'

Hugh was silent for a moment. It wasn't 'like this' at all, he
reflected. Or was it?

'And the concerto's finished, is it?' asked Denis.

'I'm half-way through the orchestration. No problems now.'

'That's wonderful, Hugh.'

'I wish it seemed wonderful to me.'

'Maybe you'd like to stay with us for a while when you get back?
When do rehearsals start?'

'Too soon, Denis. I've spent a fortune in xeroxing and sent off short
scores to Boris and to Katey. That should give them time to get into it.'

'Looking forward to it immensely, Hugh, I must say. But just now
life must go on.'

'Yes, of course, Denis. Thanks again for all that you've done.'

'Don't mention it. And don't forget we've got a sofa-bed here.'

'I might just take you up on that, Denis. Thanks.'

'Bye, then.'

'Goodbye.'

If they had a sofa-bed, why hadn't the Heathfields offered it before? Dorothy's antagonism, probably. Some obscure loyalty to Daisy. And why offer it now? Did they think he was cracking up? How desperate had he sounded on the telephone, asking Denis to search all over New York for someone he'd never met who might not even be there? It must indeed have sounded frantic, the sort of wild appeal from the depths of an obsession that friends ignore at their peril, but which sets them to awed gossip or head-shaking concern.

Hugh had no reason to stay in Dexter. He had lunched with Moffat in the faculty plaza and visited the electronic workshop. Prinzhorn had arranged for him to receive his cheque, a procedure complicated by his not having a social security number. He had politely declined an invitation to a graduate soirée. He could, as it were, quietly tiptoe away and nobody would notice that he had gone, just as nobody had noticed him arrive.

When he returned the keys to Jed, the dog Sam was for once within sight, behaving as though he might actually belong to the caretaker.

'You're on your way then, laddie,' said Jed, who could not have been more than ten years older than Hugh.

'That's right,' said Hugh.

'Did your friend find you?' said Jed, pocketing the keys.

Hugh's heart moved a foot out of place.

'Have you seen her?' he asked. 'When was this?'

Jed spat on the ground.

'The nigger wench?' he said. 'Hell no, I didn't mean her.'

Jed observed Hugh's furious blush, and laughed shortly, lifting his jaw slightly as if he was inviting Hugh to hit it. Sam came nosing round, sensing the tension between the two men.

'No,' continued Jed emphatically, and with a tone of grudging conciliation. 'I didn't mean your lady friend. No disrespect, laddie. Fellow was asking about you.'

Hugh could barely conceal his disgust and anger.

'Who was he?'

'How should I know?' returned Jed. 'City fellow, I reckon. Maybe he wasn't looking for you after all.'

'What did he say? What did he look like?'

'City fellow, like I said. Didn't say much.'

Jed seemed anxious to go. Sam was raising dust round his feet, and licking up the gob of his spittle on the ground.

'Well, what did he say?' asked Hugh, in open exasperation at last.

'Don't worry,' leered Jed, in what he must have intended to be a gesture of conspiratorial friendship. 'I didn't tell him nothing.'

And before Hugh could find a way of saying to Jed that there was nothing to tell (and find a way of saying it, moreover, which didn't involve counterproductive temper) Jed was gone, the craven Sam following openly, knowing that his summer family was no longer available.

The decision to fly back to New York not from Dexter but from San Antonio was easy enough to make in view of the mere few hours' journey it took by bus, but Hugh was very uncertain about how he was to find the Baroness there. He became more and more convinced that she was there after all. It was the way that their journey south had triggered her account of her youth, her grandfather's guitar, the attentions of Sam, her mother's marriage to Jack Gerald and their move to San Antonio. Hugh had no means of knowing if the Geralds were still there, or how to be certain of finding them, but it was worth trying. How long might it have been since Gin had left home for New York? It could be more than six years. But it was so near to her. It was so near, and all in her mind.

Hugh dozed in the bus, half listening to a drunk in the seat behind him talking to an incredibly polite and long-suffering Australian student.

'People,' the drunk was saying. 'People are the greatest commodity in the world.'

In his dream, Hugh was travelling at night by Greyhound. The recently vacated seat next to him was filled at some point as he dozed by an oppressively heavy and lolling man. Hugh was afraid that the man had put all his stuff, his jersey, headset and portfolio, at the back, but then he felt it reassuringly beneath his shoulder and elbow as he leaned against the headrest and window. The man was a nuisance. He got outside, playing the fool, and Hugh hoped that the driver would leave him behind. Why did Hugh have to be outside as well? He was annoyed at being woken up. They had been approaching a wire fence, and Hugh was convinced that they would hit it. It was desert country, tussocks of dry grass and small sandy declivities that made him stumble. To get back to the bus Hugh had to push through thin bare trees, their whip-like branches trailing to the ground. The driver looped back a snake: a detached gesture, part of the service, but Hugh was afraid of more snakes. Simon was there, being covered with sparks which Hugh had to blow and brush off him as he rolled down the sandy bank. Simon was wearing a headscarf of black silk, like a babushka. 'I'll take care of him,' Hugh called out, lifting him in his arms. He was as small as a child. Hugh dreamed that he was dreaming and slept through the next stop. When he woke he was cramped, and the bus was moving off again.

'Do you know what πr^2 is?' the drunk was saying behind him. 'Radius of a circle.'

The bus proceeded at the relatively stately 55 miles per hour required by law. Hugh saw a sign for NACOGDOCHES. Wasn't that the town that Groucho, visiting in vaudeville and getting a frosty reception, dared to say from the footlights was full of roaches?

'It's the area of a circle,' said the Australian student.

'Yeah,' said the drunk. 'What did I say?'

Hugh felt that he had been travelling for a lifetime and perhaps was going round in circles, too.

At San Antonio he left his case in a bus-station locker, and walked the few blocks to the Alamo, which he imagined to be the tourist centre of the city. He was right. The place of heroic massacre, a baroque

136

Hispanic façade, was a much photographed gateway to the state's history, a long account of the subjugation of local Indians through the agency of missions such as the Alamo itself originally was; of struggles for national freedom (Mexico from Spain, Texas from Mexico); of the seizure of land; of the creation of wealth and the military power needed to protect it like the casket displaying a jewel; and above all of the frontier spirit that fired the makeshift army of the Alamo to its defence. It was the recklessness of opportunism. Hugh stood in the long-secularised nave of the mission of San Antonio de Valero among the dusty muskets and portraits looking at the most blatant invitation to legalised theft that could be imagined, in the form of a printed handbill:

> Now is the time to ensure a fortune in
> Land: To all who remain in Texas during the
> War will be allowed 1280 Acres.
>
> New Orleans
April 23rd, 1836.

Indeed, thought Hugh, people are in some ways the greatest commodity in the world. But other people are always to be used. It is the merest good fortune if it should happen in the process that the exploited have any sort of a chance to advance themselves.

Love perhaps was really like this, the rare intuition of mutual advantage playing like history upon a bedrock of biological need. And love itself was also the hidden wealth of history. The incredible 267,338 square miles of this state had grown rich through little more than 150 years on a succession of green money, black money and grey money (cattle, oil and the computers necessary to the space programme). Throughout this sequence, in its essence inexpressible in currency, was a core of pink. Pink had no monuments of its own, though it lent its civilising touches to the baronial mansions built in retirement by the veterans of the Chisholm Trail.

Hugh could not bear for long to contemplate the processed records of such violent development, where every act of exclusion or accession contributed its stylised image to toothmugs, diaries, pencils and combs, and all the trivial domestic booty of tourism. But in the search for Jack Gerald, who lived by such process of stylisation, he felt it necessary to become at least the pretence of a tourist.

He asked for Gerald at The Heart of Texas, an entertainment complex on the other side of the Alamo Plaza. The girl in charge was unhelpful until Hugh said that he thought that Gerald ran trips to some kind of Indian monument out of town.

'Oh sure,' she said at last. 'You mean the Scattle Stones.'

'That's it,' said Hugh.

'The tour office is just a couple of blocks down the Plaza.'

'Thanks.'

'You're welcome.'

Hugh walked along the streetcar tracks till he came to the office. He knew when he had reached it, for there, unexpectedly but unsurprisingly, was the Baroness's record-sleeve in the window, together with the record company's poster with her photograph. The tour office was also a kind of run-down store, selling the obligatory historical toothmugs, diaries, pencils and combs and Davy Crockett caps. The Davy Crockett cap had been a fad in England twenty-five years earlier, and not even the fact that Crockett himself had died in the siege of the Alamo could lend the article a fresh glamour or relieve it of its tawdriness. In these surroundings Gin's singing face (eyes closed, mouth drawn down and back) seemed like an image of pathetic struggle or survival, as culturally irrelevant as the portrait of a head of state in some seedy colonial outpost.

The store was long and narrow with a booth at one end behind which sat a boy with a prominent Adam's apple.

'Next bus leaves in twenty minutes,' said the boy. 'Twelve dollars round trip, including admission.'

'I was looking for Mr Gerald,' said Hugh.

'Mr Gerald ain't here,' said the boy.

'Do you know where he is?' asked Hugh.

The boy, with his arms crossed in front of his skinny chest, was simultaneously scratching his ribs with both hands. The Adam's apple rose and fell as he spoke with the precise dipping thrust of a sewing-machine needle, giving his inappropriately deep voice the effect of some piece of bionic engineering.

'Nope,' he growled, as the whole front of his throat disappeared between his collarbones.

'I was wondering where I might find him,' said Hugh.

Without turning his head the boy called out through a half-open door to a room at the back:

'Mona? Fellow here wants to know where he can find Jack.'

An old woman wearing lipstick and tartan shorts appeared in the door behind him. She looked Hugh up and down.

'What's it about, mister? I just made the return last week, if that's what you want. Didn't I, Steve?'

'Sure thing, Mona.'

'It's in the mail, mister.'

Hugh shook his head.

'No, no,' he said. 'I just want to see him privately.'

The old woman thrust out her lower lip as she appraised him.

'You must be from out of town,' she said. 'What business you got with Jack Gerald?'

'Well,' said Hugh, confused by this inquisition. 'It's about his stepdaughter, actually.'

'Is that so, actually,' said the old woman. The boy sniggered. 'Say, are you a reporter or something? You a promoter?'

She had her eyes thoroughly narrowed by now, and her hands on her hips, as she stared at him. Hugh had the feeling that he might be sent packing at any moment if he didn't establish some status.

'I write music,' he said.

'Gee,' said the boy. 'I got a real winner I just finished last week. Maybe going to play it at the Riverside soon.'

The old woman's suspicion was diverted.

'They'll never let you play that old poky ramble at the Riverside,' she said scornfully.

The boy, who had been tilting back in his chair happily, blushed and sat up with a clatter.

'Maybe they will,' he muttered. 'Maybe they will at that.'

'I ain't never heard anything like that at the Riverside,' she said.

'Hell, you never been there,' the boy replied.

'I been there plenty,' said the old woman. 'Hey, mister, you want to go there. You'll hear some good music at the Riverside.'

'I probably won't have time,' said Hugh. 'But I'd like to find Mr Gerald.'

The old woman suddenly lost interest.

'He'll be out at the Stones this afternoon,' she said. 'You'd better take the tour out there.'

'He won't be at the Stones, Mona,' said the boy. 'Why should he be at the Stones?'

'He's out at the Stones because Daniels got round to delivering the timber.'

'Yeah?' cried the boy incredulously, his Adam's apple flying up into his chin. 'And what the hell got into him? What got into Daniels, for Christ's sake? He delivered the timber? My God!'

He slapped the counter, and looked all round him in exaggerated disbelief. Then he laughed at his own performance.

'When you're through, Steve,' said the old woman, returning to the back room, 'you can give the man a tag.'

'Sure, sure,' said the boy, still smiling to himself. 'That'll be twelve dollars.'

He made an entry in a book, and handed Hugh his tag. In that split second before seeing it, as though with the weird prescience of dreams, Hugh knew what it would look like. He knew what it was, knew he had seen one before.

It was made of dull tin, stamped with a crude decorative frieze and the letters 'SS' in the middle.

18

That quality in life that we find alienating, either because it is unpredictable or bears no relation to our purposes, or because on reflection it can't be made to form a credible narrative of our life, is often mistakenly called dreamlike. In truth, dreams are the purest form of emotion's unquestionable consequence. It is precisely because we make no forecasts in dreams that we are never disappointed. Dreams, being the very embodiment of our anxieties and needs, can never of themselves fail to correspond to a theory of expectation or a determined programme of hope and fulfilment.

It was the same with the myths of the nameless ancestors of the Coahuiltecan Indians, carved perhaps thousands of years ago in sandstone. These shallow, linear, connected images and symbols presented themselves with the density and regularity of pattern or decoration. At some points near the top of the twenty-foot slabs, where the incisions had most weathered, modern tradition had reinforced the images with paint. The viewing platform was set at a short distance, serving also as a protective barrier. Viewing glasses in the style of beach telescopes were also provided, thus vastly increasing for the spectator in the private darkness of the eyepiece the sense of eavesdropping on the collective dreams of the tribe.

These dreams, though beyond the construction of the paying tourist for whom the platform led inevitably to the racks of postcards and souvenirs that placated his curiosity, had a meaning which scholars had once confidently ascertained.

When the Sky God was tired of hunting the stars he settled down in one place with the First Mother and gave her a daughter so beautiful that he fell in love with her. The daughter was proud and at first would not be wooed. The seed of the Sky God fell upon the ground and scuttled away in the shape of a scorpion. For six more seasons the Sky God wooed his daughter, and in the same way created the spider, the mosquito, the bullfrog, the rattlesnake, the jackal and the vulture. The Sky God threw down all his gold before her, and slowly she warmed towards him. The Sky God threw down all his silver before her, and she melted before him. From their union arose the first blade of corn. But the First Mother was jealous of their union, and angry with her daughter. One day, when the Sky God had once again set out to hunt the stars, she called to the animals and begged from each of them a gift. The spider gave her his eyes, the mosquito his body, the bullfrog his skin, the rattlesnake his arms and legs, the jackal his genitals, and the vulture his hair. She asked the scorpion for his poison, but the scorpion would not give it to her and hid in the desert. Out of all the things that the animals had given her she made a man. And that is why the spider is blind and why the mosquito is invisible. That is why the bullfrog is naked and why the rattlesnake can only wriggle on the ground. That is why the jackal is a howling scavenger, and why the vulture is bald. The scorpion was punished by being made to be an enemy to himself, but all the rest were enemies to man. The First Mother gave her daughter to man to be punished in her turn, and to be controlled by him. Man took charge of her and of the blade of corn, which he reared and multiplied. As well as the enmity of the animals, man incurred the enmity of the Sky God who had to be placated with offerings of corn. If the Sky God was pleased with the offering, he would return in the new year to make love to his daughter. But he was only allowed to make love to her once: after that he was sent away to hunt the stars until his offspring was strong enough to stand, and the First Mother was content.

The modern representatives of the First Mother's creation filed past this legend, wondering at the size of the stones and how they had been up-ended. Then they all took photographs from the one vantage point that revealed their full height without the impediment of the viewing platform. This point was just to one side of, and a little in front of the kiosk where the tags were inspected.

Hugh realised the point of the tags: the embossed frieze and the style of lettering was a stylistic approximation of the design of the stones. The handling and retention of the metal rectangles seemed to lend a special aura of authority and authenticity to the whole trip, which a ticket stub would not have done. Jack Gerald was certainly a shrewd operator.

'And why would she come back here?' he asked, when Hugh had located him on the site directing some building work. He had a measuring-rule in his hand with which he was checking the dimensions of some lengths of wood stacked on the ground. He looked with sudden directness at Hugh as he straightened up and folded the rule.

'And why should I tell you if she had?' he added, putting the rule into the front pocket of his shirt. He was a heavy man, with a good-natured, slightly vacant expression. He had shaken Hugh's hand with great politeness and had appeared to take his account of his 'friendship' with Gin as it was intended: a professional relationship of some kind, musical business to be pursued with urgency.

Hugh had nothing to say to that.

Gerald laughed, and made a dismissive gesture with his hand.

'Now don't mistake me,' he said, moving round the piles of timber. 'I'm ready to help you all I can. I can see you're on the level.'

Hugh followed him, stumbling a little on the littered ground.

'Yes, indeed,' said Gerald. 'I can see that by the way you don't feel no need to identify yourself.'

A man selecting lengths of wood interrupted them with some question which Gerald briefly answered.

'If you weren't what you say you are, you'd know you had to prove you were. You'd be shoving all kinds of goddamn documents at me. Wouldn't you, hey?'

Gerald laughed again, and turned to look at Hugh directly. The laugh was not the kind of laugh that transforms all the muscles of the face with its deep involuntary emotion, and it quickly faded. Hugh felt himself challenged.

'Smart thinking, hey?' said Gerald, not waiting for an answer. 'I've learned to think smart in this business. Can't miss a thing, or you soon go under.'

'That must be true,' said Hugh, weakly.

'More than anything else,' said Gerald, 'you get to recognise the man wants something, won't say right out what it is. Man conducting a survey, wants to sell me some insurance. Another man comes to sell me something I might want, he's a tax man. Or take another instance.'

They began, at Gerald's direction, to walk back towards the area of the stones.

'A man says he wants to promote my stepdaughter, makes out she sings real good. I know, and he knows I know, that he's just chasing tail. I don't have to tell him, and he sure ain't telling me.'

Hugh could not look at Gerald, but did not need to as they were walking side by side. The stones were near enough now to reassert their presence. Their vibrant angular account of the sexual aetiology of agriculture had been produced by men very different in resources from Jack Gerald, but their mode of thinking provided a crude and crucial link across the centuries.

'They started around ten years ago,' Gerald continued, 'like wasps round a honeypot. Came to the Riverside to hear her. Came to the house. Got her mother mad.'

As Hugh dared to glance up at Gerald as they walked, he saw him run the tip of his tongue along his lower lip. His eyes were fixed. Hugh felt his embarrassment suddenly lift, for of the two men it was Jack Gerald who was in the victimised grip of his imagination. It was Gerald who had perhaps suffered as many years of Gin's challenging proximity as Hugh had days. It was Gerald who was (how could this be?) most tortured by her absence. And Hugh immediately saw how this could be so.

'What's singing anyway?' Gerald muttered. 'She never used to sing. Jimmy used to sing more than she did. I gave him his first sax when he was thirteen. It was her meatbox singing, that's what it was. All girls' singing comes from between their legs.'

He stopped, as though realising that he had been half talking to himself. They stood there, within sight of the stones, alone together. The girl at the kiosk came out as if to walk towards them, but stopped. The herded tourists had disappeared, the last shutter dropped.

Hugh did not know what to say.

'I think she's a very great singer,' he said, knowing that this, though appropriate, serious, corrective, was not quite the right thing to say.

Gerald turned and smiled again, and this time there was an involuntary gleam of the genuine in it. It was a proud pleasure in Hugh's observation, a recognition of its professional objectivity, a kind of relief that Hugh had directed the conversation back into manageable channels, but it was, finally, mastered by an overwhelming sadness, a long-suffered sadness, at his stepdaughter's absconded talents. Whether these talents were musical or sexual, it did not seem to matter. The girl had removed to a different sphere of existence. None of his understanding of her genius had any point any more, for it was clear finally that he did, despite himself, understand it: it was simply that he had no control over it, and had never had any control.

'Now you've missed the bus,' said Gerald.

'I can get the next one presumably?' said Hugh.

'Next bus won't get here for an hour, hour and a half. You got over a two-hour wait.'

'Oh,' said Hugh. He looked at his watch, and made calculations about his airline reservation. His hopes of cancelling it had faded, and now time was short.

'Perhaps I could get a taxi?' he wondered.

'Hell, no. That'd cost you,' said Gerald. 'Wait here a while and I'll run you back.'

'There's no need . . .' began Hugh.

'It's OK,' said Gerald. 'I'm due back in town. Guy didn't sent me all I ordered.'

He set off back to the construction area, the flesh that filled his shirt a mobile and pneumatic bulge above a two-inch-thick belt. The girl from the kiosk took another step forwards and called out: 'Gerry?' But he either did not hear, or pretended not to hear. She looked at

145

Hugh briefly in appraisal. She was tall, and wore a sleeveless white blouse and slacks that were designed not to meet each other. A thin gold chain hung across her stomach, with a pendant adjacent to her navel like a bath plug pulled out. Her hair was pulled up into sluttish bunches. Hugh felt that he had never been looked at so directly in his life. He had smiled at first, but no smile was forthcoming from her. Finally she turned and walked back to her kiosk as uncertainly as if she were on a plank six feet above the ground. Her platform shoes were deeper than anything he had seen Gin wearing.

It was only after she had turned away that he realised that she must be about twelve years old.

Jack Gerald not only drove Hugh back, but made a detour to visit the only Spanish aqueduct still extant in the States and insisted on taking him for a drink at one of the terrace bars on the Paseo del Rio. His generous mood seemed like a kind of self-exoneration. He drank one bourbon quickly, and ordered another, while Hugh nursed a Chablis. Where else in the world, Hugh thought, would they serve a glass of chilled white wine with an apple segment stuck on the rim? For the first time that day, hot and sticky from his fruitless quest, he felt he could relax a little.

'One day I'm going to buy into this development,' said Gerald, taking out his wallet. Hugh thought for a moment that he was about to demonstrate that he had the wherewithal to do so, but he was simply paying the waitress. 'This is where the money is. Five miles of riverwalk, all lit up at night. You can't keep the tourists away.'

He was right. The place was crowded. A gondola passed by with a family of eight having a meal on it. The waiter was flambé-ing a lobster.

Gerald still had his wallet open.

'This is Jimmy,' he said, passing over a photograph.

Hugh looked at it without expecting to be interested, but was riveted by the shy challenge of the camera-glance and the curl of the upper lip. It was a tangible reminder of Gin, not least because of the boy's colour, Hugh not having known nor seriously speculated about whether Jack Gerald was black or not. Nor, having discovered that he wasn't, had Hugh needed to appraise his physical presence in Gin's family further. But now that he had seen Gin's features standing in her half-brother's face, and could attempt to subtract from it the features of his companion at that moment still going through things in his wallet, he had the means to visualise the crucial member that he had not yet met, and might never meet – Gin's mother.

It felt like some Mendelian calculation of heredity, or the palaeontologist's excited guess.

'Lookie here,' said Jack Gerald, handing over a clipping from his wallet. 'What do you make of this?'

It was a box-ad cut from a journal of some kind, a quality monthly perhaps, judging from the smoothness and weight of the paper.

Jimmy sent me this a year, maybe eighteen months ago,' said Gerald. 'He hadn't been in New York so long.'

Hugh read the clipping.

'SCATTLE STONES
$20 for your photograph of the Scattle Stones, San Antonio, Texas! Any condition. $20 bill by return. You may have forgotten till now, but you know you've been there in the last 15 years, and your loved one has taken your picture in front of this great Indian monument. Hunt it out now. $20 just for a quick look in your bureau. BOX B4107.'

'He was surprised, huh?' said Gerald. 'I was sure surprised. I mean, I could have sent in a whole crateful of postcards. Why should they want such things? They can get photographs of the stones. The stones are sure as hell famous. They can get photographs.'

'Did you send any photographs?' asked Hugh.

Gerald shrugged.

'Never have got round to it,' he said. 'There's a trick in it somewhere, you bet. Didn't want to get involved.'

Hugh handed back the photograph and the clipping.

'Your son's a musician too, then, is he?' he asked.

147

'Sure,' said Gerald, without great conviction. 'Jimmy's doing OK. Nice-looking boy, huh?'

'You must be very proud of him.'

'Yeah.'

Gerald swigged his drink and looked about him. Hugh wanted to ask him every kind of thing about Gin and couldn't. A little girl at the next table was looking at him with great solemnity. She seemed Chinese at first, but Hugh realised that she must be of Indian descent. Her parents were giving her a Coke. He smiled at her, but she stared back sadly and refused to smile.

'About Gin . . .' began Hugh.

'Yeah,' interrupted Gerald. 'You tell her we keep thinking of her. When you see her, tell her we'd like to see her some time.'

'But I've been trying to explain,' said Hugh. 'I don't know where she is.'

'Girl like that's unpredictable,' said Gerald. He seemed anxious to go now. He had finished his bourbon, and kept adjusting a neatly folded bill he had left under his glass as a tip. 'She's a successful woman now. Could be any place. Jimmy will know, I bet. Look him up when you're back in New York. I'll give you his number.'

Hugh wrote down Jimmy's number without enthusiasm. He knew he was not going to get anything more out of Gerald. The lift, the drink, the tourist chat were, he suddenly realised, a diversion. He had been successfully diverted from his quest. Gerald knew it, and was ready to wind up the uneasy relationship.

Hugh was furious at his own weakness. He had not even had a plain answer to his original question. Gin could be at home with her mother at that moment, in a resentful retreat, wanting him to be sent away. Somehow he did not think so, for in that case Gerald would surely have had the assurance simply to send him packing.

But perhaps this was the shrewd operator's way to send someone packing, reckoned to be more effective, worth the little time and expense?

Hugh finished his wine. He felt drained of will, hot, tired, controlled now by his booked flight, ready to submit to its impending departure from Texas.

'Know what?' said Jack Gerald cheerfully, as they stood up to go. 'There's five miles of this river to one mile of city. Its first name meant "Drunken old man going home at night" in the Indian language.'

The little girl still refused to smile. It's not just me, thought Hugh. She's not going to smile at anything. It's as though she's waiting for something, something she knows isn't ever going to happen.

The little girl pushed away her Coke deliberately with the back of her wrist.

19

'I'm losing you, horns, I'm losing you!'

The strings were massively busy in a surging complexity towards the end of the second movement. Katey's third and fourth fingers slid further and further towards her defiant chin as her pitch soared. Boris's baton stirred the air in front of him as though the concerto were a sauce that shouldn't be allowed to stick.

'Now that's too much,' he shouted wearily above the eloquent din.

The violin's climactic melody retreated in a little cluster of runs and triplets before its final assault on the summits, and Katey momentarily lost control of her intonation.

'Shit,' she hissed.

Boris tapped his stand, and again more loudly. The orchestra broke off eventually, and there were some murmurs of disappointment.

'OK, people,' said Boris. 'Things are coming apart. Strings, you weren't together from 85. Please watch me. You're doing great, Katey.'

Katey shrugged. She was standing with feet apart, her violin and her bow held loosely in each extended hand, rolling her head around on her neck, her eyes closed.

'Hugh,' called Boris to the back of the hall. 'Are you sure you need two horns here?'

One of the horn players made a ribald remark and a ripple of laughter spread from the wind section. The leader, pretending not to hear, leaned forward and sternly pencilled in an instruction on his part.

'Hugh, dear,' said Boris, smiling round at the orchestra, 'are you sleeping through this simply beautiful tune?'

The laughter increased. Katey wandered off to the side, practising her high notes pianissimo.

'Do we have the composer here today?' called Boris in mock concern. 'Sonia, can you see if Mr Howard is on the floor somewhere back there?'

Hugh collected himself.

'I'm sorry, Boris,' he said, coming forward from the corner where he had been sitting. 'I didn't catch what you were saying at first.'

'Two horns, Hugh,' explained Boris. 'They're frightened of playing too loud, so they play too quietly and start to lose their notes. One horn could play this whole passage piano. Wouldn't that be enough?'

'All right,' said Hugh, willingly. 'Just as you like.'

'Suits me,' said the second horn. 'But I still get paid.'

'Everybody gets paid,' said Boris. 'Even I get paid.'

Katey strolled towards them, her fingers still working on the strings.

'I really like this movement,' she said. 'It's beautiful, but it's so sad, you know? After the first movement, all that anger, it seems like it needs an answer. This wonderful tune, it isn't an answer at all. It just goes away, you know? It just floats off.'

'Katey, sweetheart,' said Boris. 'Are you embarking on a lecture? I don't think this is the right occasion for a lecture.'

'I was just going to suggest,' said Katey, flushing, 'that this whole recapitulation could be taken slower, maybe. What do you think?'

The last remark, avoiding the question of how she should address him, was directed so particularly at Hugh that for some reason he found himself startled. The very turn of her head and avoidance of a name seemed suddenly intimate.

'That's a very interesting point,' he said, conscious of an involuntary stiffness.

She played a few phrases, and smiled at him.

'See?' she said. 'Now it's sort of lost.'

'Lost?' said Boris. 'Katey, I wish I could understand what you're talking about.'

'Hugh understands me,' protested Katey. 'It's kind of lost and doesn't come home. I always think of the music coming home at the end of a movement. This should just sort of, sort of wander. And go to sleep in the barn.'

'In the barn?' cried Boris. 'Would you believe it, people, we've got a poetry session going on up front here.'

'A touch slower,' said Katey, obstinately.

'I think she's right, Boris,' said Hugh.

'Right?' said Boris, in a pretence of manic despair. 'Of course she's right. Slower. Faster, Katey's always right. Needn't play all the notes as written, of course, but tempo, tempo, it's that feminine touch.'

'Up yours, Boris,' said Katey coldly.

Boris lifted his baton.

'We'll take this again from 70,' he announced. 'One horn in this section, and a little slower. Andante quasi adagio.'

They resumed playing.

The rehearsal of the concerto had come upon Hugh with the stealth and speed of all significant dates. He had never been so late before in supplying parts, so that the inspiration of Texas, bringing particular relief upon completion, was still his predominant mood, an aftermath of creativity. He had still not made that psychological leap from the private satisfaction to the public accountability that was necessary for his effective cooperation at rehearsal. The realisation of his sounds on the platform was almost an intrusion, like finding Boris reading the loose pages of score on his desk, turning over an engagement diary, reading letters.

For he could not dissociate the concerto, even the earlier movements, from the lake at Dexter and all that he had found and lost there. After parting from Gin, he now understood, he had meted out the emotional punishment to himself of shutting out the possibility of finding her again and not letting her go. He had diverted his loss into his music with a willing connivance, and now that the concerto was completed it was too late.

Or was it? He had renewed his efforts to find her on returning to New York. After Denis's visit, the neighbour Myrna Robinson was no longer forwarding mail to Dexter. Indeed, some of it had already been returned by Jed and had rejoined the bundle which Myrna kept on the chest of drawers in her hall. When Hugh suggested that one of the letters might contain a clue to her whereabouts, Myrna was indignant.

'I ain't going to let you open none of these letters,' she said. 'Why, that would be a terrible thing to do.'

'Why do you think she hasn't given you another forwarding address, then,' asked Hugh.

'She'll be biding her time,' said Myrna.

'Have you any idea where she might be?'

Myrna was sullen and unfriendly.

'All I know is she went off with you,' was all she would say.

Goldbein was more helpful. He put Hugh on to her real agent, whose impressive-sounding Park Avenue address turned out to be a couple of rooms in an upper floor of a building whose size, shabbiness and noise made it seem like the service area of an airport terminal. The agent was a middle-aged woman with flat scraped hair and ferocious efficiency. She would say nothing to Hugh until he revealed all the details that he could remember of the arrangements for *The Freddy Connor Show*, and proved that he was who he said he was by producing a clipping of a review of *Beatrice and Benedick*, and the cheque from Prinzhorn, which he had not yet managed to launder. He suspected that the agent thought that he was in the process of stealing the Baroness from her. She also gave the impression that the Baroness was not always reliable, and that she was not best pleased with her not having turned up for Freddy Connor. These opportunities occurred when they occurred, and didn't always occur again.

'She doesn't always take the best advice,' were her last words.

In these interviews, and in his conversations with the Heathfields, Hugh began to feel that he was being accused of something. It is natural, in any case, for the things we most regret to present themselves as being, however irrationally, our fault. Even some decisive conspiracy of events, or some congenital deficiency, over which our reason tells us we have no control, can begin to look like the outcome of error, simply because our natural state of guilt requires its ready symbols. We willed it, therefore we deserve it. Or we perceive it to be so, and thus it is so.

Some sort of direct accusation like Tikki Crail's was enough to induce in Hugh a real sense of victimisation. He had been at the Heathfields' for a couple of days when she rang.

'Oh,' she said. 'You *are* back, then.'

Sensing the unusual grievance in her tone, Hugh imagined that it was because he had not expressed his gratitude for the loan of the Crail 'ranch', or reported back on the state of things there, or about the safe delivery of the Cadillac. But the Crails were somewhere in Tuscany at that moment (or were they in Stratford?) and he had not thought it necessary to contact Tikki. He started to make amends, but she was not interested.

'Hugh,' she interrupted. 'Peter's apartment!'

She made the announcement dramatically, as though it were the answer to a riddle. Before Hugh could begin to thank her for the use of that as well (though sensed that this was not the point) she launched into a series of extremely polite accusations.

'Of course, you can't have left the apartment like that. I *said* so to the janitor, but he made me feel that you might have done, and that made me feel just awful.'

'What do you mean, Tikki? Like what?'

'Oh, you know. Drawers all open, one of them on the bed. Things on the floor.'

'You mean you've had a break-in?' said Hugh, appalled. 'No, of course I didn't leave it like that.'

'No, I'm sure you didn't, Hugh, how could you have done?'

Tikki sounded unrelieved, as though the business might have been most easily cleared up if he had admitted to rummaging through Peter's things and leaving in a hurry.

'Was anything missing?'

'Oh no,' replied Tikki. 'At least Peter doesn't think so. And the janitor says he found the door unlocked. So nobody broke in exactly.'

'When was this?'

'Oh, Peter only went back there at the end of last week. I telephoned the ranch, but you'd left already.'

'Oh dear,' said Hugh. 'I am sorry. Nothing damaged, I hope?'

'Well, no,' said Tikki. 'That's the funny thing. I mean it doesn't seem to amount to anything, does it? But Peter was upset. Hugh, *could* you have forgotten to lock the apartment when you left?'

Hugh briefly thought back to that afternoon of erotic anticipation, escape and hectic arrangements. He was sure that he had locked up, because he was under instructions to return the keys to the janitor. They were in his hand. He had used them. It occurred to him that the janitor himself had a perfect opportunity to prowl and put the blame elsewhere, but Tikki would have none of it. Why should he prowl so messily, she pointed out? Besides, it was ridiculous. He was such a nice man, wasn't he? Hugh supposed that he was, and expressed his puzzlement and commiserations once more. Tikki was perfectly friendly when she rang off, but Hugh felt that he was under a cloud nonetheless.

He told all this to Denis Heathfield one evening when Dorothy was out and he felt that he could stay in without being in their way. Denis had poured a second drink, and seemed to want company.

'I wouldn't worry, uncle,' he said cheerfully. 'It's the classic solution. The butler did it.'

'In Gin's case they think I did it.'

'So I see,' said Denis solemnly. 'The last person to see the victim alive. Very suspicious.'

'Don't, Denis. It's not funny.'

'So you keep telling me, my dear fellow. But you mustn't take it all so seriously. The sufferer of the classic *Liebeskrankheit* is ripe for paranoia, you know. Everything, but everything, is grist to his mill.'

'What about the prowler at Dexter?' said Hugh. 'Perhaps he's taken Gin off somewhere.'

'In broad daylight? In front of the airport?'

'He left that tag, the Scattle Stones tag. It upset her.'

'Hugh, it seems more likely that it was hers, doesn't it? I mean, did she say it wasn't? Did she wonder where it had come from?'

'Not exactly.'

'There you are. Anyway, suppose there was somebody. Maybe she simply went off with him. You say you'd quarrelled.'

'I did not say we'd quarrelled,' objected Hugh.

'Well, you had, hadn't you? She was leaving?'

'Not for ever,' said Hugh. 'It wasn't like that.'

Wasn't it like that, he thought? How much like that did it have to be? Gin's intuition that there was no future in the long history of their essential separateness was part of her cheerful strength and independence. He on the other hand had allowed them to separate as he had allowed them to come together, with an acceptance of fatality. Standing on the sidelines of his own life, he accepted both the rules and the to-and-fro of actual play. But this difference between them had hurt them in those last days, he knew. He had failed her.

'She hoped for something from me, Denis,' he said. 'I think she was frightened of something.'

'Something, something. Life and love, perhaps,' said Denis. 'Anyway, you said that her father didn't say . . .'

'Stepfather.'

'You said that her stepfather might have been hedging.'

'I don't think he was, really.'

'Hugh, she could be anywhere. You don't know enough about her.'

'I'd just like to find her. I think I should go to the police.'

'Don't be ridiculous, Hugh. They'd laugh in your face.'

Hugh shrugged.

'I think she would have let Myrna know where she was. I think she would have let *me* know. We weren't finished. We were talking. We were in the middle of talking about it, for God's sake!'

Denis's answer to this outburst was to pour him another drink.

'The rehearsals will take your mind off it,' he said. 'And maybe soon she'll send you a letter that will explain it all.'

'Nobody knows where I am,' complained Hugh. 'Perhaps she did write. Perhaps she wrote to Riverside Drive and the prowler stole her letter.'

'Wouldn't she write to you at the Ballet?'

'I don't think so.'

Still, the next day, when he collected his accumulated mail from Johnny Tierentanz, he could not help his eager expectation of the sight of her handwriting as he uncovered each envelope after self-denyingly reading the letters in turn. There was nothing from her, but the last letter was from Daisy.

20

'. . . I might have known you'd never ring and I do know that you got the letter because John Tierentanz was very proud of the way he'd managed to forward all your letters when *I* rang *him*. It's not so difficult, you know, all direct dialling and it doesn't cost the earth. You just didn't want to ring, did you, and jolly well weren't going to. It's not that I mind selling shares, but it isn't exactly the right moment to do it, as Whitehead keeps telling me, and I did think you still had some in your building society and could ask them to issue a cheque to Simon directly. But you didn't ring, so I'm selling the shares because if I don't Simon will almost certainly not get Tinsel Street and will end up on some druggy's floor. Why don't you ever *do* anything? Anything important, I mean. I thought you did actually care about

Simon at least. Perhaps you've used the money up buzzing about all over the States. Aren't they paying you anything, or have you mucked all that up as usual? I know you like to see yourself as a super-efficient work-machine operating in your ivory tower as though ivory-towerism was perfectly O K if you use up a ream of paper a week and your telephone bill is £250 a quarter. Well, believe me, it isn't. The ivory tower has a basement, you know, where real life has to go on in its mucky way. I don't know about work-machine, more like an ice-machine. Cold, cold, cold. You only melt with Simon, as though only he was worthy of your attention, handing on an image of yourself. That's why I couldn't understand you just doing nothing about the money. You know we'd agreed. I thought you'd been so reasonable. For once, you'd really been reasonable. For Simon, of course. He'd do it for Simon. The machine would slow down for him. But no, it was too much to expect. The sounds from the basement don't reach quite that high, do they? The ice-man isn't going to melt after all. I suppose you're really disappointed with life, aren't you? It doesn't quite measure up to the ice-machine, does it? Those perfect shapes, bring them to the basement and they're just little puddles of dirty water. Well, most of us have to slop about in dirt all our lives. It's all we can do, trying to sort it out. Dirty money, dirty blood, dirty sex. But you want everything sterilised. You'd like it all arranged nicely, set out for you, just so that you can ignore it. You don't *want* anything, actually. You just want it to be there so that you can take no notice of it. If it hasn't got a shape, it's no good. You have to make a shape of it and it has to be your shape. No other shape is quite good enough. And it must be clean. And cold. Oh, so cold! Then you can just about admit it to your inner sanctum. Into the ivory tower. Into the ice-machine. But I don't believe you really love anything. You certainly don't love your parents. You've never loved me. I thought you loved Simon, but he didn't turn out to be an image of you at all, did he? What a disappointment. You were so hurt when he showed no interest in music. You didn't see that he might have done if you hadn't made so much of it, expecting him to turn up to concerts, making him learn the cello. That beastly cello! You were so impatient with him, weren't you? Why couldn't you accept that those sounds were what Simon produced in the thing? It wasn't what *you* expected. You wanted the music of the spheres, and all you got was a stuck pig. But it was Simon's stuck pig, and it came from the basement, that real warm place where we all struggle to do what we can. Oh no, you wanted the best, and Simon wasn't good enough. He couldn't put on your super-efficient ice-mask and produce ice-music. Simon did his best, and his best was splashing about in basement puddles, and you just couldn't accept it. You couldn't accept anything he did. You couldn't accept his moped any more than you could accept his dirty nappies. You could hardly accept his penis, especially when the time came that he might actually use it. God forbid! The poor boy had failed with the stuck pig. How was he bloody well going to manage with a penis? *You* couldn't manage, so you couldn't bear the thought that Simon might be able to. That was the worst sort of basement stuff. You had to put on an ice-mask and scrape ice-music on your viola. Oh yes, it was a fine sound, I grant you that, but did you ever work out what you were really doing poking that bow across that gut? Look at the *shape* of the thing, for God's sake. Talk about sublimation. You could learn to play the viola. How long did it take you? Twelve years? Twelve years, backwards and forwards across that vibrating hole? But you could never learn to play *me*. The ice-mask had to slip a bit for that to happen, and you can't let that mask slip a millimetre, can you? Because do you know what's beneath that mask? Beneath that damned mask of yours you're all jelly. A jelly-man. You're afraid of everything, and jealous, too. You're really jealous of Simon, when all's said and done. You're jealous of his height, and his looks. You're jealous of Tinsel Street, and jealous of Sally. That's because you're jealous of his penis. And that's why you don't really want to give him any more money. You're a jealous jelly-man, who's afraid of the only real thing you've ever made and won't lift a finger. Well, I've sold the shares, and Tinsel Street will be all right if we're lucky and there's still time, and you can bloody well stay in America for ever, and nobody I know will ever miss you. We don't want anything from you, and certainly won't ask you again . . .'

21

After a frustrating and demoralising session with the desk sergeant, who gave the appearance of believing nothing that he was told and writing too little of it down, Hugh was summoned back to the precinct headquarters within hours, and ushered into the presence of Lieutenant Heaney.

Heaney was standing by the window, looking out into the shadowy well formed by the adjacent buildings. Pigeons waddled incongruously across a concrete ledge that spanned this well. There was no hint of the sunlight that seemed inescapable outside.

He turned to greet Hugh, who saw that he was holding the statement he had made that morning. He was a small man, with a neutral and precise manner that could pass as polite or threatening as occasion demanded. His mouth in repose possessed a kind of comic primness, the more unnerving for being topped by a heavy moustache.

'Mr Howard?' he asked, holding out his hand.

Their interview was so cordial that Hugh could not but think that somewhere the sergeant was in disgrace for not taking him seriously enough. Lieutenant Heaney insisted on hearing a new and more detailed statement, which a police stenographer was brought in to take down. Hugh was able to add to what he had said that morning the result of a telephone call to Gin's half-brother Jimmy, for his call had at last been answered.

After so many unanswered calls Hugh had felt suddenly unprepared. Jimmy had told him nothing, and he could think of no tactic for getting behind the sullen and protective barrier of his expressionless voice.

'You're the Englishman,' Jimmy had said. At the time Hugh could not tell if this was a polite acknowledgment of identity or a kind of threat. Jimmy had not sounded friendly. He had not been in touch with Gin for months, he said. He also wanted to know where Hugh was staying.

Lieutenant Heaney allowed all this to be taken down, leaning back in his chair and occasionally running the top of his forefinger beneath his moustache.

'You said nothing about the call to Miss Gerald's brother to Sergeant Schutz,' he remarked.

When he heard that Hugh had only received the call that day, he simply nodded. Hugh signed the statement, and the stenographer left the room with the carbon copy, presumably to create a file among the thousands of files that fed the routine of the precinct. From television serials Hugh had expected to find wire cages full of gum-chewing prostitutes, sentimental drunks being interviewed, harassed men in shirt-sleeves and shoulder-holsters, and a vast deal of eccentricity and camaraderie. But the police headquarters was in essence simply an office, conducting the usual business of offices.

'So, Mr Howard,' said Heaney, with the new statement in front of him on the desk. 'Let me ask you: what do you think all this amounts to?'

He might have been Hugh's accountant. But to his accountant Hugh could more or less say: 'You tell me. That's what I'm paying you for.' To Lieutenant Heaney he could say very little.

'I don't know,' he said. 'I just feel that something's wrong. Nobody knows where she is.'

'How do you know that nobody knows?'

'I don't know anybody who does know.'

'That's not the same thing. She must know people that you don't know, and they presumably don't know you.'

Heaney leaned forward across the desk, with a suggestive gleam in his eye.

'Suppose,' he said. 'Just suppose that she was still with you. Don't you think there might be friends of hers who would be worried about her? Three weeks gone? Nobody knows about you.'

'She left the forwarding address with her neighbour.'

'Sure,' said Heaney. 'But I'm not saying she was obliged to. This is a free country, Mr Howard. She can do what she likes.'

'I think she felt . . . threatened, perhaps exploited. There was this prowler. She just disappeared at the airport. She hasn't fulfilled any of her engagements. Why shouldn't she appear on *The Freddy Connor Show*? It was a big chance for her.'

'Exploited?' queried Heaney. 'She sounds pretty independent to me. Sounds as though she does what she likes.'

'I'm sure it was a kind of escape,' said Hugh. 'She wanted me to take her away, and she didn't want anyone to know.'

'So?' smiled Heaney. 'Maybe now she doesn't want you to know. I can understand your feelings. Maybe your pride is hurt.'

'Oh yes, all that,' said Hugh ruefully. 'But the point is that somebody did know. Her brother knew about me, though he said that she hadn't been in touch for months. Someone followed us out to Dexter.'

'A long way to go,' observed Heaney. He looked down at the statement, and pondered. 'Why couldn't her father have told him that you'd been around asking questions?'

Hugh saw that this was indeed perfectly likely, and wondered why it hadn't occurred to him before.

'And this prowler,' continued Heaney. 'He didn't take anything?'

'Not as far as I know.'

'You say he was watching you?'

'And asking about me.'

'Asking about you by name?'

'I don't know.'

Heaney sighed, and pushed the statement to one side of his desk.

'Well, Mr Howard,' he said. 'There's a lot here that you don't know.'

'That's why I've come to you.'

'What exactly do you expect us to do about it?'

'What do you do when someone is missing?'

'To be very frank, Mr Howard, there's not a lot that we can do. Seems to me on what we've got here there's just about nothing we can do. Nothing yet, anyway. We'll have to wait awhile.'

'But I'm not going to be in the States much longer,' said Hugh in alarm.

'We've got your statement, Mr Howard,' said Heaney. 'That shouldn't present any problem. Unless, of course, you know more than you've told us.'

'But I want to know what's happened to her,' said Hugh.

'We can arrange to let you know if she turns up.'

Hugh could hardly tell whether Heaney was interested or not. He seemed agreeable, but distant. He came up with no practical suggestions. He seemed to be expecting Hugh to tell him more, but made no serious effort to extract information from him. At the same time there was a kind of meticulous intensity about his conduct of the interview, and Hugh wondered why he had been called back in the first place if the police had no intention of trying to trace her. After he'd left, he felt just as despondent as when he'd finished with Sergeant Schutz earlier in the day.

Staying with the Heathfields had its small disadvantages. Denis was a night creature, moving equally from his study to the living room or from the living room to the kitchen, usually with a drink in his hand. Dorothy was nervous and orderly, unhappy if she didn't know the numbers for meals. They coexisted peaceably, like orbiting planets, but Hugh's presence seemed to bring their different habits into confrontation. If Denis poured Hugh a drink and disappeared, Dorothy would be sure to poke her head round the door and say: 'Oh, have you started already?' When Hugh cleared up after a meal, drying glasses with a fresh paper towel for each one as he had seen Dorothy do, Denis would take them from him and say: 'Oh, just bung these in the machine.' Hugh knew very well that Dorothy could not possibly want him there. On one occasion he thought he overheard her talking about him ('Doesn't he have a job to go to?') and he never knew how much she knew about the Baroness. He reserved that subject for Denis alone out of respect for (or was it somehow fear of?) Dorothy's long-standing friendship with Daisy.

Indeed, now that he was back in New York where his relationship with Gin had been secret or only potential, it was almost as though he had never known her, for so few of the people he knew had ever been aware of it. He supposed that it would get back to the Crails eventually, through Jed, but not yet. Olive was the most diligent gossip he had met, but for that reason her information was probably discounted by her friends, and in any case she really knew very little. Denis was his only confidant.

It was Denis who noticed the television programme.

'Well, uncle,' he said, pouring himself his breakfast coffee. 'I don't think you've much to worry about. She's on TV tonight.'

Hugh's feelings were compounded of puzzlement, animal excitement and disbelief. There was an aesthetic element to the mystification that he had hardly experienced since childhood, when the behaviour of grown-ups on whom he depended seemed wilful, unpredictable and therefore admirable. But in this case he had a foretaste of hidden purposes which excluded him.

At first he naturally thought of *The Freddy Connor Show*, but the programme was one of a series about singers. He almost immediately realised that it must be pre-recorded, but he looked forward to it as to a posthumous revelation and watched it as eagerly, and with as much sense of hopeless regret, as a war widow opening a delayed letter from the front.

The format of the programme was a song and an interview, the minimum that could be expected. Nobody had been to any trouble. There was no editorial interference. No one made a criticism or a generalisation. It made English television seem astonishingly highbrow.

None of the Baroness's material had been specially filmed. The song looked as though it were part of some tribute to an earlier singer, or perhaps from a programme about the blues, and it was hard to tell if she were in period costume or not, since the style of dress that Hugh had most seen her in was so 1940ish in any case. Here she was boldly draped in nightclub diamanté, in front of an orchestra who all wore unnaturally brilliantined hair. She seemed younger, less certain of herself. The song was raunchier than any that Hugh had heard her sing, and was backed by suggestive tremolos from grouped trombones or cornets, with a slack percussive undertow from the rhythm section whose drummer, whenever he came into shot, was chewing and grinning and looking pleased with himself. The Baroness belted out the song as though addressing the last man left alive:

> 'Put your cards upon the table.
> Let's see the kind of man you are.
> Isn't it true you think you've got it made
> Because I go too far?
>
> I'm off my guard
> And it isn't funny.
> It's not too hard
> To clean me, honey.
> Just deal a card
> And take my money.
>
> All you need to do is play me.
> Call my bid, I'll lose for sure.
> Listen to me now, no need to cheat
> Because I go too far.
>
> When I've got plenty
> It's a kind of ache.
> I twist at twenty,
> That's my mistake.
> Then the table's empty
> And everything's at stake.
>
> I've got the heart to lose a million.
> That's my heart a-knocking at the door.
> You let me in, you hear? You've nothing to lose
> Because I go too far.'

Hugh could have listened to this all night, but it seemed to be over almost as soon as it had started. There was so much in it of Gin that he recognised and understood that its musical difference, or the range of mood and gesture that she employed to project it, seemed a perfectly natural extension of what was already established about her in his mind. Musical variety was a function of her own personality, which most came to life in response to its challenges.

The interview, however, was a revelation.

Or rather, it was a disturbing reminder of a scene that he very well knew was fixed in his memory, but which he kept half-consciously repressing. The interview was not with Gin alone, but with Gin and Sammy West. It even conveyed the strong likelihood that it was extracted from an interview with Sammy West, for they were sitting on the same sofa, and Sammy was significantly nearer to the camera. The Baroness sat apart, not unhappy but disengaged. Hugh could imagine her fingers busy with her knitting: here they lay in her lap stiff and patient, as though sculpted. Sammy looked pleased with himself, glowing in the aura of jokes extemporised, the apparently new topic of Gin educing from him a serious tone which was accompanied by a clearing of the throat and the leaning forward to reach an ashtray. The relationship revealed was that distant and undemonstrative one that had impressed itself at the Crails' party. Hugh had wanted to believe that it was one of singer and songwriter as it was being presented here, or at least one of pupil and mentor. The mentor spoke proprietorially, the chin suddenly raised to settle more comfortably in the collar, one shoulder drawn back, ash forever aimed inaccurately at the ashtray in front of him. The pupil spoke briefly, as though rehearsed, and neither looked at the other. Something was wrong with this. It was too guarded, the issues musically uninteresting, the staging-posts of the career so unexceptionable. Only a certain amount could be said, it seemed, as if by the control of invisible strings.

Almost as soon as it had begun, the interview was over, but in that short space of time Hugh came to face what he knew he had really known all along, that Gin and Sammy West were, had been, still were perhaps, in some strange and disagreeably ill-sorted sense, lovers.

22

When Hugh left the Heathfields' apartment the next morning, he had the feeling that he was being followed. He could imagine himself as part of a classic film sequence in which a man in a hat detached himself from a lamppost and threw down a half-smoked cigarette. In several quiet streets he sensed that he was not walking alone, that someone was keeping pace at an unseen distance.

He had obtained Sammy West's address from Olive Dempster, since it was ex-directory.

'Hugh Howard!' she had exclaimed. 'Now you see him, now you don't!'

'I've been in Texas, Olive.'

'Of course, of course,' she had replied. 'It's the coming place. When not here, in Texas. What does anyone do in Texas?'

Hugh told her about his lectures.

'It's too bad,' she had said. 'Everyone disappears as soon as you want them. I'm supposed to do a piece on Gore Vidal, and he's in Europe. Dan Fleischman discovered he has an appendix. And everyone's looking for the Baroness.'

Hugh had tried not to sound too concerned.

'Why?'

'Nowhere to be found, dear, that's why. She missed a recording session, and I've never seen Hooky Foster so mad. I don't suppose you ran off with her, did you, Hugh, you devil?'

'I haven't seen her, Olive,' lied Hugh.

'I wish someone would run off with me,' Olive complained. 'I can understand wanting to give everything up. Too much pressure.'

'You manage quite well, Olive.'

'Oh, me? I'm as tough as they come. Someone like the Baroness, though. Too famous, too soon. Hard to get it right.'

Hugh risked the question that was haunting him.

'Doesn't Sammy West know where she is?'

'Sammy West? I expect so. There's not much that old goat doesn't know.'

'As a matter of fact, Olive, I rather wanted West's address, if you have it.'

'Sure, I've got it.'

Olive gave him the address and telephone number.

'What kind of get-together are you planning on? I wouldn't have thought you two had much in common.'

Hugh thought in a flash of sickening insight of what they probably had in common, and of how little in fact he had had of it.

'Nothing important, Olive,' he had said.

It seemed to him extraordinary, now that he was back in New York, that no one except Denis, and Myrna Robinson of course, seemed to have any idea about Gin's accompanying him to Dexter. Of all the people who might have discovered or suspected something, Olive was the most likely. Then there was the sullen but somehow compliant Yellow. What had Gin told him? Yellow had not been in evidence when Hugh had visited Willa's Place, and Goldbein, come to think of it, had not shown any great anxiety about the Baroness's absence ('I can get other singers. She's never been reliable'). Who did care? Presumably Bob Gordon, too, would get another singer. What about the public? What about the press? How long did it take for it to be recognised that someone had disappeared?

Sammy West's apartment building had the impregnability of great wealth: double glass doors, a vigilant man in uniform. Hugh was now used to Manhattan's automatic self-protectiveness; Gin's Shaker, no doubt wary behind his newspaper, the maligned janitor at Peter's Riverside Drive apartment. This man was, by contrast, openly on duty. You could not enter the building without making yourself known to him. Even the apartment mailboxes and buzzers were behind the outer door, which was locked. And the man had an easy air, bright-eyed. He might have been on a terrace, watching a horse race. And he wore a gun.

167

As Hugh approached the glass door, these suddenly evident facts combined with the more certain knowledge that he really didn't know what he was going to say to Sammy West, or how he was going to say it, made him stop in hesitation. For a moment, as he faced the building, his eyes met those of the man in uniform, and Hugh turned his hesitation into a more theatrically deliberate change of plan. He even pretended to look at his watch. He turned round, looked down the street, then strode on.

On his return, within two minutes, on the other side of the street and hating himself for his indecisiveness, Hugh saw two men come quickly out of the building and look up and down the street on their side. They stood for a moment uncertainly craning, back to back, immobile against a small trickle of passers-by. For a second Hugh watched this scene with an aesthetic detachment. Like much that occurred on the sidewalks of Manhattan, it was contained, self-absorbed and eminently watchable. So much so, that it was some moments before Hugh realised that because he knew the men they must know him, and that it was him they were looking for.

One of the men was Yellow, and the other was Gin's brother Jimmy.

He had not time to examine the strange motives that made him turn and walk quietly away: half fear, half guilt? From either of the men he might, in theory, have welcomed the opportunity of extracting information. Together, they seemed to defy that possibility, not least because they were so anxious to find him. It was not, he felt sure, because they had something to tell him.

He unhurriedly turned the first corner, hoping that the pair would have split up and pursued him in both directions on the other side of the street, not imagining that he would still be directly opposite the apartment block. He didn't dare to look round, since if they were to catch up with him it would surely be in his interests not to be thought to be deliberately evading them.

But since he was deliberately evading them, what did he think they were after him for?

His mind was confused on this point, as it was already distracted by the body's compulsive escape. He had acted as instinctively as an animal startled in some inquisitive approach. His feet moved with the automatic guile of a quarry. But the mind worked to explain the situation, even in the fullness of his being a victim within it.

He had not made himself known, but his hesitation had been enough to alert the doorman, who must therefore have been earlier primed by Sammy West to look out for him. Was this credible? Did Sammy expect him, then? Had Olive Dempster been whispering? And why, as the crowning puzzle, had it been Jimmy and Yellow who had burst out of the building on Sammy's behalf, for all the world like the incapable but obedient henchmen of some gangster?

Hugh already had begun to feel obscurely responsible for the loss that challenged him. That was a natural consequence of the low moments when he became convinced that it was deserved. Now there were other players in the game: he might be called to account in ways that would not boost his indulged *Schadenfreude*, ways that would not be at all pleasant for him. He remembered Jimmy's words: 'You're the Englishman.' It could not have been Gin who had described him thus if it were true that brother and sister had not met for months. Now it seemed without doubt that it was Yellow who was the source of information about him, and if Yellow was the source of information, lacking any of the discretion that Gin in her trust must have attributed to him, then Sammy West knew quite a bit more about Hugh than he liked.

His original intuition that Gin was not after all missing, but was back again in Sammy's clutches, seemed now invalid. Why? The reason was, he told himself, that the pair had not spilled so precipitately on to the street simply to tell him that Gin was sitting in Sammy's apartment, incommunicado. And yet, if Yellow was a betrayer of Gin's trust, that betrayal was of long standing. Hugh could not quite remember how much Yellow was supposed to know or not know. He had seemed to be a willing messenger kept in essential ignorance of the matters on which he ran errands. No doubt he knew a great deal more than anyone thought, and what he didn't know could always be extracted with threats from those, like Myrna, who did.

Hugh found himself in Washington Square, a place altogether altered since the days of Henry James's Catherine Sloper. Now it was an informal pleasure garden, a meeting place of trick cyclists, lovers and chess fiends. Youths brandished stereophonic radios the size of suitcases, the volume turned up full. Secretaries ate sandwiches on the grass.

Hugh had no idea if he were being followed, and decided to stop in the vicinity of one of the chess games to find out. There was safety in numbers. It was, as he soon discovered, less a private contest than a form of street theatre. He sat on the end of a bench, mingling with the audience. He kept an eye on the path down which he had come for Jimmy and Yellow while listening to the dialogue of the players.

Their ruse was to appear to be unwilling to play. The younger man was a big Greek, continually distracted by the needs of his dog and the urgency of some other, unspecified business which in theory required him. His challenger was critical, grudging, and apparently the more concentrated player. The stake was ten dollars, but the Greek seemed uninterested in money. He played carelessly, and with a scandalous disregard for the rules of the game, mis-setting the clock and edging captured pieces back on to the board. His opponent, when not arguing about procedure, was continually threatening to leave. Hugh soon perceived how they made their money: a third partner, a young man in thick spectacles, took unlikely side-bets which their erratic play usually won for him. His innocent sophomoric chatter as he collected the money they would all no doubt later share dispelled all possible objection. In any case, the spectators were riveted by the outrageous cheating and wild combinative play of the combatants, and by their continuous mock-heroic dialogue:

'You're dying, Tony.'

'Am I dying?'

'Yes, you're dying.'

'I'm dying? That's what I'm doing? What about this?'

'What that? What are you doing?'

'That's what I'm doing. Am I there?'

'What do you call this?'

'Tell me. Am I there?'

'I don't know, doh.'

'I'm there. What are you doing now?'

'Was your pawn there? I don't remember it being there.'

'What are you doing?'

'The pawn wasn't there.'

'What are you doing in America, Erica?'

'You moved that pawn.'

'It isn't true, doo.'

'You moved it.'

'Noo.'

'You're dying, Tony.'

And Tony died. And the young man in glasses collected from several onlookers. There was no sign of Yellow and Jimmy.

Behind the benches a man was collecting empty beer cans for the five-cent return that a trash-conscious culture required the beer companies to offer. No one who drank beer collected the five cents, ever, but this man made a living from a ballooning plastic bag full of them.

A cross-looking man with a snub nose and a bad shaving rash was refusing to pay the man with glasses. He seemed vaguely familiar to Hugh. The man with glasses laughed disbelievingly.

'You've got to pay, man,' he said, looking round. 'What will all these people think?'

'I know what they'll think,' said snub-nose. 'They'll think he ditched the game, so you could collect. That's what they'll think.'

'Oh yeah,' said the man with glasses. 'You want your face busted?'

'Try it,' said snub-nose.

The Greek, who was rapidly setting up the pieces for another game, sensed trouble and sent the man with glasses off in search of a bowl of water for his dog.

Hugh left the chess players and soon found himself in Bleecker Street, suddenly thirsty, hungry and tired. He ordered a pastrami sandwich and beer at a sidewalk café. He kept his eye on his food, irrationally feeling himself more invisible if he did so. Nobody walked the sort of distances he had been walking, down from Park Avenue to Greenwich Village, pursued, far from a subway, incompetent at hailing a cab. He felt craven and ridiculous.

When he had paid he stood up and for the first time glanced into the street, his eye taken by an enormous transvestite waiting by a fruit barrow for the traffic to thin. Several people were staring, and a boy starting up a motorbike made some loud remark as the transvestite, 200 pounds of mince and powder, began to cross the street. Hugh was making up a tip in change, though he knew he should have left a dollar bill. When he looked up again he saw Yellow on the opposite side of the street in the theatrical space left by the transvestite.

Hugh hurriedly brushed past several tables to reach the gap in the iron railing that protected the café from the sidewalk. This brought him almost into contact with the transvestite, who half-turned as though accosted. Someone in the café behind him laughed. The boy succeeded in starting the engine, and began a slow turn in the street.

Hugh was aware of all these movements, and his own, as though they were elaborately rehearsed, as in a film of a planned robbery where every member of the gang has a tiny, unlikely but crucial part to play in the scenario of observation, delay and impediment.

He turned left out of the café, and immediately left again, thinking to head north for Washington Square. There was safety in numbers, indeed, but safety from what? And Bleecker Street, with its tourist pull, was as crowded as anywhere he had passed that morning. Why hadn't he stayed there? For now suddenly he was in a perfectly deserted back street, almost half of one side of which was the blank brick surface of the back end of an art gallery. Were those footsteps behind him? He could hardly believe it, since despite his fright something told him that the man he had seen outside the café could not really have been Yellow.

But if it was? The back street stretched ahead, not clearly leading anywhere in particular. Hugh took the next left turn, hoping to rejoin Bleecker Street after a while and stay in Bleecker Street until he could find a cab. This was a mistake. The turn was into an alley filled with cardboard boxes.

Physical fear converted the whole of his body into a vortex of

impressions sensed and recollected. Idiotic phrases insisted themselves ('What're you doing in America, Erica?') and he thought
sharply and regretfully of his most unexpected and absorbing sexual
moments with Gin. The footsteps were still there, close behind him.
His head thundered, shoulders and neck cringing in vulnerability.

His feet continued to move, leadenly and unconvincingly, as
though there might be some useful doorway behind the cardboard
boxes ('It isn't true, doo'). There was nothing.

When the hand grasped his shoulder, he reacted in desperation. His
body uncoiled like a spring, turning and knocking away the hand in
one movement. He heard a voice say: 'Hey, wait a minute,' and hands
came in again to grasp both his upper arms.

In knocking away the hand, Hugh knew that he must have lightly
hit Yellow in the face, but now he could see that it was not Yellow at
all. It was the man with the snub-nose who had argued about his chess
bet in Washington Square.

'Don't move,' said snub-nose. He had pushed Hugh back against
the cardboard boxes where he leaned, slightly off-balance. Snub-nose
had a gun out, not pointing it at Hugh, but held away from his body as
he eased the arm inside his jacket sleeve and rubbed his shoulder with
his other hand. Hugh staggered against the boxes and tried to right
himself.

'Don't move!' shouted snub-nose. 'For God's sake, Howard,
you're leading me one hell of a dance. You'd better come into the
precinct before we do each other an injury.'

23

'Let's see what we've got here,' said Lieutenant Heaney, in his
accountant's voice. He might have been about to itemise the contents
of a vagrant's suitcase. Hugh sat in front of him, confused and abject,

noticing again the clumsy rendezvous of the amorous pigeons on the concrete bridge outside his window. Somewhere in the outer office the snub-nosed detective was no doubt laughingly recounting his adventures of that morning, hoping for more significant duties in the afternoon.

'I'm sorry about this morning,' said Hugh.

Heaney shrugged.

'Detective Rance can look after himself,' he said.

'I'd no idea I was being followed,' said Hugh.

'Then you sound to have been giving a very good imitation of a man being followed,' said Heaney, smiling briefly.

'I mean, by one of your men.'

'Uh-huh?' said Heaney. 'You don't see why we should be interested in your movements?'

'Not really,' said Hugh, surprised by his own daring. 'I mean, I don't see how it can affect your investigation.'

'Our investigation,' pondered Heaney, stroking his moustache and squeezing it as though it were damp and needed wringing out. 'Yes, the investigation. You'd be surprised what an investigation can uncover, Mr Howard. There's always more to it than meets the eye.'

He looked directly at Hugh.

'I hope you weren't inconvenienced this morning by Detective Rance?' he asked suddenly.

Hugh felt that he was being toyed with.

'No,' he said lamely. 'Not at all.'

'There's no need to be polite, Mr Howard,' said Heaney. 'You thought you were being followed by somebody, then?'

'Yes,' replied Hugh, 'as I told Detective Rance.'

'Sure,' said Heaney. 'We'd better get another statement.'

He made no move to call the stenographer.

'And why did you go to Mr West's apartment this morning?'

'I thought he might know where Miss Gerald was.'

'Let me get this straight,' said Heaney. '*You* thought that *he* might know?'

'Yes,' said Hugh.

'Why?'

The question was direct, abrupt, and somehow unanswerable.

'He was . . .' Hugh fumbled. 'I mean, they worked together.'

Heaney smiled condescendingly, and walked to the edge of the desk. Behind him the pigeons fluttered in their vertiginous courtship, and Heaney glanced at them as if at a significant emblem of a point that he need not make, like a lecturer with an over-abundance of slides.

'Well now,' Heaney repeated. 'What have we got here? We have a report of a missing person.'

He paused, returned to his chair, and sat down.

'And then,' he continued, lighting a cigarette, 'just a few days later, at a different precinct, we have another report of a missing person.'

He shook the match out, and placed it carefully in an ashtray.

'And it's the same missing person. It takes time to make the connection, you understand, and normally missing persons are neither here nor there. I don't intend a pun. Simply, Mr Howard, that missing persons are too daily to worry about overmuch.'

Hugh was astonished.

'Who else reported her?' he asked.

Lieutenant Heaney held up his hand. Hugh noticed that he held the cigarette between the third and fourth finger.

'A moment please, Mr Howard,' he smiled. 'I haven't revealed your statement to the other party, so I won't reveal his statement to you. And why not? I will tell you. I think there is no collusion here. Sometimes, you know, a family – simply to make a fuss, to get something done – will make different reports. Most cases, it's obvious who goes to the police: mother, sister, lover. So here I ask: what do we have? We have two reports, two men. Do we have two lovers? That's not unusual. Do they suspect each other of funny business? That's not so unusual either.'

Hugh began to object, but Heaney silenced him.

'Please, Mr Howard,' he said. 'Listen to my thinking. It's a large part of my job. Detective Rance and men like him go out into the streets and get politely roughed up in Greenwich Village. It's exciting for them. Me, I sit here and do the thinking.'

He drew on his cigarette.

'Now neither of these reports mentions that the lady in question has recently been in the hospital. A material fact, you might think. At least more material than the mysterious prowler.'

'There was a prowler,' said Hugh defiantly.

'I'm not saying there wasn't,' said Heaney. 'But checking on your prowler is difficult for us. Checking New York hospitals is one of the things we do.'

He waited, as if for Hugh's comment.

'I forgot to mention the hospital,' said Hugh. 'She asked me to pick her up there.'

'She asked you?' repeated Heaney. He picked up a paper from his desk. 'You signed for her release before she had finished treatment. I have a statement from Dr Saul Listener that you also brought her in.'

'No, no,' said Hugh, remembering the hostile doctor. Why should the doctor have made that claim? 'I did sign something when she left, but I didn't know she'd gone in.'

'Dr Listener says that you were a frequent visitor, and were very nervous and anxious to get away,' continued Heaney. 'Do you know what she was in for?'

'She didn't want to tell me,' said Hugh. 'She seemed all right.'

'She seemed all right?' Heaney raised his eyebrows.

'Well,' said Hugh. 'She had bruises on her ankles.'

'Bruises?' broke in Heaney emphatically. 'On her ankles?' He made it sound faintly ridiculous. 'That's not what I gathered from Dr Listener.'

'What did he say?' asked Hugh.

'This is confidential information,' said Heaney. 'Anyway, I would have thought you would have found out after you sprung her from hospital. If you didn't have very good reason to know already.'

'I didn't spring her,' objected Hugh. 'She was leaving. She wasn't compelled to stay.'

'Her neighbour says she didn't look well.'

'I don't suppose she did. She seemed tired. She was fine in Texas.'

'You drove her straight to Texas?'

'She wanted to go immediately.'

Heaney pondered.

'You collected her from hospital and took her straight to Texas,' he said. 'Pretty abrupt, huh?'

'Well,' said Hugh. 'I think I made that all quite clear when I saw you before. She was frightened of something.'

'Sure she wasn't frightened of you?'

Hugh shook his head in exasperation.

'OK, OK,' said Heaney. 'I'm not saying I don't believe you. Some fellows, though, look as though they wouldn't hurt a fly, quiet types like you, they're the ones who figure in the worst cases of abuse.'

In his deepest being, Hugh took fright at the word 'abuse'. He did not want to think of what it might refer to. He did not even want to think about thinking of it. In some strange way it seemed to suggest an inadequacy in himself that went further than what he now saw as an unnecessary timidity in finding out from Gin herself what had been the matter.

'Such files are available to us in any case,' Heaney went on. 'There may be charges. Tell me, did Miss Gerald mention her brother?'

'Her half brother? Not particularly. I mean, she told me a lot about her family.'

'Are they close?'

Hugh thought of the photograph in Jack Gerald's wallet, the lip and the jaw that were so like Gin's. He thought of the man who had spilled out of Sammy West's apartment with Yellow, searching the sidewalk with an animal quickness. He remembered the words on the telephone: 'You're the Englishman.' He realised that he knew nothing about him whatever.

He shrugged.

'I think perhaps he works for West', he said. 'He was one of the men looking for me this morning.'

'How hard to find are you, Mr Howard?' asked Heaney. 'I thought you were famous.'

'I'm not sure that many people know where I'm staying.'

'Does Miss Gerald know?'

'She could find me,' said Hugh, with a prickle of uncertainty and panic.

'In that case anyone can find you, Mr Howard,' said Heaney. 'And if you've got nothing to hide, you've got nothing to worry about.'

'Of course I've got nothing to hide.'

'Let me know if Jimmy Gerald gives you any trouble. We have a file on him, as it happens.'

'What has he done?'

'Nothing that should concern you greatly,' said Heaney. 'Nothing that should concern you personally, a man of your tastes.'

'You're not telling me very much, are you?'

'I think that makes us about even, Mr Howard.'

'What happens now?'

Hugh realised that for the last few minutes Lieutenant Heaney had been gradually showing him to the door. And that he had either extracted the information he required, or conveyed the information that he wanted Hugh to have. Which was it? Hugh also knew very well that the whole business was obscure, uneventful and inconclusive from the point of view of the police. Denis had said that they would laugh in his face. They had not done that, but perhaps they were laughing behind his back.

As if to confirm it, Hugh saw Detective Rance through the glass partition sitting on a desk and holding out his arms wide in the middle of recounting some anecdote to another man in shirt-sleeves. He looked up and caught Hugh's eye, dropped his arms, and muttered something. The other man smiled.

'We can't make anything happen,' said Lieutenant Heaney, his hand on the doorknob. 'Things that happen, they're going to happen anyway. Much of what happens isn't very pretty.'

'Will I hear from you?'

'I don't think you'll be hearing from us. Look, Mr Howard. People are disappearing all the time. It's their privilege. It's a free society.'

Hugh nodded, and Lieutenant Heaney put a hand on his shoulder. 'Girl like that,' he said, 'maybe needs to escape for a while. If anything more does happen, then we can act.'

24

Escaping for a while, Hugh reflected later, was what everyone comes round to. Nothing is so perfect that it cannot be wilfully spoiled by the desire to stand outside that perfection and disbelieve it for an instant. He thought of the Milton Baxter song that Gin had sung at Dexter:

> 'There's always time to claim there's time to
> Find the time to say to you
> All that needs saying
> Before I shrug and climb to
> Some cold and distant view.'

Was there a difference between saying and living? Did there have to be both? Wasn't that like the realisation that you are happy which means that the happiness has come to an end? Was there a difference between escaping and giving up? Was there much difference between either of these and Hugh's own brand of stoical acceptance of whatever dirty deals fate had in store for him? A kind of stoicism that some might call cowardice? The resolutions always came too late. The understanding always came too late, a shrug and a smile followed by one hypersecond of moral scrutiny like a shaft of torchlight swung into a dark cave of forgotten hoards.

He didn't even understand his own escapes, so how could he hope to understand Gin's? The escape from Mary Meadows was the kind that required pursuit, a failed challenge. The escape from Daisy was a misplaced yielding to her own supposed desires, a failed gift. The escape from Gin was pure disbelief in perfection, the artist's guilty resort to self-consciousness. The escape from Katey pure fear, the middle-aged man's self-righteous excuse.

The escape from Katey? Oh yes, that little number was ringing all right. He could see it coming. He had no need to be jealous or suspicious of Boris, who now stood outside the charmed circle of composer and soloist, impotent to do anything except bring them fruitfully together, like a pander. Hugh was in a way ashamed to offer his concerto to the girl. Her playing of it forced her to the creation of feelings of which she became the willing accomplice. To the emotion of the score she brought a physical actuality which miraculously restored the erotic basis of that emotion, as in a nude painting the body of the model conveys the painter's handling of pigment that without it would simply be so much pigment, the vision broken up again into mere behaviour of colour. Who was the Svengali now?

And yet at the same time Hugh could feel that he was himself only the trustee of this emotion, that he was handing something over from Gin to Katey that did not belong to him and which had cost a great effort of understanding. When he had lunch with Katey a couple of times during rehearsals so that she could tell him about her interpretation, he felt powerless to disagree with anything that she proposed, like a biographer in the bosom of his subject's family. He could always so easily feel that only the emotions of other people were fully valid, and that this gave them not only a secret understanding of each other, but a right to impose the resolved conclusions of those emotions on himself. Hadn't he too easily accepted Daisy's proposal of separation? Hadn't it been the Baroness who had done the wooing? Was he not even now waiting for Katey to make a move? So much for escape. Might as well call it exile, or limbo.

When they came out of the sandwich bar one day, she took his arm like a suddenly nostalgic grown-up daughter. Hugh at once froze and basked in this intimate yet socially acceptable gesture. It was outrageous. It was possible. He felt faithless, abject, thrilled at the touch. Then almost as suddenly she removed it, preferring to hug her violin case rather than carry it in her free hand on such a crowded street. Or perhaps she felt that the gesture was not quite right. Who knows? As a further distraction from the contact she had initiated she pulled him into an amusement arcade. Hugh could not stop his ears against the siren voice he knew he would find there. When Katey heard it she paused in their unrewarded drift along a tide-line of fruit machines and looked at him sharply.

'Ama-zing!'

He raised his eyebrows and smiled quizzically at her in recognition of her identification of the motif.

'You old poacher!' she exclaimed. 'So this is where you get your ideas from?'

'Not all of them,' said Hugh, showing her how it worked.

'God, it's disgusting,' she said. 'It's the most blatantly chauvinist game I've ever seen. I hope you get your hand stuck in that thing. Is that your pulse rate?'

She looked at him again with fresh curiosity.

'It's your company that does it,' said Hugh.

Katey snorted.

'I bet,' she said. 'Saving Dolly Parton from King Kong, more likely.'

'I think King Kong is meant to be saving Dolly Parton from me, actually.'

Hugh was hardly concentrating on the game, and lost easily to King Kong.

'Not up to your usual standard, H. Hovarc,' purred *Amazing*, with all the unintended malice and monotone of speech synthesis.

'What did it say?' cried Katey in alarm. 'What did it call you?'

'It seems to know who I am,' said Hugh, astounded at the technology that could produce such an effect. 'This glove thing must have recorded my fingerprint or something.'

'Hovarc?' she laughed. 'It makes you sound Czech.'

'Try again, H. Hovarc,' insisted *Amazing*. 'Bills may be changed at the side of the machine.'

'Oh, no,' said Hugh. He shook his head at the machine and spoke loudly to it as if to an insistent Arab beggar. 'No bills. Enough. No dollars.'

'Borrow from your girl friend,' droned *Amazing* encouragingly.

'Help,' said Katey. 'Let's get out of here.'

'Don't go away,' said *Amazing*. 'I take American Express, Master-card . . .'

Back in the street it was Hugh who took Katey's arm and she did not resist. Blinking in the sunlight, she shuddered slightly.

'What a weird machine,' she said. 'It'll be writing music before long.'

'I can think of some things it will never do,' said Hugh, squeezing her arm.

It's no good, he thought. He could not tell what Katey was thinking. If he went any further he would probably appal her, for this was not the dimension in which they were fated to encounter each other. They continued down the busy street in silence.

There was a name he could not remember, which belonged to one of his dreams. It was, he thought, a place. Or perhaps it was a state of being. In any case, it presented itself as a sign of fear, wonder and attraction. And Gin was there. That was where she precisely was. She was revealed in the dream to have irrevocably joined the underworld of the unavailable. It was like a secret political or religious commitment, to be spoken of in danger. It was like that exclusive party of the dead, to be spoken of with awe and blank regret. In his dream, despite this mystery, the mystery of the unremembered name and its syllables, it was, of course, neither. It was merely the being absent and beyond access.

When he saw Gin in the street it immediately consigned the accessible Katey to the unacceptably quotidian world in which romance was a comedy that occurred to other people. His heart pounded. He answered some casual question of Katey's with he knew not what nonsense. *Amazing*'s chrome glove would have sent the red needle flickering way beyond the highest calibrations. He was ready to accuse, to weep, to make a scene. He was ready to be forgiven, to forswear his concerto. He would fight time and its irreversible changes with the confidence and touching valour of a Don Quixote. He would do anything. And nothing. He was ashamed and afraid. He released Katey's arm, and at the same moment saw that it was not, of course, Gin, not even someone very like her. It was an illusion.

And the distance between his arm and Katey's was yet another betrayal.

Illusions kept him on edge. When Dorothy answered the telephone one evening, instead of quietly arguing with it for ten minutes she came into the living room where Hugh was reading and said: 'It's one of your girl friends.'

She might just as well have said that it was the President, perhaps asking for a complimentary ticket for his concerto. He took the receiver from her carefully, as though it were only half assembled.

It was Olive Dempster.

'Hugh dear,' she cried abruptly. 'You're taking me out to dinner.'

'I am, Olive?'

'Sammy West has issued a summons. He's longing to see you.'

I'll bet he is, thought Hugh.

'I don't think I want to go,' he said.

'Nonsense,' said Olive firmly. 'You'll have to go, to escort me. Nobody refuses Sammy West. It's tomorrow at eight.'

You mean, thought Hugh, that you've been invited to escort me, to make sure that I go.

'What did he say?' he asked.

'What do you mean, what did he say,' replied Olive. 'He's giving a dinner party and he wants us to go. I told him I'd given you his address, but he said he hadn't seen you. So he's inviting you round. Look, Hugh, most people would sell their grandmother to get invited by Sammy West.'

'At twenty-four hours' notice?'

'Hugh Howard, you've got to do this thing. I'm relying on you.'

Hugh agreed in the end. He hadn't seriously intended to decline. He knew that he had to see West. He knew that West knew it. It was written into the cartoon scenario: the pursued mouse tiptoes out of his hole in fascination to dine with the fat cat, a moment of grinning hospitality before the chase resumes, the firework tied to the tail, the shotgun aimed at the skirting-board. But was the invitation a warning or a boast? If it was West who had made that other report to the police, was it genuine or was it a ruse to get Hugh into trouble? If it was to get him into trouble, how could West have been sure that Gin's hospitalisation would have been so easily connected with Hugh and not with himself? Yellow, of course; Yellow was the link. Gin had trusted him, but he was not trustable. Nor, felt Hugh with a shudder of apprehension, was Sammy West. Perhaps he had made the report simply to cover himself in some way.

Whatever his motive, there was no doubt that his investigations, both in New York and Dexter, had revealed quite enough to turn him into a monster of jealousy. Was Hugh jealous? Was Hugh jealous enough? Did he mind enough, or were all his feelings distilled into the now imminent and self-sufficient concerto, that worshipped cannibal fetish of significant sounds? There was a thing about loneliness, he thought, as he went back to the Heathfields' living room: it is only a deficient quality of love that makes us lonely.

25

It was as though the curtain had gone up in a theatre where a dinner party was already in progress, guests working full tilt at polite disagreement and cold roast beef with no knowledge of how they got there. Feared or long-expected events had this power to concentrate the mind. Everything else was mere scene-setting, and every apparently chance remark the negligible chatter of extras. Now, thought Hugh, or at least soon, I will get my cue. Something significant will be said. Something will be revealed.

He had no doubt that the party was entirely created for his benefit. Its style impressed him: candles, flowers, Crown Derby, the plentiful brownish burgundy transmitting its inches from cut glass decanters. But the physical ambience, like the ad hoc company, wore the air of careless familiarity. West was not particularly out to impress. If he gave a dinner at all, he would give one like this. The fixtures of the dining room suggested as much. The effect was of the transportation of rare English country-house lumber into expensive utilitarian living space. Even the furniture seemed decorative only. The gilt-framed portrait of a Whig politico might have concealed a safe. The canterbury was empty, the Regency escritoire shut. The greatest concession to vulgarity was the completely mirrored ceiling, which not only doubled the height of the room but when looked at appeared to trap the diners not at the horizontal distance of a stage but at the vertical one of an aquarium: one glance during a lull in the conversation and one felt first amused and then trapped, immediately anxious to swim upwards to safety. Or would it be downwards?

The ceiling reflected the hair and working hands of the hastily assembled guests: Olive on Sammy's right, gesticulating actively; Hooky Foster, a bald dome comparatively still; Bob Gordon, eating steadily, looking lost without his tenor saxophone; Hugh's face, staring upwards into the ceiling; the grizzled crewcut of Slim Santini, the painter, boyfriend of Bob; Chuck Peters, the adoring youth of the Crail party; Tanya Czejarek, her glass for ever at her lips and the other hand apparently on Chuck's knee; and at the head of the table, opposite Hugh, Sammy himself.

'And what do you see in the pool of Narcissus?' asked Sammy suddenly.

'I don't know exactly,' laughed Hugh. 'I feel that down here perhaps we are the reflection and that's the reality.' His apologetic shrug could not disguise his tenseness.

'I keep forgetting that it's there,' said Olive. 'This steak is so good.'

'You don't know it's there,' stammered Chuck, 'unless you look. Like Bishop Berkeley.'

He found himself stared at, and blushed.

'You know,' he explained lamely. 'Is the world there if there's no one to look at it?'

'I don't know about bishops,' said Sammy. 'They may love

185

themselves too, for all I know. Are you taking freshman philosophy, Charles?'

Chuck blushed even more deeply, almost the shade of the very rare beef which was now circulating for second helpings in a flat white dish with raised pottery sprigs of smaragdine parsley round the edge. Hugh helped himself to another of the oily slices that crowded the plate like limp leather spectacle cases. The salad (iceberg, asparagus, walnuts) followed.

'Such a sad story,' proclaimed Olive. 'You're right. It's just like love. You don't know it's there unless you look.'

So they all looked up at the ceiling, their white faces like the opening fronds of an anemone. Hugh noticed that Tanya had removed her predatory hand.

'Did you say Bishop Berkeley?' asked Sammy. 'Looks more like Busby Berkeley to me.'

'So sad,' repeated Olive.

'Why sad?' protested Tanya. 'Why sad? Is not sad.'

'He fell in love with himself, for God's sake.'

'I thought you meant the ceiling.'

'We're all in love with ourselves,' said Hooky Foster. 'It's the only love that lasts.'

'*Die Liebe dauert, oder dauert nicht,*' murmured Hugh.

'Oh sure,' laughed Bob Gordon, uncomprehendingly.

'Love lasts, or else it doesn't last,' translated Sammy. 'Brecht, set by the misnamed, the divine Kurt Weill.'

'Oh, Weill, yeah,' said Gordon. 'We have an arrangement of "Speak Low".'

'Didn't Laurindo Almeida play that?' asked Chuck eagerly. He was looking more at Sammy than at Gordon. Sammy was looking elsewhere.

'Ours is better,' said Gordon.

'So it doesn't last,' said Sammy.

'Sometimes it doesn't begin,' said Olive.

They had finished the beef and salad. Hooky Foster asked Slim about an exhibition of his paintings opening at the Feldman Galleries.

Tanya was saying something inaudible to Chuck. Hugh tensed himself for the removal of the plates, for to his surprise and deep embarrassment they were being served by none other than Jimmy Gerald, impassive and unremarked in a white coat, as though he had been a butler every minute of his working life. Was he not known to any of these people? To Olive? Was his resemblance to Gin not immediately obvious to anyone?

The chatter continued while the plates were cleared. Tanya leaned back and lit a cigarette. Olive was saying that she had once lived on Mercer Street where the Feldman Galleries were to be found. Sammy smiled benevolently at the company. Jimmy filled the wine glasses.

It was clear that he had rendered himself invisible. As a guest, his features would surely have been remarked on. As butler, he was ignored.

Sammy's smile, radiant and goblin-like, was beamed through the conversation directly at Hugh, and yet in a strange way he was not really looking at Hugh. His expression was a kind of abstracted rictus of forced amiability. The pouches and crevices of his visage glowed with the effort of maintaining it. It was an expression that brought hostly benignity and good will more closely to potential hostility than any expression Hugh had ever seen.

The pudding was a large bowl of raspberries and a large bowl of wild strawberries and a large bowl of thick Greek yoghurt. Olive helped herself to all three and passed the bowl to Hooky Foster.

'How can you eat both together, Olive,' smiled Sammy. 'It's like mixing claret and burgundy.'

Olive raised both palms in mock surrender.

'OK, OK, I'm a slobnik,' she said. 'To me it tastes good.'

'I've never had these before,' said Chuck.

'Which are you eating?' cried Olive. 'Don't eat them both together.'

'Ah, Sammy,' said Tanya dreamily. 'We have eaten so well.'

'Thank you.'

Olive was resolute.

'There are worse things,' she said, 'than mixing claret and burgundy.'

'Such as, Olive?' asked Sammy, lifting his upper lip clear of the full panelled length of his canines.

'Whopperburgers?' suggested Olive. 'Elder abuse? Mayor Goode?'

'A good try, Olive,' he said.

There then followed a discussion of the remarkable degree of support for Mayor W. Wilson Goode of Philadelphia, who had recently dropped a bomb on a recalcitrant group of squatters, destroying three blocks of houses and killing twenty people. The city council had voted 9–8 not to investigate the incident.

With their social consciences salved, they rose from the table and returned to the living room. Coffee was waiting for them.

Tanya seemed restless. The general silence of Bob and Slim, which had been slightly oppressive during the meal, became focused in a virtual withdrawal as Bob took Slim on a small tour of Sammy's paintings. Sammy talked privately with Hooky Foster. Olive was investigating some liqueurs and explaining them to Chuck.

As Hugh stood in the centre of the room with his coffee, looking about him and wondering if Sammy's curiosity was satisfied, he saw on the mantelpiece a pair of Gin's earrings. The gold hoops and little creamy slabs of plastic were unmistakeable; they gave him such an immediate and irrational sense of her presence that he turned round as if he expected her to be standing in the doorway. At that moment Jimmy came in with a fresh pot of coffee which he left on the small table. He immediately left again without looking at Hugh.

What a fiendish masquerade! thought Hugh.

The earrings were Gin's. He was sure that he had seen her wearing them. But he could not remember if she had worn them in Texas. On the whole, he felt with a sense of disappointment, she had not worn earrings in Texas. They lay on the mantelpiece, between a Stafford-shire dog and some outsize papier-mâché cherries, for all the world like a little Christmas puzzle of identical pieces to be extracted from each other. Removed from the ears in what spirit? But deliberately left for the amusement of guests.

Or as a challenge.

Sammy's attitude was withdrawn, uninquisitive, oddly contained. It was as though having finally managed to summon Hugh to his presence he was content simply to have him there rather than anywhere else, as if to prevent him doing harm. But this surely could not last. Hugh knew that something had to be settled that evening.

Tanya was at his side, mooching. She laid her clasped hands on his shoulder, and her chin on her hands and looked him in the eyes.

'Not many men I can do that to,' she said. 'You are more my size, Hugh. A nice size, Hugh.'

Hugh smiled at her with an effort of friendly stoicism.

'More than who, Tanya?' he asked.

She shrugged.

'It doesn't matter,' she said. 'You're all the same.'

She followed Hugh's gaze and saw the earrings. She detached herself with a squeeze of his shoulder and with her other hand picked one of them up. It dangled, a ghostly decoration, at the end of her painted fingers.

She smiled quizzically at Hugh, with eyebrows raised. It was as much a smile of conspiracy as of interrogation, and it told Hugh nothing. If they had been alone he would have asked her directly what she knew about Sammy and the Baroness, but they were not alone. As it was, Hugh wondered with unease if Sammy had noticed her lifting the earring, which was now back with its twin on the mantelpiece. Hugh was glad they were not alone. He felt in distinct danger from her lipsticked mouth, a hungry mournful thing the same shape and almost as thin as her eyebrows. She was having little luck tonight.

Sammy could not have noticed. He was standing by the piano with Hooky Foster, picking out a tune, and Hooky was playing phrases and asking him questions. The piano was a medium-sized white grand, covered with flowers and photographs of people who were famous twenty years ago. Chuck looked up eagerly.

'Have you written any new songs, Mr West?' he asked.

'Every day before breakfast,' grinned Sammy.

Tanya had joined Olive on the sofa, and was pouring more coffee. Bob and Slim were now in the hall, still looking at pictures.

'Will you play something?' asked Chuck.

Sammy protested that it was a rule of his never to bore his own guests, but he was, of course, soon persuaded. He sat down and tried a succession of chords as though to see if the piano, like a neglected machine, were still capable of efficiently changing keys.

'As a matter of fact, you'll have heard them all before,' he said, above the chords.

'Never mind that,' said Olive. 'Play!'

Sammy continued to protest, or so Hugh thought. In fact, his style of singing was so conversational and unvocalised that he was well into the refrain of 'When You're Looking Around for Love' before Hugh realised that he had started. It was one of the songs on the Baroness's tape, and he knew her version well. He expected to be outraged, but how could he be outraged by the composer of the song?

> 'The merchandise is on the shelf.
> I know because I put it there myself:
> Am I too bold?
> But if you touch it I say broken,
> If you break it I say sold.'

Without the instrumental timbres of the backing on the track that Hugh knew, the song sounded too direct. In Sammy's hoarse catarrhal rendering it stressed argument rather than emotion. His piano style seemed at once rudimentary and ostentatious. And yet it was undeniably the song that Hugh loved, and there was much in it that he was fascinated to acknowledge as authentic: intervals that the Baroness had cheerfully jettisoned, a tempo that indicated elegance rather than indulged regret.

> 'You can have anything on earth
> And every little glance is worth
> Its weight in gold.
> But if you touch it I say broken,
> If you break it I say sold.'

190

In Sammy's version the brief verses were grudgingly thrown out in the course of a more extended structure of melody on the piano. It was guarded, introspective, offhand.

> 'Some ask for it with their tongue,
> Some with their heart; for everyone is young
> Until they're old.
> But if you touch it I say broken,
> If you break it I say sold.'

Chuck was rapt. Tanya had not touched her fresh cup of coffee and lay back against the sofa, her eyes closed. Olive tapped her fingers. Hooky Foster stood by the piano, his arms folded. Hugh wandered out into the hall.

'Sammy's begun, I see,' said Bob Gordon. 'We'll be here all night.'

'He's good, isn't he?' said Slim.

'Sure he's good,' replied Bob. 'He's been good for a hundred years. He's historical.'

'I must go to the bathroom,' said Hugh.

'Yeah,' said Bob. 'He can have that effect on people. It's down the passage.'

The apartment, like many in New York, was arranged in two main clusters of rooms connected by a very long passage, like dumbbells. The kitchen was in the same cluster as the reception rooms. Hugh could hear the muffled clatter of dishes where Jimmy was presumably washing up. With the latest words of the song in his ears he walked down the dark passage.

> 'Is there something you don't see?
> Take all the time you like. Feel free.
> It won't get cold.
> But if you touch it I say broken,
> If you break it I say sold.'

The words faded to indistinctness. The first room Hugh tried, because it was lit, although dimly, turned out to be some sort of study. He retreated, and tried the next door. This was the lavatory, and he

191

took advantage of it. It was humiliatingly filled with photographs by Robert Mapplethorpe.

When he came out the tune could still be heard. The piano's distance made it sound melancholy: Sammy could easily have been playing to himself alone. Even though he could not quite hear them, Hugh knew the words of the last verse.

> 'You're blowing hot, you're blowing cool.
> Make your mind up. There's this rule
> That I uphold:
> If you touch it I say broken,
> If you break it I say sold.'

The dimness of the passage and the height of the ceilings, Hugh's solitude and the continuing music, thematically appropriate but subdued, like a soundtrack, gave him a sense of strange dramatised purpose. On an impulse he stood again on the threshold of the study and pushed the door even further open. The song had ceased. He heard distant voices, and was about to leave when the piano started up again. Sammy had his audience. He had only just begun, indeed. Hugh would not be missed for a while, surely?

26

The room was like a shrine. The walls were covered with more posters and signed photographs than Hugh had ever seen outside a celebrity restaurant. The concealed wall-lighting had the air of never being turned off, like a vestal flame. Or was it turned on for guests? There seemed to be nowhere for more than one person to sit down, no surface to work on except a small bureau which was itself covered with trophies, including, Hugh noticed with a small shock of delayed recognition and ungrudging respect, the erect impassive ikon of an

Oscar. What had Sammy got his Oscar for, Hugh wondered. It must, of course, have been for the film of *Silver Dollar*, of which there were many other memorabilia in the room, including an immense poster with the laughing faces of Howard Keel and Ethel Merman at least three times life size. There were framed programmes, record-sleeve designs, the original of a first-night cartoon by Hirschfeld. Many of the photographs were of the kind that link performance with celebration, that capture the public moments of private lives and the private moments of public lives. There was Bob Hope on the set of *Fairway Hotel*. There were Sammy and Ethel Merman cheek to cheek in a restaurant with waiters solemnly lined up behind them like private detectives. There was Fran Maxwell dressed as Dilly in *Silver Dollar*, inscribed: 'Sammy, darling, a chance in a million.' There was what must have been the chorus of *More's the City* with linked arms on a posed shopping spree on the streets of Manhattan: the young Liz Crail was among them, wearing a tight belt and a tiny hat. And everywhere was Sammy, reaping the rewards of fame: Sammy with the Kennedys, Sammy in a ten-gallon hat, a young Sammy with a young Judy Garland (of course, Hugh remembered, she had starred in the stage production of *How do you do da?*), an older Sammy with the young Rock Hudson, Sammy signing a contract, Sammy in a large fur coat descending from an aeroplane, Sammy receiving his Oscar, Sammy receiving kisses, Sammy with his arm round Fran Maxwell, Sammy with dark hair and more of it, smiling a smile that was the same smile but more sexually rapacious. The photographs were in no particular order, unless they were deliberately contrived to suggest the variety and vagaries of show business over the last half century, with, at the core, the one consistent, reliable, immortal factor – the genius of Sammy West. There was only one thing that puzzled Hugh.

Where were the photographs of the Baroness?

As if in answer to that question Hugh came upon a table in the corner on which was an album, and a large manila envelope, and on top of these another pair of the Baroness's earrings. This pair, similar in style to the others but with green discs and gold hoops, did not look as though they had just been taken off. They looked, rather, as though they had been collected or expropriated. Or, Hugh felt, laid out to tease. First one pair, then the other, like clues in a treasure hunt. On an impulse he pocketed them.

The envelope contained prints of Dan Fleischman's shots of the Baroness for *Nightbird*. They were, in accordance with Dan's fast film and surreptitious manner, intimate, grainy, elusive in mood. Gin's alternate amusement, suspicion and delight on that occasion had been trapped in the shutter as cunningly as the camera could freeze the wings of a hovering hummingbird. The informal angles of the head, blurred hands, dawning smiles, showed her as a kind of hopeful wraith haunting her own dressing room. In one of the photographs Dan's haste had included in a corner the mirror-reflected attendant heads of Goldbein and himself, the one impassive and the other foolishly mesmerised. The photographs were too good for a scandal sheet, and Hugh guessed that unless a scandal broke they would never be used.

Was Gin's disappearance a scandal? Did it belong to the world of defeat and manipulation, or was it a sudden brave defiance of all that, as Denis, and as Lieutenant Heaney seemed to think? Sammy's appetite for fame and power may have led him into some strange corners. How responsible had he been, for example, for Fran Maxwell's meteor-like burnout? Judy Garland had killed herself, too. No, that was ridiculous. Theirs was a world in which many could not stand the pace, and those who did, like Sammy, simply by surviving acquired the flamboyant aura of the inhuman.

The album was of the flip-over kind which could contain a multitude of snapshots. Hugh inserted his finger like a card dealer turning over half a spread deck. Beneath it was the image of an overweight woman in T-shirt and Bermuda shorts, staring defiantly at the loving eye of the camera. It was nobody that Hugh knew, but behind her, in full splendour, were the Scattle Stones.

He quickly looked at random in the album: all the photographs were of the Scattle Stones, all from the same angle and from the same point, where their full height could be accommodated in the viewfinder. Common to all the photographs were the Stones, a beaming or scowling tourist or two, and in between, to one side in the middle distance, the kiosk where the tags were collected. The photographs were different sizes, the seasons varied, the growth of the vegetation and the state of the site, too. But the photographs were arranged in chronological order, and the administration of the Stones revealed a steady advance: the building of paths, the erection of a viewing platform (no more than a shadow in many of the photographs), the painting of the kiosk, improvement in the fencing. But this was not the point. Nor was the array of posed spouses and families.

In almost all the photographs the young Virginia was on duty at the kiosk.

She stood by it in ankle-socks, weighed down by a leather collecting bag. She sat inside it on a high stool. She sat in it with the door closed, leaning out on its ledge. Her arm lay along the ledge in the sunlight. Her arm was raised, toying with the window-strut. She was half-hidden by tourists. She directed tourists, her finger pointing, eyes squinting against the sun. She was bringing in the rack of postcards at the end of the day. She stood in shorts. The kiosk door was half open. It was shut. She wore a red check dress. She leaned out of the window, like a train passenger, curious at an unexpected halt. Her back was turned to the camera. Her profile, half in shadow. She was reading a book. She took the tags. She took money for postcards. She frowned. Her head was bowed as she looked for change. She was hidden by a tall man at the head of a small queue. She stood at some distance in front of the kiosk talking to Jack Gerald, who had his hands on his hips. Her arms were folded on the ledge. She counted postcards. She took the tags. Her hair was in pigtailed braids. The red check dress fitted her too tightly.

Hugh moved his fingernail slowly upwards against the edges of the plastic pouches that contained the photographs. They dropped back one by one, and as in some primitive cinematograph Gin's life at the Scattle Stones was haltingly recreated. A hundred unknown Kodaks had retrieved one insignificant but memorable routine in the forgotten adolescence of someone who was loved enough for them to be imagined, pursued and paid for, so that they would each yield their share of this memory. It was a miracle, like the discovery of a lost notation of ballet. It bore the same relationship to time that the intermittent radio images from a Jupiter probe bore to space. The weight of her body, the shadowed angles of her limbs, the deepening beauty of her face, the elusive grace of her movement, were like something previously unknown. The movement in stillness was unearthly.

Hugh did not hear Jimmy come into the room until he spoke.

'You find what you were looking for in here, mister?'

Hugh laughed in embarrassment.

'It's quite a career, isn't it?' he said. 'I was just looking at all these photographs.'

'I can see what you're doing.'

Jimmy shut the door behind him and came further into the room. He was still wearing his white coat, but it was undone, revealing a large silver engraved buckle on his trouser belt.

'You fed well tonight, mister? You sure as hell were scared as a rabbit when you came round.'

He chuckled softly.

'Scared as a rabbit,' he repeated. 'Now you turn up dinner company, neat as you please and eager to nose around.'

'Jimmy, I'm concerned about your sister,' said Hugh, suddenly risking directness.

'Oh, it's Jimmy is it? I don't think we were introduced.'

'I want to know where she is.'

'No, you don't want to know where she is. You know where she is.'

'Did she go home?' asked Hugh. 'Did your father tell you about me? Did she tell you?'

'You ask a lot of questions for a little man,' said Jimmy. 'Everyone knows about you nosing around. Don't need no telling.'

He sat in the only chair and looked up at Hugh, his thumbs hooked into his belt. His face was a mask of defiance, but Hugh sensed that he was nervous.

'Jimmy, I admire your sister very much,' he began.

'Ad-mire,' grinned Jimmy. 'That's a fine word. That's the best thing I ever did hear. You want your piece of her ass like anyone else.'

Hugh felt himself blushing.

'What can you do for her, man?' asked Jimmy. 'She's doing fine. She don't need you.'

Hugh was silent. Everything he thought: that she didn't need anybody, that she had loved him, that it was none of Jimmy's business, was unsayable. At that moment, whatever else it had been or might be again, it was Jimmy's business and he was making it his business. What did he want from Hugh? The lip that so resembled Gin's curled with a cruel and unresponding hostility that made a sinister mockery of her mischievous smile.

'Mr West reckons on having some fun with you tonight,' he said, giggling.

Hugh was suddenly out of patience.

'Fun,' he said. 'Is this his fun, too?'

He held out the album of photographs. Jimmy barely looked at it.

'Was this your idea? Advertising for these photographs?'

'Sure it was my idea. It kept the old man happy.'

'Why did West want these photographs? It's because he couldn't have Gin, isn't it?'

Hugh knew with a sinking heart that this was not so. Jimmy laughed at him.

'What do you want me to say? That he loves her like a pappy? He wants every little piece of her, man. He wants the meat and the gravy. I tell you, there's nothing he doesn't want from her, and he can pay for it, too.'

'And you helped him to get it?'

'You ain't in a position to say things like that.'

'You're a pimp,' said Hugh recklessly.

'You're a rash man, mister,' said Jimmy, sitting up in the chair.

'You pimped for your own sister!'

Jimmy leaped up. The smile had gone from his face. He came up and stood close to Hugh, his breath an indefinable sweet taint. His large hand reached between Hugh's legs and gripped.

'You had better learn to keep your mouth shut,' he hissed. The fingers probed gently. 'You can do nothing for her.'

The pain shot up into Hugh's abdomen as Jimmy's fingers and thumb found what they were looking for. He tried to push him away, but any movement at all made it worse.

'Every little piece,' sneered Jimmy. 'He'll say to her, real sweet, and he really is a sweet old man, isn't he? He'll say, "Come here and sit on my knee, honey." And she'll laugh at him and say some sassy thing, you know? And then he'll tell me to leave the room, and I'll leave the room, and they're in there, you know, real quiet, and I'll listen at the door. There are things that old man wants no woman going to give him for free.'

All the time Jimmy's fingers kneaded away, and Hugh, his face clenched and averted, did not know whether it was the pain itself he resented or the intimacy of this practised torture, the outrageous violation of the privacy of his body. The album of photographs had fallen from his hand, and some had spilled out on the floor.

'That's what it's all about, mister. Payola. No one makes it without putting out. What did you think?'

'Please,' whispered Hugh. 'Please stop.' He thought he was going to be sick.

'Well,' said Jimmy, detaching his hand and stepping back. 'I guess we've had our fun already.'

Hugh was doubled over. He wanted to weep, to hide. He had not felt such humiliation, rage and unnecessary pain since he was at school. He crept out of the room and went into the lavatory where he knelt at the bowl, spitting a thread of bile, and wondering if he had been damaged.

Jimmy's voice came from outside the lavatory door.

'When you're finished in there, I reckon you'd better leave, Mr Howard.'

Hugh said nothing.

'You'll get nothing from him,' said Jimmy after a while. There was another pause. 'She ain't nothing without him.'

Then Hugh heard him walking away down the passage. The lazy tinkle of the piano could still be heard from the civilised end of the apartment. Hugh forced himself to stand up and control his trembling. He knew that he had to return to the living room as though nothing had happened. He knew also that he had come as close to an explanation as he would ever come. The Baroness had walked right through and out of the trap sprung for her, of that he was sure. And she had had to do it on her own.

Backman had puzzled him. Her agent was a woman and she had proved, in any case, that she was her own agent. He was not Goldbein. He was not Yellow. Even the vile Sammy was somehow exonerated, for Hugh, having found himself sympathetically tuned to the enthralling whine and thrum of his obsession, had a dawning sense of their appalling kinship. Backman was all these. He was all men. He was an idea. But most particularly he was embodied in the puppyish opportunism of her own half-brother.

What Jimmy had meant to say was surely that Sammy was nothing without the Baroness? For it was the old man's need that gave him his own jaunty and precarious power. But it was not true. When Hugh came out of the lavatory and began to walk tenderly down the passage, Sammy's playing, for all the lavish sentimentality of its interpretation, reminded him of the perennial power of art to abstract itself from the passions that feed it. Jimmy had no power over that, and therefore had no real power over either of them. Chord after chord resolved the vagrant tensions of hope, desire and foreboding into mere ripples on the surface of the pool of Narcissus. Sammy was playing 'Tell It Me Again'.

27

And at last the baton was raised. The audience who had travelled through the early evening from unlikely and unknown occupations, who had presented tickets they had actually bought, who had settled

themselves in anticipation, were now about to pay attention to the
ego of one man. The expensive orchestra had assembled. Someone
who received a salary to do so arranged for the lights to dim. Boris's
tie was a centimetre crooked, his encouraging smile at the orchestra a
shade more alert and wide-eyed than it had been at rehearsal,
communicating an infinitesimal nuance of mock-panic and helpless
conspiracy. And the baton descended.

Almost as soon as it had begun, Hugh knew that it would be over
too quickly for him to capture whatever secrets it might still be
concealing from him.

Katey, oblivious of everyone and everything, was already
crouched and punishing the strings. She stood there in a long red
dress that appeared to glue her to the floor, working away like a
boxer at a punch-ball, the jaw thrust out, the bottom lip turned back
over her teeth in concentration, the eyebrows occasionally lifted in a
fastidious concern when the scurry of quavers reached a peak from
which they eased themselves into a descending pretence at the
melody.

The concerto appeared to be seamless. That was the strange
alchemy of music. It was buoyant with its own life, like a garment
long toiled over in the fitting, troublesome with tucks and hems, now
ghosted by the wind into the simulacrum of a human shape. Hugh
wanted to let his thoughts ride on it, as if its waves of sound would
urge him in the direction which he could never in reality take, and
beach him upon some decision about his future.

He knew that he could love Katey, too. He knew that such love was
nothing like the myth that is made of it. The music was. Music gave
the dim negotiations of gender a new clarity. It was symbolised in the
feminine violin which was speaking, under Hugh's charmed direction, the eloquent reproaches of all women. Daisy had been right
about such symbolism: those stretched vibrations had a depth that
went beyond voice into sex. The true violin soloist would be a man,
for a man would add to the drama of the soloist's engagement with
the orchestra the primary instrumental drama of sensual utterance.
Was Hugh so incapable of evoking this response? He did not think

that Daisy was right, but he could not think of Daisy without anguish. The finality of her letter frightened him. It lay undigested in his mind, the embodiment of unredeemed regrets.

The long, disappearing melody in the second movement took on the character of this regret. It was like paying out a rope steadily and suddenly finding that it isn't after all attached to anything, or that you are about to lose hold for good. The music connived at this, eloquently. Hugh stood by amazed at the uncontrollable process of loss. It was like wasting a whole life drifting in dreams. And like a wasted life, the concerto would soon be over.

The third movement answered the second by proposing that there is always a life somewhere else. It was the life that no one could ever know. It was the life that was always hidden. It was a guess. It was an exploration. It was a portrait of Gin as a bird of passage.

He had failed as a St George, but he knew he was now finished with the nightmare of not having done anything. So long as the scrolled wooden voice scraped its abandoned blue notes of mutual reproach, the real nightingale was nowhere and everywhere. Had his love for Gin been a distraction? Had it diverted him from something else of mysterious importance which his music in its abstraction attempted to describe in vain? If so, it had also been a gift. And he had exploited it like his own gift. And perhaps there really existed nothing at all apart from these spoiled chances.

The concerto was Hugh's own removal, his own disappearance. It was his answer, his own blues. But he had no idea where it had taken him to. As the last notes were played, he was choked with his own existence. It went beyond success or failure.

All over the concert-hall hand met hand in response to its conclusion. Almost at the first sound from the audience, Hugh knew what the response would be. He saw Boris smiling. He saw Katey drained, surprised, woken by Boris to her real self, handed to the audience, kissed, the orchestra bidden to stand. He himself was called to the platform.

It always comes too late, our immense good fortune. Or is realised much too late. Its aftermath, like applause, is a surprised and grateful recognition that exalts and distances.

We stand in decisive and generous homage, the eyes bright with praise. Our whole life recedes into a finally visible perspective. Only by losing it do we ever see it there.

Hugh slowly came to understand that the concerto was the best thing that he had ever written, but from that moment he knew that it was not good enough.